ASTRAY

ALSO BY AMY CHRISTINE PARKER

Gated

AMY CHRISTINE PARKER

RANDOM HOUSE NEW YORK

 Published in the United States by Random House Children's Books, a division of Random House LLC, a Penguin Random House Company, New York.

Visit us on the Web! randomhouse.com/teens

Educators and librarians, for a variety of teaching tools, visit us at RHTeachersLibrarians.com

Library of Congress Cataloging-in-Publication Data
Parker, Amy Christine.
Astray / Amy Christine Parker.—First edition.
p. cm.
Summary: Lyla thought she was free from the survivalist Community, but it is hard to break the hold their leader Pioneer has even though he is in jail—and he is planning to use his powerful influence to get his revenge on Lyla and the town.
ISBN 978-0-449-81602-8 (trade)—ISBN 978-0-449-81604-2 (ebook)
1. Survivalism—Juvenile fiction. 2. Cults—Juvenile fiction. 3. Religious leaders—Juvenile fiction. 4. Charisma (Personality trait)—Juvenile fiction. 5. Deprogramming—Juvenile fiction. [1. Utopias—Fiction. 2. Survival—Fiction. 3. Cults—Fiction. 4. Religious leaders—Fiction.] I. Title.
PZ7.P22165Ast 2014 813.6—dc23 2013034047

Printed in the United States of America
10 9 8 7 6 5 4 3 2 1
First Edition

For Jay, always

ASTRAY

A good shepherd doesn't lie down when
one of his sheep is still astray.
—Pioneer, leader of the Community

ONE

It's been a month since the world was supposed to end. By now you'd think I wouldn't wake up every morning in a panic with the Community's alarm echoing in my ears and my breath coming so fast that I'm not actually taking in any oxygen.

But I do.

Maybe it's because somewhere deep inside I can't believe that the apocalypse isn't still looming over every horizon. My family and our leader, Pioneer, warned me about it every waking moment of my life from the time I turned five. How can I suddenly just switch gears and believe that it was all a lie?

I wipe the condensation from the bathroom mirror and stare at the swipe of my reflection that's visible. I ran the shower long enough to slow my breathing back down, to stop my body from trembling visibly, but inside I'm still thrumming with a nervousness I can't soothe—not with a hundred showers. It doesn't help that this bathroom still feels foreign to me, that the place I live in now is not my home and that the people who live here with me are barely more than strangers.

"Lyla, we don't have much time. My dad's already left," Cody says from outside the door in a low voice.

I begin to quickly dry off. Cody's dad is the sheriff, the person who raided the Community's development, Mandrodage Meadows, just before Pioneer sealed us underground to wait for the apocalypse. Today he's going to transfer Pioneer from the hospital to the county jail, and Cody and I are going to watch him.

"Be right there." I put my mouth close to the door so I won't have to talk too loud. Cody's mom and sister are still sleeping. If they wake up before we can manage to get out of the house, we won't be allowed to go. I can't say that I'd blame them for stopping us. None of us knows how I'll react to seeing Pioneer for the first time since I shot him, not even me.

"Lyla, for real, hurry," Cody says. He taps the door for emphasis.

"Okay!"

I tug on a pair of Cody's jeans and his baggiest sweatshirt. Pulling my hair into a tight bun and covering it with one of his baseball caps, I check the mirror one last time and try to find some speck of courage in my expression, but my face is all pale terror.

Can I really do this?

I try a few guy-like slouches. With any luck, once Cody

finishes giving me a fake beard and I cover my too-shapely body, I'll be believable enough as a guy to fool Pioneer, the sheriff, and anyone else we run into. I don't want anyone other than Cody to know that I'm there. I'm not sure I can face Pioneer otherwise.

I hurry out of the bathroom. Cody looks at me and smiles. I have to look away, because I'm unnerved enough right now. I can't deal with the circus that happens in my stomach whenever he looks at me like that.

"Not bad. You're not dude-like just yet, but we'll fix that." He grabs my hand and leads me downstairs and then into the basement. We tiptoe to the far corner where Cody keeps all of his monster projects and makeup tools. He pulls over a metal stool and I perch on it. My hands land in my lap and I rub my thumbs across my jeans. I breathe in and out.

"Ready?" Cody's all shiny-eyed and eager. I've just given him a way to practice what he loves. I'm his personal special-effects project this morning. Oh, who am I kidding? I'm his personal project in a lot of ways. He doesn't seem to mind, but it's bothering me more and more. Who wants to be the most broken person in the room all the time? That's why I'm going to the hospital today, to start repairing the damage that Pioneer did to me. Seeing him again is the first step.

"Yeah," I say. I watch as he picks up what looks like a tube made out of dark brown hair and unrolls it. He holds it up to my face and compares it to my real hair color.

"Close enough." He's not really talking to me as much as himself. He cuts off a few inches of the hair and fans it out between his fingers before laying it across the table beside me. I glance down at the Wolfman head he's been working on and the severed limbs beyond it. It's realistic enough that most people would probably get grossed out just looking at it, but I don't. Once you've seen real blood and gore, the fake stuff isn't all that believable, no matter how good it is.

Cody leans over and grabs the TV remote off the table. "This'll go faster if you watch something," he says as he turns on the TV and hands me the remote. I'm pretty sure that he's not worried about me being bored. He's trying to get me to stop thinking about Pioneer. The only problem is that ever since I left Mandrodage Meadows, I haven't been able to do that. When I close my eyes, Pioneer's there. I'm back in the stable reliving the moment right after I shot him. I see the blood blooming across his dingy white shirt all over again. Sometimes I think I can even catch the coppery scent of his blood in the air. And the blood of my best friend, Marie. Pioneer slit her throat so he could "send her to be with the Brethren in a better place." There isn't a TV show that can compete with those memories. Still, I scan through the channels.

Suddenly, like my thoughts conjured him up, Pioneer's face fills up the screen. It feels like my heart freezes up. He's staring right at me. I turn up the volume.

"Alan Cross, who now calls himself Pioneer, along with his followers spent the last ten years isolated in an apocalyptic compound."

Cody grabs the remote out of my lap—I must have dropped it, but I don't remember it falling. "That's enough of—"

"No, wait! I . . . I need to see this," I say, even though part of me wants to cover my ears and squeeze my eyes shut. If I can't deal with seeing Pioneer on a television screen, how can I expect to do it in person?

Pioneer's face fades and a new image of the hospital flashes across the screen. Gathered on the sidewalk just outside the entrance are my friends. They're huddled together on their knees, their hands upturned toward the sky—every one of them in the exact same position. They smile at the camera. The look on their faces . . . it's eerie how happy they seem. My stomach roils and I have to swallow to keep from gagging.

". . . his followers say that they will continue to show up at the hospital until Pioneer is released."

Julie's face fills up the screen. She grins widely at the camera. "He's alive! Pioneer should've died, but he didn't." She looks over at Mr. Brown, who is standing nearby, and he beams at her.

The man holding the microphone gestures to the way she's sitting. "You're all kneeling. Why?"

Julie laughs, a high-pitched, tinkly one that sounds nothing like the sound she makes whenever she finds something truly funny. I hate it. "We kneel because we want to show Pioneer our obedience and renewed faith."

The interviewer tries to look serious, but he's having a hard time.

Julie looks at him and her mouth twists. Her grin turns into a smirk. "You'll remember this moment—when you refused to see the miracle of his survival. On earth's last day you won't be mocking us anymore. You'll know he was right—that you're gonna die."

"Totally deluded, the idiot." Cody shakes his head angrily and taps hair onto my chin. I don't look at him, because I don't know what to say. I believed in Pioneer once . . . does that make me an idiot too? I bite my lip and try to focus on the screen so I won't cry.

". . . they have begun to share their message publicly on YouTube through taped sermons Pioneer gave in the last ten years."

Footage of Pioneer standing in front of our old clubhouse pops up. I suck in a breath. I can see myself in the background. This past me smiles as Pioneer walks toward her and holds out his hand. I watch as she leans her cheek into his palm. My heart starts to hurt. Even though I don't want to, part of me misses that girl and her belief. I haven't felt sure about anything at all since I left the Community. My mouth tastes sour and I look away, up at Cody. Has he spotted the old me?

"The end is coming, isn't it?" I watch as my parents, my friends, and Past Me nod and clap.

Cody lets out a disgusted sigh and I stand up and lunge over the table to hit the TV's power button, getting beard hair stuck to my shirt in the process. I slam back into my seat and hold my head in my hands. I don't know what's worse, the fact that Past Me was nodding right along with everyone else . . . or the fact that Present Me still has an inexplicable urge to. My brain feels like it's split in half and Past Me and Present Me haven't decided who's in charge yet. Maybe seeing Pioneer today is a mistake. Maybe it'll tip the balance in Past Me's favor. I start to shake; I can't help it. I am suddenly overcome by nerves.

"We don't have to do this, you know. I could go by myself and tell you all about it afterward." Cody studies my face. He touches my cheek with his fingertips. They're warm. I move away almost by reflex. It isn't because I don't want him to touch me. Pioneer always told us to steer clear of Outsiders, and my body still hasn't figured out how to make disobeying him a regular habit. I guess this means that Past Me still has the upper hand. It makes me want to punch something.

If my recoiling from his touch bothers Cody, he doesn't show it. Instead he picks up more hair and starts filling in my beard.

I don't know if I should apologize or just ignore what's just happened. After a moment of silence, I choose ignoring. "I need to see him. Make sure." I don't finish this sentence. I'll just sound weird. After I shot him twice in the chest, almost exactly in the heart, I was sure he would die, but he didn't—even after lots of complications. I can't seem to stop myself from wondering if maybe he really is what he says he is. How else could he have survived it all? If I can't see Pioneer as just a man instead of some kind of messiah, I'll never get rid of the part of me who still wants to believe in him.

Cody pats the last bit of beard hair in place. He steps back and studies my face. "Not bad."

He spins me around in the stool by my shoulders and hands me a mirror. I don't look like me at all. In a strange sort of way, I look like a younger version of my dad. I've never seen bits of him in my face before.

Dad.

I wince at my reflection. I don't miss my parents most of the time, because I try not to think about them. I need this time away to figure things out, but then something like this happens and I feel my chest hollow out, my stomach constrict. I turn away from the mirror. No more staring at myself this morning.

Cody starts tapping spirit gum onto his own jawline. He's working faster. We gave ourselves two hours before we needed to leave, but we're quickly running out of time. Pioneer's transfer is scheduled for less than an hour from now. I watch as Cody presses a lighter set of hairs onto his chin. His beard is longer—wilder than the one he gave me. In a matter of ten more minutes, he's done.

Cody walks over to his bed and pulls on a thick sweatshirt before he adjusts the Mel's Trucking Company cap on top of his head—the one that he picked up at the thrift store. He grabs two camouflage coats and we pull them on as we head out the side door that leads to the backyard.

Here we go.

Cody leads me to his car, parked out on the curb by the mailbox. We slip inside, both of us cringing as the rusty driver's-side door groans open loudly enough to startle some birds out of the trees beside the house. It feels like the houses, trees, even the birds are watching us, waiting to see if I'll go through with this. I settle into the passenger seat before I can change my mind, and Cody pulls the car out of park, lets it roll down the tiny hill toward the end of the street before parking it again and starting it up.

It's not quite six in the morning. The streets are mostly empty, making the town seem deserted. I'm shaking hard now, enough that it's obvious to Cody. He keeps shifting his eyes from the road to me and back again. Every minute that passes, it gets harder and harder to fight the urge to ask Cody to turn the car around.

Finally, Cody slows and pulls the car onto the road that leads to the hospital. I can see the parking lot now and most of the hospital itself, looming large in front of us. Everywhere I look there are news vans and people. The sheriff's plan to keep Pioneer's transfer low-key has failed. It looks like a large chunk of the town is heading toward the wide stretch of sidewalk and lawn leading up to the hospital's side entrance. The Community is still there. I can see Mr. Brown from where I sit.

"They won't know it's you. Lyla, it's almost better that all these people are here." Cody parks the car and gathers me into his arms.

I'm rigid. Frozen.

Cody's mouth is beside my ear. "You don't have to do this."

I want him to stop saying that. I *do* have to do this. I pull myself out of his arms and open the car door. The wind whips inside and makes my eyes sting.

"C'mon," I say. We get out of the car and walk toward the hospital. The crowd buzzes with chatter and excitement. I can feel the air humming with it.

In a few minutes most of these people will have their first glimpse of what they're certain is a monster disguised as a man. They're one hundred percent convinced of it.

Now I want to be too.

I am a miracle. I am the messiah. After seeing what I've survived, how could you possibly believe otherwise?

—Pioneer

TWO

My parents are here.

I try not to reel backward when I see them. For a split second I forget that I'm in disguise. I hug myself—a very un-guy-like pose. I've visited with them every week during our counseling sessions; seeing them today shouldn't shock me. It's just that the rest of the Community wasn't around when we met, and so, stupidly, I'd been hoping that they were starting to rethink their involvement in it. I didn't expect them to be on their knees too.

The last time I was with the Community and my parents at the same time was when we went back to Mandrodage Meadows, stood around the Silo, and watched the sun go down on what was supposed to be the last day. My family's counselor, Mrs. Rosen, said I needed a break from them—that they needed a break from me—while we all made sense of what Pioneer did to us. That's why I'm with Cody and his family. It's temporary, but I'm thankful that they took me in at all. Mrs. Rosen was right—I needed to get away from the Community. My head feels clearer in their absence. I only wish my parents had taken some time away too.

I stare at my mom. She's kneeling just behind a line of deputies. Her face is turned toward the hospital doors, to where Pioneer will come out. Even if I weren't in disguise, I doubt she'd see me. All of her attention is reserved for Pioneer.

Unbelievably.

Still.

Beside Mom, my dad looks a bit lost and confused. There's something sure in my mom's expression that's lacking in his, but his eyes are trained on the doors too. Beyond them I can see my Intended, Will, and my old friends Brian, Heather, and Julie. Will's eyes pass over me without stopping. I let out a breath for what feels like the first time since I saw everyone. If my best friend—the boy I was supposed to marry—doesn't know it's me, no one else will either. Brian glares in my direction and my heart squeezes a bit in my chest, but then I realize that he's glaring at everyone, not me specifically. He's lost the most out of all of us. His Intended, Marie, and his dad both died the day of the raid—Marie inside the Silo and his dad outside on the development wall defending it. Brian doesn't blame Pioneer for their deaths. He blames me and the sheriff and every single Outsider that was at the raid.

Brian's eyes settle on the people just in front of him now. I follow his gaze to a group of people standing there.

They've got their hands up around their mouths, barely disguising the smirks on their faces as they stare at Brian and the others. I watch as Brian gets off his knees and puffs out his chest. I move forward to get a better look. He says something and the deputy closest to where he is turns around, shakes his head at him. The smirkers start to laugh and I see another deputy move in to flank the group. Brian's chin juts out and his eyes narrow even more. He's always had a temper, but now it's like he's about to blow. What if he loses it and tries something? If the deputy has to subdue him, the rest of the Community will rush to Brian's defense. This could get bad fast. I clear my throat and prepare to yell, but then I don't know who to warn—the deputy, the smirkers, or Brian.

Before I can make a sound, a guy a little older than Brian steps up behind him and puts a hand on his shoulder. Even though he isn't from the Community, Brian doesn't shrug him off. I study the man a little closer. He seems to know Brian and the others. None of them seem very concerned that he's standing with them. I don't understand it. They've shunned all of the Outsiders as much as possible, even the counselors. Who is he?

He's dressed in camouflage pants and a thick black coat. His hair is close-cropped. Everything about him says military to me. Is he somehow with the deputies? But then I notice the way he's looking at them, his body squared off like he's expecting them to attack Brian too. He doesn't like the deputies either.

Cody follows my gaze and stares at the guy next to Brian and the five or so other guys also dressed in camo who are now beside him. "Those Freedom Rangers are kind of an intense-looking bunch, aren't they?"

I nod. They certainly look more hardcore than I thought they would.

The sheriff's mentioned this militia group several times, and every time his face looked pinched like he swallowed something bitter. They call themselves a civil liberties group, but the sheriff said most of them are "nothing more than a bunch of cowboy wannabes," big on guns and making their own rules. I'm not sure if he's right. I also heard that when they showed up after the raid on our development made national headlines, they came armed with both laptops and guns. They spent the first few days setting up a web page and blog for the Community where they asked people to donate what they could to help get the group back on its feet. They managed to raise enough money in the first four weeks after the raid hit the papers to rent a large section of farmland on the outskirts of town, put a bunch of used mobile homes on it for everyone to live in, hire a lawyer to help get Brian, Julie, Will, and the others out of the foster homes that the state put them in, and raise some money for Pioneer's defense.

I'm surprised that Pioneer and the others would let Outsiders support them. We were always taught to avoid Outsiders at all costs. Now my friends and family are standing shoulder to shoulder with some.

"Wonder how comfortable your, um, group is with having them camp out with them on the same land . . . since they're Outsiders and all." Cody keeps studying them, his eyes squinting against the sunrise. It's funny how closely his thoughts echo mine.

Cody's never once used the word "cult" to describe the Community, even though every other Outsider I've met has. I've never told him that I don't like the term, that just saying it makes me feel like my throat is closing up, but somehow he must sense it. Whenever I notice him being careful with his words, it makes me want to kiss him. He doesn't manage it all the time—like earlier when he called Julie an idiot, but he tries and that's enough. I lean into him, then remember my manly disguise and smile at him instead, but I'm not sure he can see it through my beard.

I go back to studying the Rangers. I'll get to see them up close this week when I go visit my parents. Mrs. Rosen scheduled our next session in their new "home" to see if I can start to feel comfortable there. Her goal is to have me begin living with my parents again before next summer. Will and all the other kids from the Community were given back to their parents right after the Rangers hired that lawyer and the foster-care people determined that the only immediate threat to them was Pioneer. I'm the only one who didn't want to go back. I still don't.

I shift from one foot to the other. Cody glances at his watch. "They're running late. Probably because of the crowd," he says. I blow on my frozen fingers and nod.

In the space between the Community and where Cody and I are standing is a crowd of news people. So far most of them have been wandering around, talking on phones and sipping at Styrofoam cups full of coffee, but all at once they start rushing around. The cameramen hoist cameras over their shoulders.

The deputies in front of them put their hands up. "Stay behind the barricades!" they shout almost in unison.

From behind the reporters there's a short burst of sirens as an ambulance pulls up to the sidewalk. Pioneer will have to go right by the press and us to get to it. I'll be almost close enough to reach out and touch him if I want to. My heart starts beating a little faster and I clench my teeth to keep them from chattering. He'll be brought out any minute now.

Across from us my friends and family stand in unison and burst into a chant, the one we said just before every meal and meeting in Mandrodage Meadows.

The Brethren will save us.
Pioneer guides and protects us.
We will look to them alone
In all that we do
In all that we say
In all that we believe.

Their faces are upturned toward the hospital doors and I realize mine is too. My lips are mouthing the words with them. Cody gapes at me. I joined in without even knowing I was doing it. I dip my chin and glance around to make sure that no one else saw me, but all eyes are on the Community. Several people shake their heads, give the Community lots of space like maybe if they touch them they'll catch whatever it is that they have and start chanting too; others start to laugh. From somewhere close by I hear two women talking.

"They're certifiably insane. Didn't I tell you? And we're supposed to allow our kids to be exposed to that?" She makes a disgusted sound. "They won't get within five feet of our boys if I can help it."

I turn around to see who's talking. It's a woman in a brown quilted coat with a white knit scarf wound tightly around her neck. Her face is red from cold, anger, lack of air, or all three. The woman with her is nodding absently, her eyes still glued to the Community. She looks scared to death.

I grimace. All of the kids from the Community—me included—are set to begin Outsider school tomorrow. Culver Creek High. I'd been wondering why no one tried to make us go earlier. Now I guess I know. The Outsiders don't like us either. *Interesting.*

As soon as the Community members say the last line, they start the chant over again. The news crews train their cameras on them, and several reporters start talking into their microphones in hushed tones I can't quite make out. By the time the chant gets repeated for a third time, the air feels charged in the same way it does before a wicked thunderstorm.

The hospital doors open and Cody's dad, Sheriff Crowley, appears, surrounded by five deputies. They linger in the doorway a minute eyeing the crowd. Finally two of the deputies trot up to join the ones holding the news people and everyone else at bay. The crowd presses into them. The Freedom Rangers start shouting.

"No raid without cause!"

"Owning firearms is American, police brutality is not!"

They seem to have their own chants too.

"Deluded—the bunch of them," Cody says under his breath. "Dad didn't open fire, their so-called victims did."

I don't know what to say to this. Part of me still has this knee-jerk need to defend my Community. We weren't trying to hurt people. We were trying to protect ourselves. But then I think about our target practices, about the men destroying all of our animals—my horse Indy—before we went into the Silo, about Pioneer locking me in the Silo's cell and murdering Marie, and I wish they'd raided us sooner. How long before I stop having to remind myself of all this? How long before I'll be free?

There's more movement by the hospital's doors. I can see a group of people silhouetted behind the glass now.

It's time.

The doors open wide one more time and a line of deputies comes out. The sheriff watches as they pass him and then he falls into step behind them. As they get closer, I get my first glimpse of Pioneer. He's in a wheelchair. His hair has gone from salt and pepper to almost completely white in only a few months. He's thinner than he used to be, almost skeletal. It should make him look frail, but instead it makes him look fierce. His eyes are flashes of fire against the gray of his skin, which is stretched so tight across his face and neck that it makes him seem over-alert. He smiles when he sees Will and the others.

I study Pioneer's chest. I can't see the bandages underneath the blankets wrapped around him. I wish that I could. I shot him twice. In the chest. At close range. The bullets missed his heart by only millimeters. He should be dead. He should have died before he ever made it to the hospital. Every doctor and nurse said so. They wouldn't come right out and call it a miracle, but I think sometimes even they wonder if it was. I want to see the wound, to place my fingers on it and feel the puckering skin and stitches. I need to prove to myself that he's every bit as human as I am. But instead I'm trying to imagine the wounds, trying to see past the robe-like effect of the blankets that have him looking exactly like a prophet should.

"Pioneer!" A chorus of calls goes up from the reporters. I wish they wouldn't call him that too.

Pioneer looks directly at the cameras. He smiles softly, almost shyly. He folds his hands in his lap and nods as if giving them the okay to ask him questions. His hands are cuffed. I hadn't noticed at first. Pioneer fiddles with the metal around his wrists.

I watch as Cody's dad tries to hurry Pioneer's wheelchair forward. The wheel has caught on the sidewalk and they have to tilt the chair to maneuver it forward. I can tell by the set of the sheriff's jaw that he wants this transfer over with.

"Pioneer!" a woman in a long black coat yells from beside a line of cameramen and deputies. "Your deadline for the end of the world passed over a month ago. What happened?" There's laughter from the crowd now, mocking grins.

Pioneer's smile slips just a little. It's so slight a change that I'm not sure anyone else has noticed. He stares the woman down for a half second longer than is comfortable for her—or anyone else—before he speaks. "Precisely what should have happened."

This isn't the answer anyone was expecting, I think, because suddenly it's quiet.

"The end began. The betrayal of one of my own, the raid, the deaths that followed, all of this was part of the Brethren's plan." He chuckles a little as if he can't believe how stupid she is. "My family is about to face a time of great persecution. I'm about to be thrown in their jail. They've labeled all of us as crazy." He turns so that he's looking at my parents and the others. "So they can bury the truth with their lies. They're trying to take me from you. They think it will make you weak. They think you'll be easier to corrupt. The Brethren are letting it happen. They're waiting to see what you'll do. But I can see that you still believe. I've all but risen from the dead, haven't I? I'm a bona fide miracle."

The sheriff starts rolling him forward again, but Pioneer plants both feet on the ground, stopping the chair. "Family, keep your faith in me! Cling to the truth. Don't let them deceive you like they did our Little Owl."

The sheriff and two deputies get in Pioneer's face and yell at him to put his feet up. The Community presses closer to the deputies who are trying to keep a space between them and Pioneer. The deputies hold their ground, but barely. Most of the Community is crying and reaching for Pioneer. I see more than one of the deputies put their hands on their guns.

Cody puts his hand on my back. Around us people start jostling to the left, moving in toward Pioneer for a closer look. From somewhere behind me a woman protests loudly. "Hey! Stop pushing. Back up!"

"Don't listen to the lies they feed you about me, brothers and sisters! Stay strong in your beliefs. Lean on one another." Pioneer settles back into his chair as if he's the one who's decided that it's time to move forward.

I'm closer to him now, pressed up against the deputy in front of me, my chin resting just above his outstretched arm. I didn't mean to get this close, but the people behind me keep squishing me forward. Once again, the deputy yells at them to get back.

Without warning, Pioneer's face swivels in my direction. He stares straight at me and I forget to breathe. I can't move. The whole world disappears and it's just his face, those eyes staring directly into mine.

"Little Owl," he says.

Oh, please, no.

"Clear the path. Now!" the sheriff shouts, oblivious to what's happening between Pioneer and me. I bite my lip and try to wiggle away from the deputy's arm, try to find a way to blend back into the crowd before Pioneer can do anything.

"I see you, Lyla Hamilton! Did you think I wouldn't recognize you? I'd know you anywhere, child," Pioneer calls out, and I freeze. "I forgive you for what you did to me. Someday soon you will realize your error and I will take you back into the circle of my arms. You're mine, Little Owl. It's not too late to ask for my forgiveness. Your family won't give up on you. *I* won't give up on you. We love you and love never gives up." His chair is moving forward now, but he's turned slightly so he can keep looking at me.

The cameramen sweep their cameras across the crowd in an attempt to find me. The sheriff's managed to keep my name out of the papers until now. I look over at him. He's searching the crowd too, his face white with anger, his mouth pressed in a tight line.

This was a mistake. I need to leave. Right now.

Pioneer raises both arms in my direction and opens his bound hands, palms up. He curls his fingers, motioning me forward, his face radiant with the promise of forgiveness.

The people around me follow the path his arms suggest and their eyes land on me.

"Is that her? The girl who shot him?"

"That's not a guy."

"He said 'Little Owl.' That's what he called her, right?"

People are murmuring all around me.

I might not have been recognized after Pioneer called me out, but sometime between Pioneer mouthing my name and his speech I started whimpering.

"Lyla . . . ," someone calls from across the sidewalk. I don't look over at my family and friends, but I can feel them staring at me.

The sheriff gives one grim look in my direction before he pushes Pioneer forward and barrels toward the waiting cavalcade of vehicles ready to escort Pioneer to the jail. The crowd around me starts to press in closer. I lean into Cody to keep from falling and he grabs my elbow and tries to move me so that he's between me and most of the crowd. I can see some of the cameramen and reporters fighting at the edges, making their way over. The deputy in front of me tilts his head and listens to a voice coming from the black thing attached to his shoulder. He grabs my hand. "This way. Quick!"

He pulls me out onto the sidewalk where Pioneer just was. We head for the hospital at a run. Cody follows. From behind me I can hear my name being called, shouted from every direction like an accusation.

Believe in me and live.
Those who don't are surely lost and doomed to death.
—Pioneer

THREE

Once we're safely inside the hospital, Cody wraps me in his arms. I bury my face in his chest. It's only when several people walk by with raised eyebrows and one of them gives us the thumbs-up sign that I remember that I still look like a guy. I take a step away from Cody and pull off my beard. Cody's face goes red all over as he helps me.

"What were you thinking?" the deputy who brought us in asks Cody. He's breathing hard.

"Take it easy, Chad," Cody says, but he looks rattled too.

"Yeah, well, your dad's gonna hit the roof over this one." Chad shakes his head. He puts his hands on his hips and walks to the doors to look out at the crowd. The vehicle that took Pioneer to jail is gone. It must have left as soon as we ran inside. But it seems as if the crowd outside hasn't thinned at all. It's like they're waiting for something. Then it hits me. They're waiting to see if I'll come back out. I can't see Will or my parents, but I feel like they're looking for me, studying the building.

The doors open again to let in another deputy. The sound of people singing follows him in. The tune is child-like and campfire-sing-along cheery, but it makes me shiver. We all fall silent at the same time and listen.

Come back to the fold. Come back to the fold.
There's not much time before your body goes cold.
The end is here, and he wants his sheep home.
There's no safe place for you to roam.
Come back to the fold. Come back to the fold.
There's not much time before your body goes cold.

I don't recognize the song, but I know they're singing it for me. *Those words.* They seem to mean that I'm now doomed like Cody and the others because I'm out of the Community, but part of me wonders if they also mean something more, something even darker. The deputies look at each other and then over at me.

The doors finally shut, but not before I hear the song starting over. My whole body starts to shake. I hurry away from the doors and lean against the far wall, slide down it until I'm huddled on the floor. My head is swimming. Pioneer's words—*"You're mine, Little Owl"*—mix with the lyrics of the song—*"before your body goes cold"*—until they're all I can think about. I was just starting to feel okay. Being at Cody's house, away from my parents and Pioneer and everyone else, had fooled me into thinking that I was stronger, that I might finally be figuring things out. Now the only thing I'm sure about is that Pioneer and the Community aren't done with me yet.

Cody sits down next to me. "You all right?"

"Barely," I mumble. I put my head on my knees and wrap my arms around my shins. I tap my feet against the linoleum and try to concentrate on the muffled thumping noise my shoes make as they strike the floor. "I thought seeing him . . . I . . . oh, what does it matter what I thought? This was stupid. It would have been smarter not to see him ever again. At all."

"No, it would have been smarter to see him through binoculars from the other side of the parking lot while wearing earplugs." Cody exhales. "I shouldn't have brought you. . . . My bad entirely." Cody picks at a piece of his own beard and balls it up between his fingers.

"All right, Steve's gonna take you home." Chad crouches down beside me. "He's parked over in the emergency lot. There are a couple of us in the halls between here and there so it's clear. We'll get you out of here safe, Lyla." He gives me a sympathetic look. It makes me want to cry.

"What about my car?" Cody asks.

Chad laughs loudly enough to make me jump. "Your dad said you won't need it for a while."

We're going to be punished. My stomach does a somersault.

"I'm so sorry. I shouldn't have asked you to do this," I say.

Cody stands up and offers me his hand. "I offered, remember?" He smiles, but there's a trace of agitation in his face. I can't tell if it's anger or fear. What will his dad do to us when we get home? I know what my parents and Pioneer would do . . . or at least a close approximation.

I put one hand to my neck, feel the uneven scar beneath my hair. "I'll tell your dad it was my idea."

Cody chuckles. "Yeah, he'll never buy that. He knows me too well."

Together we walk the hospital corridors. Every time a door opens or I hear someone's shoes clicking on the linoleum behind us, I jump. After all that just happened, I keep expecting Pioneer to pop up somehow, to find me. It's crazy and yet I can't shake the feeling that he can still see me. By the time we reach the last set of doors, my palms are clammy and my heart's pounding in my chest.

"Don't you two look . . . handsome." An older man in uniform with a seriously large belly greets us as we walk back out into the cold. The parking lot here is full of cars, but there aren't any people anywhere. I guess they're all inside the emergency waiting room caught up in their own crises. It's hard to believe that anything other than Pioneer's transport happened this morning. It feels like everyone's life should have stopped for it—maybe because mine did.

"Shut up, Steve." Cody helps me into the back of the squad car, then looks at Steve. I can see his mouth curl into a smile. "Uh, you got some chocolate on your pants there, dude."

Steve's face turns red. He looks down at the front of his pants: there's a brown smudge just to the left of the pocket. I catch a glimpse of a brown and green wrapper sticking out of the pocket before he crumples it with his hand.

"Milky Ways before seven a.m.? Can't be good for your diet," Cody says as he ducks into the car beside me.

Steve slams the door without a word and walks around the car. I can hear him muttering to himself as he makes his way to the driver's-side door. Halfway around the car he trips over something and almost falls. A string of words I've never been allowed to utter come pouring out of his mouth. Cody looks at me and we both start laughing. The fact that I can laugh after all that's happened this morning surprises me, makes me laugh even harder. We try to stop when Steve opens the door, but it's almost impossible. Steve starts up the car without turning around, without even acknowledging that we're behind him, and takes off so quick he barks the tires against the blacktop, which sets us off all over again.

I sober up faster than Cody. The closer we get to his house, the more that the prospect of our punishment and what it might be looms over my head. My hands twist in my lap. I look over at Cody, fully expecting him to look worried too, but he doesn't. He has his arm draped over the back of the seat and his eyes are closed.

He's sleeping?

How can he sleep when he knows his dad is mad at him? I can't wrap my head around it. Disobeying to this degree back in Mandrodage Meadows would have meant a major punishment—the kind that leaves a permanent scar. I put a hand on the rippled skin at the back of my neck again. I would know.

When the car slows and pulls into Cody's driveway, I have to nudge him awake. He rubs his eyes and grins at me. It makes me want to shake him. *How can he treat this so lightly?*

Steve heaves himself out of the car and yanks Cody's door open. As we get out, Cody says to him, "Seriously, lay off the chocolate. You know Meg would freak out on you if she knew." He pats Steve's chest, right over his heart. "Okay, big man?" Steve glares at him, but his mouth keeps twitching like he wants to smile in spite of himself.

"Yeah? Well, you need to quit the white knight stuff," Steve says as we walk past. "Not exactly keeping you out of trouble, is it?" He gives me a pointed look and I feel my face go hot.

I head for the front door, but hesitate once I'm there. I'm never sure if I should just go in or knock.

"Open it," Cody says from behind me. I pull open the storm door, which is always unlocked.

"Hey, your hand's shaking." Cody moves so that the storm door is resting on his back and we're both huddled together. "Are you scared?"

"You're . . . we're in trouble. Your parents . . ." I swallow and try to think of exactly how to ask him what his parents' idea of punishment is. I haven't told him or the sheriff about what our punishments were like back home. I'm not sure if I should. I know that if I do, the sheriff could take Will and the others away from the Community again. The Outsiders would see our punishments as brutal. It isn't that I don't agree, it's just that I know that separating my friends from their families will feel even more brutal to them. "Um, how mad do you think they are on a scale of one to ten?" I finally ask.

Cody's eyes widen and then he gives me the one look I absolutely hate. The one that says he's feeling sorry for me. I turn away so I don't have to see it.

"My parents will be mad, but they won't hurt you. At the worst, Dad will yell a bit and Mom will be 'disappointed.' I'll probably end up with an extra chore and no car for a bit. But you? You'll be fine. They won't punish you at all. Really."

I'm relieved, but I don't feel better, which makes no sense. I'm afraid to get punished, then disappointed because I'm not treated just like Cody? What is that? I guess maybe the special treatment emphasizes my "special project" status. I'm not family. I don't belong, not completely.

Cody takes his key out to unlock the door and smiles at me one last time before he lets us in. We practically run right into his mom. She has the phone up to her ear. Her face is still sleep swollen and her hair is sticking up on one side. She looks at Cody and then at me and shakes her head. "Get in here."

Cody and I head for the kitchen. We sit at the table and wait for his mom to follow us. She's on the phone for a minute or two more before she comes in, leans against the counter, and massages her temples. "Do you two have the slightest understanding of how stupid it was to go over there this morning?" She looks at me, and in spite of her irritation, her eyes warm a little.

Cody grabs a banana from the bowl of fruit at the center of the table. He turns it over in his hands, but doesn't peel it. "I know, we're sorry."

"All that media and Libby Dickerson with her parent group protesting. Not to mention Lyla's people. You're lucky that a riot didn't erupt! You could've been hurt. Your dad had enough to worry about out there. This wasn't the day for a stunt like this." She's talking mainly to Cody.

Cody sighs and finally peels his banana. He shoves half of it in his mouth in one bite. I watch him chew. I don't think he knows what to tell her.

"I'm sorry. It was my idea. I just . . . needed to see for myself. . . ." I trail off. She'll never understand. Pioneer isn't even Pioneer to them. He's Alan Cross, just some man with a criminal record, not a messiah.

"Believe it or not, I do get it, Lyla." Cody's mom comes over to sit with us, puts her hand on my arm. "But today wouldn't have brought you closure in the best of circumstances. It's going to take time. You have to be patient. One day, honey, you'll get it. You're such a strong girl. You'll make it through this, I don't doubt that at all." Her smile is so warm, so . . . motherly. It makes my heart hurt. My own mom wouldn't have reacted like this. Ever.

I want to cry, but I clench my teeth and hold it back. If I start, she'll be over here hugging me and smoothing my hair and that'll just make me feel worse. My family will never be anything like Cody's. While I'm happy that for the past couple of months I've been able to pretend to be a part of their family, I'm not. At some point I'll be returned to my own parents. I can't afford to get used to being treated this way.

"Okay, look, Lyla's had a trying morning, so I'm not going to belabor the point"—she stops to give us each a pointed look—"*this* time. But I won't have you two sneaking out of the house again, understand? If I feel like I can't trust you, I'll have to rethink this arrangement." She doesn't come right out and say that she means my living here, but she may as well have. I get it.

"So, that's it?" Cody looks at her hopefully.

She laughs out loud. "Uh, no. Your dad's going to assign you some shifts at the station *and* I'm drafting you both into working the Winter Festival. I still need a few attendants at the ice-skating rink."

Cody's mom is in charge of this big charity festival that the town puts on to raise money for the fire and sheriff stations. She's been busy with it ever since I started living here. Cody's been sidestepping her pointed hints that we help out. He wouldn't even let me volunteer. I can tell it pleases her that he has to help out now. I just don't see how this is really a punishment. *I've* been dying to go to the festival ever since I heard about it. It sounds like something out of a movie. I keep envisioning giant stuffed-animal prizes and carnival games. Once or twice I even fantasized that Cody and I were riding a Ferris wheel and got stuck at the top like Fern and Henry in *Charlotte's Web*—until I remembered that it was almost Christmas and way too cold for that sort of thing.

Cody groans loudly. "You can't be serious." He looks at me. "We'll spend the entire day stuffing nasty kid feet into skates."

I burst out laughing. I can't help it. Cody is totally grossed out by feet. The boy can mix up a vat of fake vomit, but he can't stomach bare toes. He's not supposed to know that I know this. His sister told me the first night that I stayed with him. Cody looks at me, then raises his face toward the ceiling and yells, "Taylor! You suck."

"Good morning to you too, little brother. Cranky much?" she yells down the stairs. I hear a door close upstairs and then the sound of running water. Taylor's a "never let them see you looking less than your best" kind of girl. She won't come down until she's completely ready for the day.

"You're getting off easy, son. Waking up to find you gone isn't something I want to go through again, understand? I've got too many gray hairs already," Cody's mom says as she gets up. She smacks his back lightly as she moves away from the table. "Now get Lyla some breakfast. I think there's some leftover egg casserole in the fridge . . . if Cody's father hasn't eaten it all." She heads down the hallway and toward the stairs.

Cody smiles at me. "See? Nothing to be scared of."

Maybe not here, but when I think about what happened this morning I can't help feeling like maybe this is the only place where that's true.

All the Outsiders can offer is persecution and disappointment. Who in their right mind would want that?

—Julie Sturdges, member of the Community

FOUR

I'm trading one disguise for another today. Yesterday it was a beard, now it's a pound of makeup and a calculatedly casual hairstyle. If I start both days in basically the same way, what are the odds that they'll turn out equally awful?

I glance at the clock on the dresser. It's six forty-five. School starts in less than an hour. My first day. Ugh. *Why did I ever think I would be able to do this?* I shake my head and try to calm down.

"I can be normal. Blend in," I tell myself. "I'll just fake it until it happens."

I run my hands down the sides of my jeans to try to get rid of the moisture on my palms.

"Stop fidgeting, Lyla!" Taylor says. It comes out sounding more like "Op idgeting, I-ya," because she has a dozen bobby pins pressed between her lips.

She grabs a thin section of my hair and begins to braid it. I watch her in the dresser's mirror before studying the work she's already completed on my face. I don't look like me. My lips are all glossy pink and my eyes have these expertly smudged lines of dark brown around them. It's like staring at a stranger, someone straight out of my best friend, Marie's, contraband magazine collection.

Marie.

Thinking about my best friend sends my stomach churning. She should be the one getting this makeover, especially since she would have appreciated it so much more. She should be going to school today too. She should still be alive. For a moment the thought of it, of her never getting the chance to have this day, overwhelms me and I can't breathe.

"Okay, I'd say you're ready. And looking rather hot, if I do say so myself." Taylor takes a step back to admire her work, and a slow grin spreads across her face.

I stare at my reflection and tug at the snug sweater she harassed me into wearing. *Am I ready?* I've never had a first day at school, at least not one I can remember. Pioneer taught us all of our subjects in the clubhouse. The high school will be huge in comparison to our tiny room there. *Can I navigate a maze of hallways and kids I've never met before?*

"School starts in half an hour!" Cody's mom calls up the stairs, her voice full of forced brightness. I can almost picture her standing at the base of the stairs, wringing her hands together the way she does every morning. She's big on being on time. It must be killing her that no one is downstairs yet, but she won't fuss—probably because she's already guessed how nervous I am.

Taylor groans and heads downstairs. I hurry over to my bed and grab the worn leather shoulder bag that used to be my dad's back when he worked as a structural engineer in New York, before my sister went missing and we moved out here with Pioneer. I'm using it as a book bag. He gave it to me at our last counseling session. It's the first present he's given me on his own . . . ever. He'd left a little note inside. *"Be strong. Don't lose yourself."* Even now I'm not sure what he meant, especially after seeing him at Pioneer's transfer. I want it to mean that I'm supposed to stay strong against Pioneer, but it's more likely that it means stay strong against all the Outsiders.

There's a small click from the hallway and then a brief flash of light. Cody's standing in the bedroom doorway with his cell phone in front of his face. His grin is so wide that the phone almost seems to rest on it.

"You look . . . wow." He pulls me into his arms. I remind myself to stay loose, not to stiffen. *He's allowed to hug me. I want him to. Pioneer isn't watching.*

"Where are you on the nervous scale?" he asks against my hair. I close my eyes and lean into his chest so that I can hear his heart and feel the warmth radiating off him.

"Um, about a ten point five."

"Thought you might be." He frowns for a second, but then his face brightens. "Would it help if you wore this?"

Cody steps back and points to the T-shirt he's

wearing—the one he had on when we met. It reminds me of him more than anything else.

"You'd let me wear it?"

"I wouldn't offer it up unless I wanted you to," he says.

I nod and he ducks out of it, then hands it to me. His chest is lean and tight, defined in every place it should be, and there's a small constellation of freckles on his left shoulder. Every time I see it, I have to fight the urge to trace it with my fingers. I'm pretty sure that if I did, I'd figure out that they make a perfect Little Dipper. He's watching me stare at him and I blush, but I don't turn away. He grins and hands me the shirt.

"Thanks." I take the shirt and wait, but he doesn't turn to leave. After a slightly awkward beat of silence, his lips twitch a little and he raises his eyebrows at me.

"Well? Aren't you gonna put it on?" He leans against his sister's dresser and crosses his arms over his chest like he's going to stick around and watch.

"Whatever, there's no way!" I laugh and push him out the door. My face is flushed all the way to my ears; I can feel them starting to burn.

"You're cute even when you're lobster colored," Cody says. He leans over and kisses my forehead, then turns to go.

I pull off my uncomfortably tight sweater and slip Cody's shirt over my head. A mixture of fresh-scented deodorant and the glue he uses when he works on his movie special-effects stuff surrounds me. I breathe it in and my body starts to relax. Now that I don't have a real home of my own to speak of, this scent and Cody himself are the closest things I have to one.

"Lyla!" Cody's mom calls.

"Almost ready," I call as I put my book bag over my shoulder. But even if I'm not, it's time.

Fifteen minutes later we're turning down the long road that leads to Culver Creek High School. I can see a large crowd of people, cars, and news vans—almost as big as the one at the hospital yesterday morning. Cameramen huddle close to the fence that surrounds the school, their cameras pointed out toward the road, at us. It looks like Cody wasn't the only one who wanted to capture images of my first day of school.

Taylor slows the car, but she can't exactly stop or turn around. There's a long row of cars behind us. She pulls down her visor and checks her face in the tiny mirror. "Looks like we're about to be on TV, you guys."

"Crap," Cody grumbles from behind me. His hand comes up and taps my shoulder. "Hey . . . duck down, okay?"

Immediately I stuff myself into the footwell. Not exactly how I pictured myself arriving on the first day. I pull my head close to the cloth seat and cover my eyes. I can't see now, but I can still hear the people outside. I don't move until the car pulls into the lot, beyond the chain-link fence that surrounds the school grounds.

I lift my head and peek out the window. The sheriff and several deputies are by the fence, near the open entrance, making sure that the media stay outside. They must be so tired of managing all of this. Taylor slows and rolls down her window and Cody's dad comes over, leans down, and peers in at us.

Cody says, "What's up with all of this?" He jerks his head toward the swarm of media pressed against the fence.

"They found out that the cult kids—sorry, Lyla, the *Meadows* kids—are starting today." The sheriff hesitates. "And with Pioneer's transfer and his first court date coming up, they're all caught up in the story again. Just park as close to the building as possible and do your best to ignore 'em. They'll hang around a day or so and then move on if they don't get what they want. Cody—I'm having your car brought around for later. Can't have you and Lyla stranded with this circus goin' on, and Taylor's gotta work after school." He leans closer to the car and points at Cody. "But you're still grounded. Head straight to the station for phone duty after dropping Lyla off this afternoon, understand?"

Cody nods with mock gravity and for a second I almost feel like laughing. He loves his car. The sheriff just made his whole day—well, almost. If he didn't have to go to the station to work after school, *then* it would have been made.

I can hear the reporters calling to us from behind the fence. The sheriff lingering at our car has made them curious about us.

"Sheriff, who's in the car?"

"Is she in there?"

"Lyla!"

"Hey, Little Owl!" When someone shouts this, a ripple of laughter spreads through the crowd. I hate reporters.

"Roll up the window and get inside," the sheriff says, purposely putting his back to the row of cameramen so that they can't get a good angle on the car or us. The reporter's questions are muffled once Taylor rolls the window back up. I get up off of the car's floor and sit low in the seat. There are groups of students gathering on the school's side of the fence now, posing for the cameras. I can't imagine why they'd want the attention. A few of the kids have noticed me and are pointing at the car; behind them the chain-link fencing bows a little as several reporters lean even harder against it, straining to see.

Taylor drives forward slowly. Students pass along either side of the car; some tap the hood and laugh, and others lean down and stare in at us. Taylor waves. She seems to be enjoying all of the attention. I just want it all to go away. I'm a sideshow and the day hasn't even really started. Is it too late to turn around?

A van is working its way up the road to the school. It's white and has long scuff marks along its sides. It rolls to a stop before it reaches the entrance when a group of people fan out across the road holding signs. I can't see what the signs say, but I don't have to. The people are yelling loud enough to be heard inside the car, even with all the windows rolled up. "No cults in our schools!"

I watch as several deputies force them off the road. One man struggles to stay and ends up in handcuffs. The shouting gets louder for a moment, but then the deputies manage to subdue the crowd and motion the van through the school's gates. I stare at it as it slowly passes us. I have enough time to get a good look at the driver. It's the same guy who was standing with Brian at the hospital. I recognize his dark black hair, trimmed tight to his scalp so that it looks like someone's peppered his head. There are lots more people behind him, their faces pressed against the glass. It's Will, Brian, and the others. They stare at me. Julie waves. Before I think better of it, I wave back. It's hard to see her as anything other than a friend . . . but the way she talked to that reporter the other morning . . . I'm not sure that I know this new version of her. Maybe that's fair. She doesn't know this new version of me either.

Suddenly there's a roar of noise from behind me. The news people have pushed the fence too hard and it's leaning forward. They're all shouting and jockeying for a better vantage point. They know that the van has the Community kids in it.

"Get back!" I hear shouts from several deputies. They rush the fence with their hands on their guns. A string of police cars stream down the road, sirens blaring.

"They called in the state police," Cody says. He shakes his head. "What a mess."

I follow the van with my eyes as it parks by the school buses. In some ways I almost wish I was in it. I still miss

Will and Julie and the others. They were my closest friends. Cody and his family have been really nice and understanding, but they can't really know what this day is like for me, for all of us. They can never understand the deep pit of mistrust we have to try to bridge just to walk in the school doors.

I turn around again. A deputy pulls the school's gate closed. I guess they'll have to keep opening and closing it all morning until all of the other students arrive. *Weird how we left one gated compound only to enter another one.* Why does the school even need a fence and gate like this? Who are they trying to keep out?

"Later. Good luck today, Lyla," Taylor says as she gathers up her things and rushes across the lot. She's got a thin cropped leather jacket on—her favorite. She refuses to wear anything warmer even if it is freezing, and so she just runs from the car every time we go out somewhere. I watch her weave through cars, her high-heeled boots clicking across the blacktop.

Cody hands me my bag and then grabs my hand and together we walk toward the large set of glass doors that lead into the school. The building reminds me a lot of the hospital, all glass and concrete. There's nothing warm or inviting about it, not like our clubhouse back home with its knotty-pine walls and large front porch lined with planters full of bright-colored flowers. Dozens of other students stream past us to the entrance. Some of them wave to Cody. All of them stare at me, not bothering to be discreet about it. At first I try smiling at them, but this seems to make them stare even more, so I concentrate on the school building again.

We have to walk past all of the school buses and then the van to get inside. I see Will looking out of one of the windows. I raise my hand to wave, hoping even after yesterday that things are still okay between us. He looks at me and his mouth turns up at the corners. I beam up at him. *I have Cody and Will to lean on today. I can do this.* But then Will's eyes drift over to where Cody's standing beside me . . . and then to Cody's hand, which is still covering mine. His smile falters. It's like watching a flower dry up and curl in on itself. I try not to fidget my hand out from under Cody's. It's too late now anyway. Maybe Will really has forgiven me for what happened with Pioneer, but that doesn't mean that he'll ever be okay about Cody. I was his Intended. He was convinced that we should get married—and I guess maybe for a time I was too, but that was before I met Cody. Now I know that we will never be anything more than just friends. I only hope that someday soon it'll be enough for him.

Will and the rest of the kids file out of the van and gather by a man in a pair of khakis that are a bit too snug around the middle and too short at the ankles. His shirt is straining at the buttons. Everything on him is too small, even the hair on his head. He's deep in discussion with a small group of women. Whatever the conversation's about, it doesn't look like a good one. He looks agitated.

I study the women. They look familiar. Especially the one talking. The white scarf and brown coat—it's that Dickerson lady. *Oh no.*

"It isn't safe to have our children around them." She folds her arms across her chest and taps one foot against the concrete. "They're brainwashed, for God's sake! They could be programmed to attack everyone. Mark my words, having them anywhere near this school—or this town for that matter—is inviting trouble."

The ladies standing with her nod their agreement.

"We'll pull our kids out, Ned. I can't leave my child here knowing that at any moment those *people* might decide to take the end of the world into their own hands." Her voice is stronger now that the others are nodding violently.

"Ladies, please, try to calm down. I've consulted their counselors and done a good bit of research. They're not a threat. We've spent the last two months making sure. They've been cleared to attend by the school board. Their leader was the dangerous one and he's behind bars. But just to put everyone at ease, I've talked to the sheriff and he's agreed to leave some deputies with us today and for as long as it takes until the Meadows kids get settled in. Your children will be perfectly safe."

Mrs. Dickerson makes a disgusted sound in her throat. "We aren't the only parents who don't want this." She gestures toward the people out past the fence holding signs. "At the next board meeting we'll be bringing it up again and at the one after that and the one after that. We won't just lie back and let this happen. You're in for a battle, Ned. We don't want them here. And if you know what's good for your career, you shouldn't either."

The man's eyebrows knit together, but he doesn't back down. "I'm sorry that you feel that way, ladies. Now you'll have to excuse me. The bell's about to ring." The man walks away from them. His lips are pressed so tightly together they've turned white.

The women's heads swivel in our direction. I don't like the way they frown at me. There is so much hate in their faces. It makes me want to hide behind Cody. Out of nowhere lyrics from that song play through my head.

Come back to the fold . . . before your body goes cold . . .
There's no safe place for you to roam . . .

Is this what they meant? Are these ladies and the people down by the fence going to come after me? After all of us?

I watch as the women shake their heads in disgust and turn away. I press my bag close to my chest and squeeze Cody's hand a little tighter.

"Principal Geddy." Cody nods in the man's direction. "Slightly clueless for the most part, but he means well. And that woman—Mrs. Dickerson—is the head of the PTA. The others are her assorted minions." Cody rolls his eyes. "She's always upset about something. A few months ago it was the snacks in the school's vending machines.

She'll find something other than you guys to rail against in a few weeks, trust me." I nod, but somehow I don't think even he believes this.

A crowd of students is starting to gather. I watch as Will and the rest of the Meadows kids huddle together, their eyes trained on the ground. They seem to be trying to ignore the growing crowd, but there's no way that they can. There are just too many of them. Brian's hands are clenched at his side—as are Will's. Heather and Julie have their arms linked. I start to move forward to say something—hi, maybe? Brian looks up when I try, and his face is so full of anger that it stops me cold. Julie sees his glare and her smile falters a little—her face turning from his to mine—before she forces it back into place.

"Lyla. We missed you on the bus," she says brightly.

I don't like the way she looks. Her eyes are so vacant. It's eerie.

Principal Geddy clears his throat loudly. He runs a hand over his rounded belly and adjusts his tie. "Okay, if I can have your attention, everyone. I'm Principal Geddy and I'd like to welcome you to Culver Creek High. Now, I realize that all of this will seem a little overwhelming at first, but we will do our best to make it as easy a transition for you as possible. So. Shall we get started?"

He looks over each of us and smiles warmly. It reminds me a little of how Pioneer used to look at us sometimes. It makes me want to back away from him.

"If you'll follow me, I'll take you inside to our media

center. Too cold to be out here much longer." He smiles so wide that his teeth show. He isn't wearing a coat like the rest of us, just a wool blazer. He tries to pull it closed around his middle, but it doesn't quite reach.

No one moves. The students and parents surrounding us are quiet. Gaping. Principal Geddy's smile slips a little and he clears his throat again. He looks around until his gaze settles on me.

"Lyla Hamilton? That's your name, isn't it?"

"Yes, sir," I say. I fight the urge to duck behind Cody.

"It's good to have you with us. Doing what you did, standing up to your . . . Pioneer?"

I cringe.

"Shows you have real leadership potential. I'd like to see you develop that while you're here. Maybe help the others to acclimate," Principal Geddy says. His head gives a little involuntary nod in the direction of the rest of the Community kids.

I almost laugh out loud. *Me,* help *them* acclimate? I'm not even sure how I'm going to acclimate myself.

Principal Geddy doesn't seem to notice my reluctance. He's too busy rushing for the door and the promise of warmth. He holds the door open for all of us, clapping several kids on the back as they pass by. Each one of them jumps and scurries away. Without their parents and Pioneer, they look so lost.

As soon as we're all inside, Principal Geddy pulls the door shut and turns to Cody. "Okay, son, bell's about to ring. You can make your way to your classes now. She'll be fine." When Cody starts to object, he cuts him off. "Leave Lyla to me, I'll take good care of her. Now go on before Mrs. Abbott marks you tardy."

I don't want him to leave, but I don't want to get him into trouble either, so I just shrug and try to look unconcerned. "I'll see you later?"

Cody nods and turns to go but stops before he's taken two steps. "I'll come get you at the end of the day. Promise."

Principal Geddy puts a hand on my back and I flinch. Cody waves once and then slowly turns and disappears into a crowd of students all rushing to get to class before the bell rings. The rest of the Meadows kids turn and follow the principal and me toward yet another set of glass double doors at the end of the hallway. I can feel their eyes on my back. My skin feels itchy and my face gets hot. I don't want to turn and actually meet their eyes in case they're glaring at me like Brian—or worse, grinning blankly like Julie. Before I left this morning, I was mostly worried about being with the Outsider kids; now I'm more worried about being with the ones I've known my whole life.

Evil is easy to spot when you're looking for it.

—Heather Lewis, member of the Community

FIVE

The media center turns out to be a library with rows and rows of books. At its center are a dozen or so rectangular tables. This is where Principal Geddy has us settle. Now, *this* place reminds me in some ways of our lesson room at the clubhouse. Same dusty paper smell mixed with hints of carpet, cloth, and leather. I've always liked this smell. Even now it has the power to calm me, but somehow I don't think it's working for anyone else. Tension radiates off of them. The quiet is complete and almost alive.

"Please, everyone, find a seat," Principal Geddy says.

I don't know where to sit. I try to catch Heather's eye, but I don't like the way she looks at me. She's got the same vacant robotic smile pasted across her face as Julie. Both of them motion me over, but I look away. I can't sit with them when they look like that. I sway in place, not sure which table to go to or if I should just settle next to the bookshelves on the floor. Finally, Will sighs and shakes his head. He uses his foot to push out the empty chair beside him. Brian's sitting on his other side, and he shoots me an annoyed look before getting up to move to Heather and Julie's table. I almost walk away and sit by myself at the far end of the room despite Will's invitation—I don't want Brian to get mad at him too—but then Principal Geddy clears his throat and cuts his eyes toward the chair next to Will. He's smiling, but underneath it I can see that he's impatient for me to sit so he can get started. I slide into the chair. Will doesn't say anything. He doesn't look at me either. He's obviously still upset about Cody. I want to talk to him about it, but I have no idea what words might make things better.

We spend the next hour listening to Geddy drone on and on about the school. His gaze passes over us continually without stopping as he talks. We make him nervous, I think. I try to listen to him, but I can't help focusing on the rows of books instead. There are so many! More than I've ever seen in one place. And on the far wall are dozens of magazines, and beyond them, computers. So many things that were once off-limits are now less than three feet away from where I sit.

When Geddy finishes talking, a woman comes over to take his place. I hadn't really noticed her before this moment. There was just too much to take in.

"My name is Mrs. Ward. I'm one of the counselors here at Culver Creek."

Will rolls his eyes. "Like we really need another one of those. I think I'm gonna puke if one more person offers to dissect my feelings." He punctuates the last two words with air quotes and I laugh softly, but it's more from relief than from what he's just said. He's still talking to me, thank God. I need him. I don't want him to ignore me like the others are. I'm not sure I could stand it.

Mrs. Ward walks over to the table closest to her and sits on top of it. She puts her feet up on the chair in front of her and leans back on her hands. The pose makes her look younger. She's wearing a pair of combat boots and her hair is short and spiky. I'm not sure if I think it's cool or if she just looks weird. She smiles at us. It's a slow, easy smile. I decide that I like her, at least more than I like Principal Geddy.

"This day is a big step. And it isn't the first one you've had to take the last few months. Your world's grown bigger and that can be terrifying and unsettling, but you aren't alone. We're here for you. To listen. To offer support when you need it. I hope that after we get to know each other a little bit, you will feel comfortable approaching me. My goal is to help you have the smoothest transition possible into our school." She hesitates and looks at each of us. "You should feel safe here. You *are* safe here."

This last bit gives me a chill. It reminds me of something Pioneer would say and I look around to see if anyone else recognizes it. But the others aren't even looking in her direction. Their eyes—every last person's—are on their tables. Even their hands are in the same position, clasped together in their laps. It's like someone ordered them to assume the same posture. Even Will. *Maybe someone has.* I try to get Will's attention.

"What are you . . . ," I start to whisper, but Mrs. Ward looks over at me and I stop. Will's eyes cut over to mine for a moment before he refocuses on the table.

Mrs. Ward stops talking. Her lips press together as she notices that no one will look at her. The room goes deadly quiet, but still no one looks up. Her eyes meet mine and I shrug my shoulders.

Principal Geddy finally steps forward and clears his throat. "Okay . . . ," he begins, but before he can get another word out, a loud buzzing sound rips through the air and these small rectangular lights on the wall by the door start flashing. The noise is so loud, so frantic. It feels as if it's cutting right through my chest. It sounds a lot like the alarm siren at Mandrodage Meadows.

Too much like it.

For a few seconds no one moves, and then the room erupts into chaos. The kids start screaming and the adults begin yelling a whole lot of words, but no one can really make them out above all of the noise. Heather and Julie and most of the other girls have left their seats and are herded together in a tight circle. Their hands are up around their ears. Their mouths are wide open. Their screaming is almost as loud as the alarms. Brian and some of the other boys have rushed over to them, knocking their chairs over in the process.

"Please, everyone! Calm down!" Mrs. Ward yells through cupped hands, but no one pays any attention. She shares a look with Principal Geddy. He rushes from the room and out into the hall, his face bright red and his chest heaving.

Mrs. Ward's eyes land on me again. I'm the only one who isn't screaming or huddling. Still, my heart is slamming against my chest. I want to be able to move, but I can't. Suddenly Mrs. Ward is next to me with her arms on my shoulders, trying to get me to look at her.

"This is nothing to be scared of. It's just the fire alarm. I'm sure it went off by mistake." She pulls me along, grabbing the other girls as she goes. Then she moves all of us toward the library's door.

Principal Geddy runs back into the room, his face beaded with sweat. "The fire alarm has been tripped but there's no fire. Please, you have to calm down!" He flaps his arms at his sides a few times like a chubby, khaki-clad bird. A bubble of laughter finds its way to my mouth and then pops out of me, startling not only me, but Mrs. Ward as well. My heart's still hammering, but the laughter has loosened my limbs and brought me back to myself a little. Another false alarm. We aren't in any danger. But these people won't be able to convince the rest of the kids. I have to do it or pretty soon they'll all run screaming from the school. I shake free of Mrs. Ward's grip and climb on top of the nearest table before I can rethink it.

"Shut up, you guys, and listen!" I yell as loudly as I

can. The room gets quieter almost immediately. I take a deep breath and keep going before I lose my nerve. "It's a false alarm. A practice, you know, like we used to have." In that moment, I have the strangest feeling that I'm back in Mandrodage Meadows, just outside the Silo door all over again.

The alarm keeps a steady rhythm as I stare out at them and they stare up at me. Finally a few of the girls loosen their grip on one another. Their faces are ashen, but they're no longer panicking.

Principal Geddy takes over once he sees that I'm not going to say anything more. "We still have to evacuate the building just in case, but there is no fire. This is not an emergency. If you'll line up behind Mrs. Ward, we'll head outside to join the rest of the students and teachers. Once we've double-checked the school, you'll be able to come back in."

We file back out the double doors we entered just an hour ago and out into the cold. We left without our coats and almost immediately we start shivering and huddling together to stay warm. Principal Geddy leads us out to a wide field just beyond the parking lot where there's a crowd of other students milling around. Most stare as we round the corner of the building, all of us in one long row, walking so close to one another that we're having a hard time not tripping over each other's feet.

"It's the apocalypse. Take cover!" some boy wails dramatically, before he crouches behind the kid in front of him in mock panic. The students around him lapse into hysterics.

"Got room for us in your shelter?" someone else calls out. More laughter follows.

Will stiffens in front of me. I can see his hands ball up into fists.

My cheeks start to burn. I search the field for Cody, but I can't find him. There are so many students. Hundreds gathered into loose rows. I've never seen so many kids in one place.

Once we're halfway across the field, I spot Taylor. Her eyes meet mine, but just as I'm about to wave at her, she turns in the opposite direction. I'm sure that she saw me, but it looks as if she wants me to think she didn't. *She's embarrassed by me.* From then on I don't look up anymore. I'm scared that I'll see Cody next and that he'll do the same thing.

"Freaks!" someone yells out of nowhere. It's like they have to keep reminding us that we're not welcome in case somehow we forgot in between this comment and the last one.

"That's enough!" a man shivering in a sweatshirt with a whistle around his neck barks.

The crowd settles a little. There are only a series of murmurs behind cupped hands. But then there's a sound above us, a plane flying directly overhead. I tilt my face up to watch it; so do Will and a few of the others. It beats looking at the other students.

"That's a play-ane," a boy across from us says loudly and much too slow. He laughs and looks at the boys next to him. "Ha! They probably thought it was their aliens finally coming to pick them up."

He's talking about the Brethren, our creators and the ones who told Pioneer that the end was coming in the first place. I hate that these kids think that our belief in the Brethren makes us stupid somehow. It bothers me. A lot. And I'm not the only one. Brian breaks free of our group and heads straight for him. The boy and his friends laugh harder. Brian is primed for a fight, I can tell. If we were back home, I'm pretty sure he'd have his gun out.

"Knock it off!" Principal Geddy hollers. The man with the whistle steps between Brian and the other boy. He pulls the boy away, practically drags him up to where Principal Geddy's standing. The boy puts his hands in his pockets and looks out at the crowd. Winks. I see Will take a step forward beside me and I put my hand on his arm to keep him from charging too.

"Brent Dickerson. You've just earned yourself a detention this afternoon." Principal Geddy stares the boy down.

"You really want to do that right now, considering how ticked my mom is already?" Brent asks, smirking.

Principal Geddy looks like he's ready to strangle him. His jaw is clenched so hard that the cords on his neck are sticking out. There's one long moment of awkward silence. Brent lazily stretches his neck from side to side. I can hear it cracking.

"Mr. Stevenson, take Brent to the office as soon as the building's clear," Principal Geddy yells. His face is so red, I'm afraid he might explode.

Mr. Stevenson starts pulling Brent away. The boys from Brent's group stare at us. One in particular catches my eye. He's standing in the group's center and he's looking at Brian like he's daring him to lose it.

"How's your first day?" he asks Brian just loud enough for most of us to hear him, but not Principal Geddy or the other adults who are all standing in a clump by the sidewalk talking in low voices.

I feel an overwhelming fury. This guy pulled the alarm. I can't prove it, but that sneer on his face . . . I *feel* like this is the truth. I just know it. I want to punch his squared-off face and that stupid cocky grin of his. *How can he think it's funny to scare us like this?*

Pioneer's words start to echo in my head. *"The world is a wicked place, full of people who want nothing more than to cause you pain. Now I ask you folks, what good can it do to rub shoulders with them? No good, that's what. They'll get in your head and twist all that's right in you until you are just like they are. Better to stay far, far away. You have to protect yourselves."*

I start to shiver and I'm not sure if it's my rage or the cold and my lack of a coat that's causing it, but I can't make it stop. Will rests both of his hands on my shoulders. He's shivering too.

I want this day to be over. I fold my arms across my

chest as the bitter air stings my face and hands. I stare out at the crowd and then look beyond them, to the woods out past the fence, trying to distract myself by focusing on the trees. I won't lose control and cry. Not now. Not ever. I bite my lip hard, hoping that the pain will keep the tears pooling in my eyes from overflowing. *Keep it together, Lyla.*

While I struggle to stay calm, a movement in the woods catches my eye. A shadowy figure is moving between the trees, coming closer to the fence. Then there's another and another. I'm pretty sure that it's a herd of deer or something at first, but then they get closer and I can see that they aren't deer at all, they're people. Mr. Brown and several other men from the Community step out into the open space between the fence and the trees. They're staring in our direction. My direction. Reflexively, I back up. The men put their hands up to the fence and lace their fingers through it. Mr. Brown nods at me. They could be here to check on the others. I silently will them to be, anyway, but the way that my heart is racing and my instincts are singing makes me doubt it. I look at the teachers and other students to see if anyone else has noticed them, but most are too busy talking and stealing glances in our direction. I turn to Will, to see if he's seen, but he is head-to-head with Brian, trying to keep him from charging the boys across from us.

But behind Will and Brian, Heather and Julie are staring at me. Very deliberately they turn and look at Mr. Brown and the others and then back at me. The girls' grins widen and their eyes shine. They press their lips together and start to hum. The tune is unmistakable. It's the one they were all singing at the hospital. My head supplies the words even if they aren't actually being sung.

Come back to the fold. Come back to the fold.
There's not much time before your body goes cold.
The end is here, and he wants his sheep home.
There's no safe place for you to roam.
Come back to the fold. Come back to the fold.
There's not much time before your body goes cold.

I want to scream, to get the attention of Principal Geddy or one of the teachers, but I can't make myself do it with *them* watching me. So instead I hunch over and turn my back on the fence. Still, I can feel their stares boring into my back.

I woke up this morning thinking that somehow this day would be a new beginning, that I would have a chance to start a new life—to finally figure out what normal is and leave the Community and Pioneer behind me. And somehow I thought that Heather and the others would let me. I'd dared to believe that the people here would be like Cody and his family, that they would make an attempt at getting to know us. It looks like I couldn't have been more wrong.

A person can't change all at once.
—Stephen King, *The Stand*

SIX

It takes almost half an hour for my body to thaw once we're allowed back inside the school. Mrs. Ward is keeping us sequestered in the library. I'm not sure if that was her plan all along or if she decided to do it around the time we all filed back into the building, but either way, we are stuck here. I can hear the heat rumbling on and off, echoing down the vents. Even so, the room is cold.

I blow on my fingers as Mrs. Ward settles onto the floor in the far corner of the library and motions for us to join her. The others stare at her, their arms folded across their chests. She looks so disappointed that I soften and sit down a few feet to her right. Will exhales, glances at the others, then slowly comes to sit beside me. I smile as he leans back against the bookshelf behind us.

"Think she'll tackle me if I make a run for it?" he asks with his eyes closed.

"Hey, you're not allowed to leave me alone here," I say, and lightly squeeze his arm.

Will opens his eyes and looks at me, his face more

serious than I was expecting. "I'd never leave you alone anywhere."

This doesn't comfort me, especially after seeing Mr. Brown and the others at the fence.

"You guys don't have to sit with me if you don't want to, but we'll be in here for a while yet. . . ." Mrs. Ward tries one more time, smiling encouragingly at the others. I focus my attention on her and not Will. Honestly, I'm grateful for the interruption.

Heather and Julie look at each other and then reluctantly find a spot across from us. Brian and a few of the other boys remain standing. The rest of the kids shuffle over and sit down close to Heather and Julie, leaving a wide space between them and Mrs. Ward. She fiddles with one of her bootlaces, then tucks her legs up to her chest. I'm not sure if she's doing it on purpose, but her posture makes her look small, nonthreatening. It's hard to see her as evil—the way Pioneer wants us to see all Outsiders. Maybe that's what she wants.

"I'm sorry that we got off to such a rocky start this morning. I'd like to promise you that what happened out there won't happen again, but I can't. I wish I could tell you that everything that your Pioneer told you about people being cruel was wrong. But I can't do that either. The truth is that everyone has the potential to be good or bad."

"We aren't here to listen to you give us a lecture on people being good or bad. We've seen firsthand what Outsiders can do," Brian interrupts. His voice has such a hard edge to it. "There isn't anything that you can say to make us see you different. You're all evil. What happened out there just proves it."

Mrs. Ward gives him a look that's all pity and understanding, and I watch Brian bristle under it. She doesn't reach out to him, but I can tell that she wants to. Instead she rearranges herself until she's sitting cross-legged. "I'm not trying to take your beliefs away from you. Really. All I'm asking is that you consider *why* you believe them." Her eyes rest on me. "Questions aren't bad, in fact they're necessary when you're trying to figure out just exactly what you stand for."

Brian shakes his head and Heather and Julie grab each other's hands and hold tight. I watch as the hand-holding catches on. In less than a minute everyone is holding hands, one long chain of defiance. Will offers his hand to me and I don't know what to do. Mrs. Ward is watching me intensely. I feel like whatever I choose to do means something—means too much. The thing is, I think I agree with Mrs. Ward, but I've isolated myself from the Community so much already. Does it make sense to do it now, especially after what happened outside?

I reach out and take Will's hand. Mrs. Ward sighs and then opens her mouth to say something more, but doesn't get the chance because the library door opens up and an older lady rushes in with a clipboard.

"Lunch," she says. She's a sturdy lady with rough hands and a ruddy face. Her hair is pulled up under a hairnet.

"Principal Geddy said it would be better if the kids ate in here." She eyeballs us. "But just this once. I can't be expected to pull together a special lunch for this lot every day and still get the rest of the school fed." The irritation and outright revulsion in her voice as she talks about us startles me even after everything that's happened. She gives Mrs. Ward a stern look. "I won't be responsible for any mess that's made. I'll send one of our ladies back in half an hour to collect what's left."

"Thank you, Marianne, we'll do our best to be tidy." Mrs. Ward smiles patiently at her. Even though she's got a nice smile and a kind face, it doesn't soften Marianne any. I wonder if it's starting to bug Mrs. Ward that no one's responding the way she wants them to.

A cart is rolled in by another cranky-looking lady in a hairnet. It's piled high with plastic-wrapped sandwiches, bottled water, and apples. Mrs. Ward asks Julie and Will to pass it all out, and soon we're settled back down on the floor, our backs leaning up against the bookshelves, our meals in our laps. I'm not sure why we don't sit at the tables. Mrs. Ward just seems to prefer the floor, I guess. She stretches out her legs across the aisle until her boots are resting close to my sneakers. She's watching me and chewing her sandwich slowly. She blushes when she realizes that I've caught her studying me. Every move I make is being dissected now, not just by her, but by everyone, even me. It ruins my appetite, so I put my food aside, stand up, and start walking along the rows of books.

I land in a row that seems to be all fiction. We only had a few shelves of books in the clubhouse, and I'd read all of those enough times that I'd memorized entire chapters. I put a finger on one of the spines and slowly pull it out. It's slightly tacky along the front and back cover, like it's been handled often. Still, I flip it open and start looking at the first page or two. It's by someone named Stephen King. There's a picture of him on the back. He looks like Mr. Brown from the Community. The resemblance is almost eerie.

"Do you like to read?" Mrs. Ward is beside me.

"Yeah," I say quietly. I flip the pages idly, forcing myself to be casual about it.

"Well, why not take that one home today?" Mrs. Ward smiles at me, takes the book before I can decide either way, and walks it up to the front of the library and around the back of the long table there. She hands it to the lady sitting behind it.

"Mrs. Connors, are the kids in the system yet? Lyla would like to check out this book."

I want to disagree. It was one thing to consider it on the shelf, but now I can feel the other kids staring at my back and the prospect of reading isn't as appealing as before.

Mrs. Connors shakes her head. "By tomorrow they will be." She stares at her computer and types something. "She can check it out under my name for now."

She types some more and then hands the book back to me. She gives me the dreaded pity look that I hate. "Take as long as you like. Since it's in my name, it won't have to come back in the usual two weeks. But see that you take good care of it. No reading in the bathtub."

I take the book and hug it tightly to my chest. My face is on fire. "Um, thanks. I promise I'll be careful."

Her face brightens. "I hope you enjoy it."

Mrs. Ward grins at both of us. I guess I've just given her her first breakthrough of the day. Behind me someone coughs and I hug the book even tighter. I have the strong urge to rush to my book bag and stuff the book inside it, but I stop myself. I don't belong to the Community anymore and yet I can't help feeling like I'm forcing myself to balance on a very thin beam all the time, trying not to lean too far in either direction: Mrs. Ward's or theirs.

I turn to go back to my spot on the floor. I tilt the book out in front of me so that I can see the title. *The Stand*. I don't know what it means, but I'm suddenly dying to find out. It feels like this book could hold secrets about what I've been missing, about what Pioneer's been keeping from us. It makes no sense, but I feel it anyway. I want to go through every row, stack book after book on this first one, and then sit down and read them all. There's so much to discover. And this is only one tiny corner of such a large world.

Principal Geddy comes back to the media center just as we're tossing the remains of our lunches into large trash cans. His eyes dart around the floor and after a minute he stoops down and picks up a smallish crumb, sighs. A few kids are still huddled against the bookshelves, their uneaten sandwiches beside them. Principal Geddy's face tightens and his mouth opens and closes, but ultimately he doesn't say anything. Maybe he's afraid to, afraid to have any of us react to his reprimand the way we did to the fire alarm. It makes for a weird sort of tension between him and us. It makes me wish someone would fake a hysterical fit just to get it out of the way, to stop him from wondering when it might happen and what he should do when it does.

Mrs. Ward passes out a series of tests. We're supposed to answer all of the questions on them to the best of our ability. They want to see what we already know so that they can put us in the right classes. I read over the questions. The English part is easy. I'm smiling by the time I finish it, but the history bits are . . . confusing. I recognize the dates of some of the historical stuff, but the possible answers we're supposed to choose from don't make sense. All of them are just wrong. And the math is like looking at another language entirely. After struggling through a few questions, I just randomly pick answers and hope for the best. Pioneer always chose what we studied. Some of us concentrated on the arts, others on math and science. By the looks of things, his lessons were very different than what the Outsiders were learning. I wonder if anyone else is realizing the same thing. I glance up at the others, but they're intent on their papers. Will is tapping his pencil on the side of his head like maybe somehow he can hammer the correct answers into it. I see very few pencils actually touch paper.

By the time we complete all of the tests—or at least pretend to—the school day is over and my head is pounding. As soon as the last bell for the day chimes, the hallway outside the library fills with students. A few students knock on the library's glass window and make faces at us as they pass. Others walk by without looking in at all. A very few smile shyly. I try not to watch them, but I can't help myself. According to Principal Geddy, tomorrow we'll be out there. With them.

I want to go back to Cody's house and shut myself up in his sister's room and try to make sense of this day, but I can't. I have a counseling session with my parents in less than an hour. My headache goes from bad to almost unbearable.

Mrs. Ward gathers up the last of our tests and we start collecting our coats and lining up by the double doors.

"What do you think about this place? About today?" Will says as he comes up beside me. He has his coat on. His hands are in his pockets like they're already cold.

"I have no idea," I say honestly, and his mouth turns up a little.

"I think it sucked . . . truly." He makes a face and I can't help smiling back at him.

Heather and Julie are watching us from the front of the line. Heather raises an eyebrow and the side of her mouth curves up. She whispers in Julie's ear. They both stare at us with unmistakable approval. Julie starts humming that creepy song again, loudly enough for me to hear; this time the tune is extra cheery. There's an unspoken "I knew it was only a matter of time" to the tone.

"So how's your new place?" I ask Will in a voice loud enough to drown out her humming.

"Not like home," he says.

Will and I squeeze through one side of the library's double doors. We haven't been this close since the night we snuck out of the Community and danced together down by the river. My nose bumps his chest, right above his heart. I breathe in sharply. It only takes a second to realize that Will doesn't smell like summertime or the fields beyond Mandrodage Meadows the way he used to. He just smells like soap and boy. That familiar scent is gone—like so many other things. Out of nowhere my eyes fill with tears. They fill up so unexpectedly and fast that I can't keep the tears from spilling out and running down my cheeks.

There goes Taylor's carefully applied makeup and my vow to never cry here, is all I can think as the tears run off my face and onto my shirt. My nose starts to run and my chest aches and then all of it—this day, this moment, all that I've lost—overwhelms me. I can't move.

Will's already through the door, but when I don't keep up, he turns back toward me. He notices that I'm crying right away. I open my mouth to explain, but he shushes me. "It's okay, I get it. Man, do I get it," he says softly, his hand coming up to touch my cheek. His eyes are rimmed in red and he swallows hard. "This . . . it's not easy."

I nod. He will always get me in a way that no one else can. It's sad and somehow comforting all at the same time.

Will's hand lingers for a moment on my cheek.

"Lyla?" It's Cody. He's walking up the hallway, his eyes on Will's hand and my face, still wet with tears. "What happened?"

Will lets his hand drop. His eyes grow distant. He rounds on Cody. "I don't know, maybe it's the weird way your friends welcomed us or maybe it's having to start her whole life over from scratch. What did you expect, for her to just blend right in?"

I don't want Will to speak for me, especially not to Cody. "I'm fine, I just had a moment there," I say, and stand between them. Neither boy looks convinced. I wipe my face. "I'm fine, really, it's just the day was . . . weird."

I want to explain, to help Cody understand, but I can't and so I have to hope that he'll get it enough to not be mad that I was so close to Will a second ago. Besides, how do I explain that Will's lack of summertime smell felt like one more death in a long line of them and it was just more than I could take? Cody wants me to be happy here with him. And I want to be that. Happy. I *need* to be. Otherwise, all that's happened was for nothing.

Cody steps closer to me. His hands are in his pockets, his backpack slung over one shoulder. He stares at Will. Will stares right back. I can feel the tension building between them. I clear my throat and they both turn in my direction. It's like they're both expecting me to do something. Choose between them, maybe? I don't want to have to. I mean, strictly speaking, I have. I chose Cody . . . and I'd do it again, but that doesn't mean that I don't want to have Will around anymore.

I squirm for a moment before I spot my salvation across the hall. The girls' restroom. *Sweet escape.* "I, um, need a second," I mumble while managing not to look at either of them. I put my head down and rush past them and straight for the door with the girl silhouette on it. I try not to let it remind me of the cardboard cutouts that we used for target practice back at Mandrodage Meadows. It's starting to feel like no matter where I go, something from my past will be waiting to blindside me. It's exhausting. I throw myself into the nearest stall and lean against the wall. I let my book bag and coat drop to the floor.

There were two girls by the mirror when I walked in. I can hear them giggling now.

"Okaaay," one girl says, her voice drawing out the word. There's another giggle from the other girl, then a brief silence. I have an overwhelming urge to peek over the top of the bathroom stall to see what they're doing out there. Instead I try to look through the narrow crack between the door and the stall. I think they're putting on makeup.

"The Winter Festival should be a blast. Kevin asked me to go with him to Ted's party after. He's having a bonfire behind his house. You're going, right?" The other girl glances at the stall I'm in and I duck out of the way, but I think she saw me anyway. I must look like a total crazy person for spying on them.

"Hey . . . everything all right in there?" The girl's voice is just outside the stall.

I lean my head back and stare at the ceiling. I study the brown watermark there, trace its shape with my eyes and try to make myself relax. "Yeah, I'm fine."

"Look, what the guys did today with the fire alarm . . . wasn't cool. Sorry if it made your first day bad and all," she says. Is she being sincere or putting me on? I can't tell.

The girls begin to whisper. I can't make out what they're saying, but then one of the girls' voices gets louder. "Uh, I've got to get my bio homework before we go. I'll wait for you by the trophy case . . . but don't take too long."

I can hear the girl's shoes click across the floor, then there's a brief burst of hallway noise before the bathroom goes quiet again. One of the girls is still in here with me.

"So, um, you're not peeing in there, are you? 'Cause if you are, I won't try to talk to you until you're, uh, done. But if you're not peeing, maybe you could come out? I just want to introduce myself."

I unlatch the door and open it, feeling a little silly for hiding.

The girl holds out her hand. "My name's Jaclyn, but most people just call me Jack."

She's got these multicolored braids scattered all around

her face like Medusa's snakes. They're sparkly too. Somehow she's managed to weave a healthy dose of glitter into each braid, but not get any on her face or clothes. She's delicate and elf-like—except for her enormous boobs—which stick out of the black sweater/tank top combo she's wearing like, well, outrageously oversized boobs. I can't even come up with a delicate description, because I can't stop staring. Her boobs are bigger than mine. This makes me strangely happy. I've never known another girl my age who was more endowed in that department. I have to work not to crack up laughing about it.

"Lyla," I say once I snap out of my boob shock and we shake hands. It seems like a ridiculous thing to do in the middle of a bathroom, and I smile.

"You're the girl living with Cody. Wait, that just came out all wrong. Living with the *Crowleys*." She smiles. "I'd ask you how your first day went, but considering the way you stormed in here, I'm pretty sure I know. Can't say it'll get better, but you probably already know that. It is survivable, though. I moved here at the beginning of last year." She says this last bit like it makes her situation and mine similar, when I'm pretty sure it doesn't. Still, it's nice to talk to someone who isn't in Cody's family or part of the Community.

"And you like it here?" I ask.

"No, I like it back in Boston. I *tolerate* here. My mom got remarried and I don't exactly get along with the guy, so she sent me to hang out with my dad for a while, but he's not exactly much better. He's Principal Geddy," she says, and rolls her eyes.

Her dad is the principal. *Weird*. I nod and smile again. I probably seem like an idiot, but I don't know what to say to her.

"So, what was it like in your . . . neighborhood? I mean, during that raid you must have been pretty scared, right?" Her question is so direct that my mouth drops open.

I shake my head. "Yeah, I guess." I walk around her and start to wash my hands. I look into the mirror. She's behind me, watching.

"Sorry—I didn't mean to overstep, but you guys are front-page news. And when I heard about it, I just couldn't even imagine what it might be like to be there." She looks at me hopefully.

For a second I consider letting my guard down and telling her, but at the last minute I change my mind. After the fire drill I'm not sure I can trust anybody in this school.

"I was thinking . . . maybe we can hang out sometime? I can show you around a little and stuff?" Jack asks.

This is what I was hoping for when I woke up and got dressed, to make new friends. My heart leaps a little, I try to be nonchalant, but I'm probably failing miserably. I don't care. "Sure."

She nods. "Good, so I'll look for you tomorrow, then. Gotta go. Aubrey's waiting for me."

I dry my hands and nod and she waves before ducking out of the bathroom. The noises from the hallway outside have dropped off. Everyone has to be headed home by now. I'm pretty sure that Will left with the others. I should be okay to go back out there.

I pull on my coat and button it, then grab my bag. My hand grazes a piece of card stock as I try to zip it closed. The note from my dad is still in the front pocket.

Be strong. Don't lose yourself.

I pull it out now and look at his message one more time before I crumple it up and throw it into the trash can. Losing myself is *exactly* what I need to do.

I believe he holds the answers to everything.
Of course I do. I have to.
—Will Richardson, member of the Community

SEVEN

By the time I leave the bathroom, the hallways are completely deserted and Cody is all alone. He's sitting on the floor, his back to the wall, legs crossed out in front of him. Spread across his legs is a sketchpad. He's so engrossed in his drawing that he doesn't even see me coming at first.

I get closer and crane my neck to see. He's drawn something that looks a little like a gargoyle with a dozen spikes running the length of its head in a deadly Mohawk. The eyes are narrowed and completely black. It's ugly and awful-looking, but I like it. I like all of his monsters—the ones on paper and the ones he molds and makes at home. I find them kind of comforting in a weird way. At least their evil is obvious. If Pioneer had looked like what he actually is deep down inside, none of us would have followed him in the first place.

I crouch down to take a closer look at his sketch.

"Hey, what do you think?" He leans the sketchpad in my direction a little.

"I like it, but I'd maybe put a little cross-hatching in here." I point to the curved underside of the creature's neck. "Add a little more texture. And his head needs more spikes."

"You think?"

"Definitely."

Drawing is one passion that we share. Granted, I mostly sketch animals, people, and landscapes, while he sketches ghouls, gargoyles, and werewolves, but still, we both get all excited about making something pop off the page.

It's nice to have someone else to draw with. Back at Mandrodage Meadows we each had something that we were good at, but once we found it, we didn't go looking for anything else—unless one of the others had the same talent and ours wasn't better. Then Pioneer would make us choose again, even if we didn't want to. He thought that when we began the New Earth with the Brethren, our Community should be as well rounded as possible. Sometimes I wonder if I'd been given the chance whether I would have found something else to love, like piano playing or singing or something. It's weird to think that I can now if I want to. But what do I try first? Instead of having too few choices, I have too many.

Cody's filling in the creature's bottom jaw, taking my suggestion and adding the extra spikes. I smile; it already looks better. Cody's pencil moves deftly across the page. "You ready to bust out of here?"

I nod. "More than ready."

"Before . . . with Will? Did he say something that got you upset?" His voice is carefully neutral, but I can feel the anger underneath. He's never liked Will. I guess there's no way he could, considering our history.

"No, actually, he was the only one who was nice to me today," I say slowly.

Cody flips his sketchpad closed and begins stuffing his art supplies into the raggedy blue backpack beside him. We walk outside. The parking lot is mostly empty. I wasn't in the bathroom all that long, but his car is one of the only ones still in the lot. Everyone must have been in a giant hurry to leave. Makes me wonder how great school can really be if everyone leaves it like the building's caught on fire. Ha! Fire. I'd almost forgotten about the fire alarm.

"Were you out on the field during the fire drill, earlier?" I ask Cody.

"Yeah." He looks uncomfortable all of a sudden.

"Did you see what happened?" I press, not sure if I really want to know, but incapable of stopping myself.

"With Brent? Guy's a loser, seriously." He shakes his head.

I was hoping that he hadn't seen it. I was hoping that somehow he didn't know. Because he didn't exactly come running over to stick up for us.

"I didn't see you out there," I say, and I can't keep the disappointment, the hurt, out of my voice.

"I wanted to come stand by you, but Mr. Goodwin

wouldn't let me. Then, before I could argue the point, it was over."

I nod, but I'm having trouble believing him.

Cody must sense this, because he stops walking and looks at me. "If I could've gotten over to where you guys were in time, I'd have shut Brent up, I swear. I know that after today it seems like everyone's determined to treat you like an outcast right along with all the other Meadows kids, but once people get to know you and see that you're not like them, they'll come around."

I know he thinks that what he's saying will make me feel better, but it doesn't. Why can't he see that in a lot of ways I will always be like the others? Leaving the Community doesn't make me different, at least not completely. I was just as devoted to Pioneer as they are. If I hadn't seen Marie die . . . maybe I still would be. But if I tell him this, will it change the way he feels about me?

We walk on in silence. Halfway through the lot Cody wraps his hand around mine. I love the way it completely covers my own. He steals a sidelong glance at me.

"All right, cut it out. Quit looking at me like I might break. I'm fine, really," I say when he keeps glancing at me.

Cody's mouth turns up at one corner and he raises an eyebrow. "Really? 'Cause your eyes are all puffy and your coat's not buttoned right."

I glance down at my coat. I missed a button somewhere along the middle. I unbutton it, then button it again. There's nothing I can do about my puffy eyes, though.

I stand by the car and inspect myself in the window while Cody unlocks the door. I have to shake off any lingering weird feelings I have about the day. Emotionally whacked out is not a good way to show up for my counseling session with my parents and Mrs. Rosen, my counselor. It'll go into overtime if any of them know today was hard for me.

Something inside the car catches my attention. There's a small, lumpy package covered in brown paper and tied up with red string lying on my seat. A present? Cody got me something for my first day. I look over the top of the car at him and grin. Sensing my stare, he glances up at me. "What?"

"When did you do this?" I ask as I open my door. I throw my bag over the seat, settle into the car, and put the package on my lap.

"Do what?" Cody plays at sounding confused as he opens the back door and puts his bag and coat on the backseat and I smile. I pull the string off and carefully unwrap the paper. I make a mental note to save it and the string—this is his first present to me, after all.

Inside the paper is a small carved wooden owl. My stomach does a quick somersault. This isn't from Cody. It's from the Community—or worse, is it possible that it's from Pioneer?

"Do what?" Cody says again as he slides into his seat and closes his door.

I let out my breath and it clouds up the air in front of

me. The air inside the car is bitterly cold. It intensifies the chill I feel looking at the owl.

"You're mine, Little Owl." Pioneer's words are so clear in my head it's like he's speaking them out loud. I'm surprised Cody can't hear it.

Cody leans over when I don't answer. He plucks the owl from the paper and stares at it. I don't need to say who it's from. I told him about my nickname. He knows immediately.

"They broke into my car?" He sounds stunned. His mouth clamps shut for a second and he looks out the windshield at the parking lot, his eyes scanning the cars and the sidewalks.

My teeth are chattering violently, which makes answering him hard. "Pioneer taught us all how to break into locked cars. He figured we might need to know . . . for the end of days." I never expected the others to use this skill on Cody and me.

I look down at the wrapping paper. There's a neatly folded piece of lined notebook paper taped to the corner. A message.

"Don't read it," Cody says. "Give it to me." He rolls down his window and the air in the car gets even colder. "C'mon, we'll throw it out."

His words snap me out of my daze.

But I can't help myself. I need to read it. I need to know for sure who left it. I unfold the note. The handwriting is Will's. I'd recognize it anywhere. He left the owl.

My breath comes out in a rush. I feel better immediately. Okay, so I don't love the nickname, but Pioneer wasn't the only one who called me Little Owl. Will sometimes did too. He was just trying to leave me a gift and didn't know how to give it to me.

"It's okay, it's from Will," I tell Cody.

"Okay? How is that okay? He broke into my car. He scared you." Cody looks at me like I've lost my mind.

I don't answer right away. I want to read the note to see if it'll help explain. There are only six short sentences scrawled across the paper.

> *You don't belong with them. They've got your thinking all twisted. You may not see it now, but you will. Come back, Lyla. Please, before it's too late. The end is still coming.*
>
> *Love,*
> *Will*

I feel my relief evaporate. I thought Will was changing, but it turns out that he's completely recommitted to Pioneer and his apocalypse again, just like everyone else. How can he? How can he when he knows what Pioneer did to me? What he did to Marie? I crumple the note up.

Cody grabs the note from me and smooths it out, reads it. I watch his jaw tighten as he does. A second later he throws it and the owl out the window. "He and I need to have a talk," he says as he starts the car. His hands are tight on the steering wheel, the knuckles white. He backs up fast and then rips out of the parking lot, driving over the owl in the process. We speed past a few lingering news vans and their crews who are still packing up from the day. A few of the people peer into the car, but they don't have time to figure out if we're newsworthy or not, Cody's going too fast.

We speed through town and onto the road that'll eventually lead us to where the Community is living now. We're both quiet, lost in our own thoughts. I don't like how angry Cody looks.

"He's just really confused about everything," I say.

"How can you defend him? What he did was *seriously* creepy. Breaking into my car. Leaving you some twisted gift he had to know would freak you out and then threatening you? You cannot be okay with this." He takes his eyes off the road and stares at me. "*Tell me* you're not okay with this."

I bite my lip. I'm not, but I can't say so—not if it makes him think it's okay to pick a fight with Will about it. It could end very badly for him if the rest of the Community gets involved. I just want to keep him safe. The last time Cody tried to defend me, back in the stables at Mandrodage Meadows, he almost got himself killed. Even if Pioneer is safely behind bars this time, Mr. Brown is still around . . . and Brian . . . and the other men. They would come to Will's defense in an instant. They wouldn't see hurting Cody as wrong, just self-defense. I shrug.

Cody shakes his head. "That's messed up, Lyla."

I stare out the window. I don't know how to respond. Cody's window is still down and the air inside the car gets even colder. I pull my legs into my chest and will my tears to go away. No matter how hard I try, I seem to keep making all the wrong choices. Figuring out how to be normal is so much harder than I thought.

There is no safety outside of the Community.
—Allison Hamilton, Lyla's mother and member of the Community

EIGHT

The road that leads to my parents' new place is uneven, hard-packed dirt—so much like the road that leads to Mandrodage Meadows that I keep expecting to see the guardhouse up ahead. Cody's car shudders over every bump as we make our way closer to the groups of trailers and the large, dilapidated barn behind it.

The sheriff says that the entire Community lives out here now, even Marie's parents. I thought for sure that after all that happened in the Silo—after what I said happened to Marie and their son, Drew—they would leave the Community forever, but even they believe Pioneer over me. Their return to Pioneer hurts me more than most of the others'—enough that I asked Mrs. Rosen about it the last time we had a one-on-one session. She told me that if they accept the truth, then they also have to accept that they are partly to blame for what happened to Marie. They're the ones who brought Drew and Marie to Mandrodage Meadows in the first place. Maybe that's how Will feels about all that happened too? This should make what just happened with the owl less upsetting, but it doesn't. It just makes me feel sad.

This is my first visit out here. We used to meet at the hospital. At first because that's where my mom was—she didn't pull herself back together right away after the raid—and later because I guess we were so used to it that no one spoke up and suggested a change. That is, until last week, when my dad announced that he would like me to come and see their home.

There are no gates or walls. There is just a barn surrounded by woods on one side and acres and acres of dead grass and half-frozen earth on the other. I study the trailers all lined up like aluminum-sided dominoes. I try to imagine how my family and friends feel about living here now, in a place so vulnerable.

In the end it doesn't matter. The truth is that they have no other options. Mandrodage Meadows is in Pioneer's name, which means that he owns the land and every house and building on it. The Community pooled its resources, every ounce of income we earned went into one account that was also in Pioneer's name, so after the raid, everything was seized and we were left with basically the clothes on our backs and not much more. If it hadn't been for the Freedom Rangers' mission to raise money online for the Community, my parents and everyone would have basically been homeless. Still, this place is barely a step above that. I think of Will, Heather, Brian, and Julie having to come back here after school today, and my stomach starts to hurt. Nothing about their lives seems good. I have Cody and his family, but what do they have?

The closer we get to the trailers, the stronger my urge to run away gets. I'm not sure why. Maybe it's because despite all of the obvious ways this place is different from Mandrodage Meadows, it seems to be startlingly similar in other ways. There are identical wooden plaques by every trailer's porch light, with the last name of each family engraved on them just like the ones on our old houses. And the barn is positioned at the end of the trailers just like our clubhouse was positioned down past our houses. And maybe it's also the way that every trailer looks exactly the same. The only way to figure out whose place is whose is to read the plaques. My parents' trailer ends up being the fourth one on the left-hand side, right in between Heather's and Will's trailers. Cody pulls to a stop beside it.

I look over at him. His eyes meet mine, and he looks so concerned, so unsure of me all of a sudden. Does he think I'm changing my mind about leaving the Community behind? That that's why I wouldn't let him confront Will? Is he right to worry? Is that older, weaker part of me winning without me even realizing it? My head starts to pound. I want to tell him to turn around and drive us out of here. But I can't. These counseling sessions aren't optional. They're required by the child welfare people assigned to the Community's case. If I miss one, they could pull me out of Cody's house.

"Look, I'm sorry about before," Cody says, his voice

still tight. "I just don't like when *they* mess with you like that."

He stresses the word "they," but he means Will. I ignore it. I don't want to start arguing with him. This is the first time we've ever come remotely close to fighting.

"Want me to stick around? Go in with you?" he asks. He still sounds tense, but he's trying to make things better between us now too. "I think I should. I don't like the idea of you being here alone." He makes a move to turn off the car.

I shake my head. "No, Mrs. Rosen is here." I point to her car. "I'll be fine. Really," I say.

Still, I'm kind of hoping that he'll insist on staying anyway, even if I am worried about him running into Will at some point, but he doesn't. Boys aren't the best mind readers.

"Dad's got me working the phones at the station while you're here. But I'll be back as soon as I can. Have Mrs. Rosen wait with you till then, okay?"

"Okay," I say, and make a show of busying myself with gathering my things. I'm trying to stall for just a few seconds longer.

"See you later," I say when I can't stall any longer.

"Hey, I'm sorry about . . . before. You know I'm just trying to protect you, right?"

I nod. That's what I was trying to do too. Protect him.

I half smile and quickly climb out of the car before he can lean over and try to kiss me goodbye. I don't want anyone here to see that. And I don't think I could kiss him back knowing that one of them could be watching. I shut the car door quickly. The thumping it makes as it connects with the car sounds overly loud. I jump. It's so quiet. I look up and down both rows of trailers. No one's outside—that I can see. The windows on most of the trailers are dark.

I walk to the end of my parents' trailer and peer around the corner at the barn. There are lights on inside. It's dark enough already that the soft yellow glow from them leaks out of a dozen cracks and spaces in the wood siding. I cock my head to the side and listen. There's a low murmuring coming from that direction, I can't make it out exactly, but the rhythm and tone is all too familiar. People are chanting in there. I almost get closer to make sure, but then I hear the trailer door creak open behind me and I turn in time to see my mom appear in the doorway, her face bright and open and warm, the way it used to be sometimes when the world was still supposed to end. I guess for her that's still the case, so maybe it makes perfect sense.

I lean over as I pass Cody's car and wave at him. He waves back and slowly starts to back up and out onto the path between the trailers. Fleetingly, I think about running after the car and away from my parents—escaping—but then my dad joins my mom at the door and calls out my name. I turn back toward the trailer and try not to think about what my mom's sudden attitude change and the chanting in the barn mean.

"Oh, honey, we've missed you so much," Mom says as

she pulls me into a gentle hug, leaving space between us like she's afraid I'll resist if she gets any closer. Her hair brushes against my cheek and the soft tickle of it triggers a thousand different flashes of memory. The nights when I had nightmares or was afraid of a storm, when she would tuck herself around me like a seashell and whisper-sing songs in my ear until I fell back asleep; the days when she would slip a note inside my pocket telling me how much she loved me; the cool cloths she used to drape across my neck while I was out tending the Community's gardens in the summer heat. But overlapping those memories are newer ones like the night of the false alarm, when she went into the Silo without me; the day I told her we needed to leave Mandrodage Meadows, the moment I begged her to go with me and she chose to stay with Pioneer—to die—instead. I can still see her face when she left the Silo that last day, so detached and disappointed. I hold on to this image. It helps keep me on alert.

I pull out of her hug and push past her into the trailer. Mrs. Rosen's not inside.

"Where's Mrs. Rosen?" I ask. "Her car's outside." It feels weird to be alone with my parents.

Dad shuts the trailer door. "Brrr, it's getting downright bitter out there. Our counseling session doesn't officially start for a few more minutes, so Mrs. Rosen walked over by the Rangers' trailers to see if she could get a clearer signal for her phone. She had to take a call from her office. Want the nickel tour while we wait for her?"

I look around me. The trailer's long and narrow, a giant rectangle chopped up into rooms. The main living area is right inside the door, with an attached kitchenette. It smells strange, like dust and mildew and something else, some kind of plastic. I don't like it. There's an old sofa with worn-to-the-stuffing arms and lumpy cushions sitting along the wall opposite the door, with a rectangular pine coffee table in front of it. By the kitchenette is a card table with three folding chairs. There's a mason jar with an evergreen branch sticking out of it, my parents' sole attempt at warming up the space. And just above the table hangs Pioneer's picture, the same one that used to hang above our old kitchen table back in Mandrodage Meadows. I look away quickly. It feels like the photo's alive somehow. *"I'm always watching over each and every one of you so I can keep you on the right path."* These words, the ones Pioneer used to say over the development's intercom system every morning after the wake-up chimes and every evening right before we went to bed, echo in my ears. I want to walk over and rip it off the wall, to stomp it into a million pieces. My hands start to sweat even though they're still cold. I ball them into fists and walk out of the kitchenette and peer down the hall.

My mom and dad come to stand on either side of me. "Back there are the bedrooms. Take a look at the first one on the left. We've made it up for you."

There's a tiny bathroom just before I get to the first bedroom. I look in just long enough to see my pale face reflected in the mirror. My eyes are too wide, my mouth clenched tight.

I peer into my bedroom. There's a narrow bed against the far wall, with my old quilt covering it and dozens of my drawings on the wall above it. I move into the room and run a finger along the squares of fabric on the quilt as I study the sketches they've put up. There's one of my parents on a picnic blanket beside the lake. There's also one of Will sitting on one of the split-rail fences by the corral with his blond hair falling across one eye. I remember when I drew that one. It was the night he kissed me for the first time. The only other one with a person in it is the single sketch I drew of my sister, Karen, when I was about ten and scared to death because I was starting to forget her face. In it she's jumping rope. I'd added her brown shoes—the ones my mom still keeps—to her feet even though she never wore them to play. It doesn't look much like her. Her body is lopsided and too long in the legs, but when I look at it, I can remember her a little better, even now.

All of the others are sketches that I did of the land in and around Mandrodage Meadows. There are ones of the clubhouse, the apple orchard where the Silo's entrance was, the cornfield just before harvest when the stalks were heavy with corn. But there aren't any of Marie or my horse Indy, even though I drew plenty of both of them.

I walk over to the small desk, the only other piece of furniture inside the room. Above it are dozens of white paper circles polka-dotting the wall like an onslaught of snowballs. There's writing on each of them. I recognize the scrawl on one of them as Will's. I lean closer. He's written *You still have my heart* on it. I look at another one. It's not in Will's handwriting, in fact none of the rest of them are. Each one has a different message written by a different hand.

You'll always belong with us.

We won't give up on you.

You are Chosen. *That doesn't change.*

I stop in front of one in particular. It's written in precise block lettering. It's Pioneer's.

You can't leave unless I let you go. And that will
never happen, Little Owl. You belong to me,
and I will find a way to bring you home.

My heart stutters in my chest. It's like he's found a way to transport himself into the room.

"Aren't they something?" Mom says brightly. "The whole Community misses you, Lyla. They wanted to let you know how much you still mean to them. They don't blame you for the raid, honey. None of us do. We understand now why things had to happen the way that they did. Someone had to kick off the end events. It was your destiny—an honor, really. We just want you to know that you don't have to feel like you're alone anymore. We forgive you and we're ready for you to come home." Her face is almost sweet and girlish-looking in the weak glow coming from the overhead light.

I don't know what to say. All I know is that nothing about these circles makes me feel better.

"But what if I don't want to come back?" I say without looking at either of them. "At least not to Pioneer and to the Brethren?"

"You don't mean that," my mom says, and the brightness in her voice turns sharp. "You're confused right now. Understandable since you've got so many Outsiders whispering in your ears, twisting the truth. But in your heart you know what's right. That's why you showed up to watch Pioneer leave the hospital and why you couldn't bring yourself to face us or him without a disguise on. You're ashamed of what you're doing. Even if you can't see the truth right now, I do. I'm your mom. It's my job to know you better than you know yourself. Pioneer's prophecies scare you. I get it. Any impending change that big and ultimately that wonderful can seem scary. . . ." She's talking so quickly that it takes my brain a moment to process what she's saying. I knew that they'd decided to believe Pioneer's story that Marie killed herself and that I blamed it on him and ended up shooting him in the stable because I had a concussion or was confused or under the sheriff and

Cody's control or traumatized or something and couldn't cope, but hearing her basically admit it to my face makes it so much more real. I think up until now I'd hoped that they'd choose to believe me eventually—once Pioneer was locked up and far away. I thought Mrs. Rosen would help them see everything differently, but now I can see that that is never going to happen.

My dad moves a little closer and I take a step back. I don't want him to touch me. For a while I thought that he believed my side of things, but obviously I was wrong. I walk over to the bed again and perch on the edge. Beside the bed is a nightstand. On top of it is a photo album. I flip it open just so I don't have to look at my parents, expecting to see more pictures from Mandrodage Meadows meant to remind me of what I've lost . . . but instead I see picture after picture of me—raking leaves with Cody's family in their backyard, standing in the window of Taylor's bedroom, watching TV with Cody in their family room. They've been watching me from just outside of Cody's house. A cold chill slides down my spine and I drop the photo album.

"Who took those?" I shout. I stare down at the photo album like it might come to life and attack me.

"It doesn't matter who took them, honey. What matters is that we haven't let you out of our sight. If you won't come home, we have no choice but to watch over you. It's not safe out there," my mom says softly.

I can't stay in the room with her for one more second. I knew that they wanted me back, but this . . . it's too much.

I push past them and hurry out into the hallway, needing to get out of here as quickly as possible. But when I get to the living room area, there's a knock on the door. Mrs. Rosen has finally arrived.

Dad steps out of the bedroom and closes the door behind him. He moves to the front door in a flash, opening it before I have a chance to think about how I can get away. Mrs. Rosen smiles at him.

"Good evening, how are you, Mr. Hamilton?" She gives the place a once-over while she waits for him to answer. "Looks as if you're settling in okay."

"Well, we didn't have much to unpack," Dad says with a pleasant chuckle, his voice brighter than normal. He looks over at me and gives me a "behave yourself" look. He wants me to pretend that I'm fine, that I didn't just see all those weird little circles of paper or that awful photo album in my room. I can't do it. I won't do it.

"You should see the other rooms, Mrs. Rosen. In fact, we should start with mine," I say. I steer her down the hall, fully expecting my dad to stop us, but he doesn't.

My mom hurries out of my room just as we pass the bathroom, practically running right into us. She looks nervous, her eyes darting from Mrs. Rosen to me and back again. "Oh, hello!" she says, in the same tone of voice that my dad just used.

"This is my room," I say before my mom can try to move us back toward the living room. I practically push Mrs. Rosen in. "There's something I want to show you." I point to the wall where all of the circles are . . . but it's empty and the photo album isn't on the nightstand anymore. It's all gone. My mom must have hidden it all as soon as she heard Mrs. Rosen come in. I should have known that they wouldn't let her see them.

"Show me what, dear?" Mrs. Rosen smiles at me before she notices my drawings hanging on the opposite wall. "Oh, these are beautiful. You have quite a talent. Do they have you signed up for art classes at the high school?"

I want to tell her about the notes and the album, about the transfer and how committed my parents still are to Pioneer, but without any real evidence, I feel like I'm not sure if she'll believe me. Would she actually search my parents' house if I asked her to?

"Lyla?" Mrs. Rosen prompts.

"What? Oh . . . I don't have my schedule yet."

"How was school today, by the way?" Dad asks from the doorway. He doesn't look directly at me, but merely in my direction. He knows what Mom just did, but he's not going to acknowledge it.

There's no way that I can sit here and watch this little show my parents are putting on for Mrs. Rosen, but I'm not sure how to expose them either. It's frustrating and scary and makes me feel completely out of control. The only thing that feels in my control is my ability to leave.

Without another word I rush past everyone, practically knocking my mom into the wall on my way. When I get to the living area, I notice that the picture of Pioneer that was just hanging above the little kitchen table is missing. She somehow managed to take that down too.

"Lyla? Your father just asked you a question," Mom says from behind me.

I turn to look at her. Mrs. Rosen, my mom, and my dad are standing there staring at me. Waiting.

Before they can stop me, I hurriedly scoop my bag and coat up off the floor and throw open the door. I take the steps two at a time and take off down the path between the trailers before cutting off to one side and into the woods. I run several yards before I stop to lean against the closest tree and try to catch my breath. I don't know where to go now. Town is miles away and Cody won't be back for at least another forty minutes or more. I look back the way I came to see if anyone followed me, but all I can see are the trailers, and beyond them, the hulking silhouette of the barn. I'm alone, but it feels like I'm being watched. Right now one of them could be out here with me, lurking in the shadows, taking more pictures. Every snapping twig or rush of wind makes me more and more certain of it.

We have no life here on this earth. No future.
So why should we care about it then?
—Brian Wallace, member of the Community

NINE

"Lyla!" My dad's voice echoes across the open area between the trailers. They're looking for me.

Other than underneath the trailers and the woods, there are very few places to hide out here. There's only this stand of trees and one other one beyond the barn. It won't be long until they figure out where I've gone. I pull my coat on and slip my book bag over my shoulder. I'm close to the barn here. I watch as the light from inside it throws shadows across the ground. It's darkest at the back end, where the light isn't bleeding through the cracks in the wood siding.

I look back to see my parents' shadows advancing between two of the trailers nearest the trees. I lunge toward the back of the barn. There's a rickety ladder attached to the wall—leading up to a hayloft maybe? It's dark and high enough from the ground that no one would see me. I veer left, grab the ladder before I can rethink it, and start climbing as fast as I can. Every few seconds I look down, expecting to see Mrs. Rosen and my parents come around the corner of the barn and spot me, but I make it to the top and into the loft without any trouble.

The light I saw from outside the barn is coming from the main space below me. I stay on my hands and knees. There isn't any chanting or singing going on now, but I do hear Mr. Brown's voice. I slide my feet forward slowly, pushing old hay out of the way as I go. It smells awful—like the hay's gotten wet and moldy a bunch of times and never dried out. I put a hand over my nose and mouth. The far end of the hayloft opens to the downstairs space. I don't want anyone below to know that I'm here. It was enough having to deal with my parents, and besides, the notes and photo album have me spooked. What will they do if they find out that I'm up here watching them? I crouch down in the hay, and try not to cringe when my hand lands in one of the damper clumps. The boards that make up the floor of the loft are spaced unevenly, and there are sizable gaps between some. I lean down and peer through one. I can see Mr. Brown. He's standing next to a television set on top of a black cart. I can see Brian, Will, Heather, Julie, and their parents too. Everyone has spread blankets across the barn floor. They're sitting cross-legged in their coats. There isn't any heat in here. I can see dozens of candles lit around the edges of the barn, sitting on top of old barrels and crates. Several camping lanterns hang from nails on some of the barn's support beams. Their flames cast dancing shadows along the walls, silhouettes of the people below.

I move onto my belly and crawl closer to the front end of the loft. I have to breathe through my mouth. Something smells rotted—gamey. Maybe an animal's died in the hay. I shake my head. I can't think about that. If I do, I'll start gagging.

It's gone quiet. I freeze. Suddenly I'm sure that something creaked behind me, but when I finally get the nerve to look, there's no one there.

"Until the Brethren return for us . . . ," Mr. Brown's voice suddenly rings out, and I jump, scattering hay across the loft. I watch as some displaced dust and hay goes over the edge and spirals down onto the crowd below.

"We have to stay the course. We have to stay together. And we will not, under any circumstances, forget who we are," Mr. Brown says.

Everyone answers him in unison, the way that they used to answer Pioneer. "We are Chosen."

"Great trials are in our future. Pioneer says that the Brethren are testing us to see if we are worthy of their favor. We must not fail. Our convictions cannot be shaken! Our path must stay true."

"Tell it to us straight, brother!" These words erupt out of someone's mouth; I can't see who's speaking, but it feels like their words carry everyone's agreement.

"I plan to, brother." Mr. Brown looks out at the crowd, to whoever spoke. "Because I'm worried. And so is Pioneer. He told me as much today during our visit. He wants to know how we can be sure that we will not fall. After all, one of us already has. Lyla fell under the sway of the Outsiders, didn't she?"

At the sound of my name, I accidentally suck in bits of hay and dust. A piece plasters itself to the back of my throat, making my eyes tear up and my lungs seize. I stuff my coat sleeve in my mouth to muffle the violent coughing fit that follows. There's silence below. I'm not sure if it's because of me or Mr. Brown's questions.

Brian stands up. "She faltered because she's weak, always has been. She doesn't belong with us. We can stand up against whatever we need to now without her trying to steer us toward the Outsiders and their lies."

Mr. Brown shakes his head. "No. She does belong with us. She's been misled, sure, but Pioneer has seen in his visions that she can be saved. You know this. But maybe you need a reminder." His voice goes sharp and even without him saying it out loud, I know he's warning Brian not to argue. "Pioneer's message for us tonight will set you straight. And if you have any questions remaining, you and I will set aside some time to talk."

Brian's anger falters a little and he blows out a breath. Mr. Brown stares him down. "*Sit down,* son."

Someone sitting on the blanket behind Brian tugs on his hand, pulls him down to a sitting position. It's the short-haired guy—the one with the military-type clothes who was driving the van. An Outsider at a Community meeting? Strange. I scan the crowd for more of the Freedom Rangers, but he seems to be the only one. Mr. Brown moves closer to Brian's blanket. He's standing right in front of the Ranger guy. "Chances are always given to those with enough of a conviction to change. Look at our new brother, Jonathan. A month ago he was just like any other Outsider. Now Pioneer and the Brethren have decided that he is worthy of redemption. He's willing to do whatever it takes to be worthy. You don't think it's possible that Lyla will realize the mistake she's made and repent too? The Brethren don't want people to perish. Those who commit to repentance are always welcome."

I stare at Jonathan. He's part of the Community? How can that even be possible? Pioneer said it was only us, it was always just our families. It doesn't make sense. Why doesn't anybody else see it?

Jonathan smiles up at Mr. Brown. His face is all angles and hard lines, so that the smile seems out of place. Mr. Brown pats his shoulder, then heads for the TV and turns it on. The screen is static and a sudden burst of white noise blasts through the air, startling everyone. A smattering of laughter follows. Mr. Brown smiles at the crowd and fiddles with the volume.

"Brian isn't the only one who has questions about our Lyla. I know there are more of you who wonder why we should take her back. Pioneer knew that you would—even before we left the Silo—and so he recorded this message to you on our last day there."

I hold my breath and move as close as I can to the edge. Pioneer left them a message about me? On our last day at Mandrodage Meadows? But I was locked up in the Silo's cell then and the shelter's doors were shut tight. How could he have guessed that I would get out? Did the Brethren give him a vision about it? I look back, out at the sky and the stars. Are the Brethren really there after all?

The TV screen goes blue and then Pioneer appears. He's in the clothes I saw him in last—his white shirt and jeans—and he's sitting cross-legged on one of the chairs in the Silo's gathering room. There's an obvious sheen of sweat on his face and his hair is wild, like he just rolled out of bed. But his expression is pure calm.

"My family. If you are watching this video, it is because the Outsiders have taken control of our shelter just like the Brethren have told me that they would. I know that I did not share this knowledge with you and I know that you may be confused. I'm sorry for that. But there was no other way for you to prove your devotion to me and to the Brethren. They wanted you to have to act on faith, their test to see if you could believe in the face of fear and doubt." His smile goes wide and warm, and even though the others know he can't see them, they smile too.

"The fact that you are gathered watching me now proves just how strong your faith has remained. Know that I never doubted your resolve, not once, and neither did the Brethren. The test of faith that you're enduring is meant to make you strong enough to endure the hardships that the *real* end will bring. What I couldn't tell you before is that the day I predicted as the end was just the kickoff event to the apocalypse. The world's final death throes won't come until the Outsiders have been given one last chance to turn from their wicked ways. Above all, the Brethren are merciful. They want to give those who truly seek it a chance to turn from their wickedness and join us before they are destroyed. There will be signs and wonders in these last days that the Outsiders won't be able to dismiss. The first of these will happen very soon."

His face grows serious, almost sad. "They are going to take me from you. They believe that without me, you won't stay united. But don't be scared. I am supposed to leave you now for a time as part of the Brethren's test. Prove to them, to me, that you won't fail and very soon we will be together again." He looks straight into the camera.

Some people are openly weeping as he talks. I watch as they huddle together and try to comfort one another.

"There is another of us that will leave for a time as well," Pioneer continues. "Our Lyla plays an important part in the last days. Just like the Outsider's Judas, her destiny is to betray me—us. The Brethren showed me this today and soon you will see it too. But this doesn't mean that she is lost to us forever. In time she will repent, but only as long as you refuse to give up on her. We are a family and we aren't complete without all of our members. It won't be easy. She has been so completely led astray. But don't lose hope. She will come home when the outside world starts to fall apart around her and she can no longer deny the truth. When she does, open your arms to her. This will not be an easy thing for some of you to do. Betrayal is hard to overlook, I know. But I'm asking you to trust me now. She belongs with us."

I don't want to hear any more. I can't. How could he know what would happen? Pioneer continues to talk, but my heart's pounding so hard that I can't hear what he's saying. Why is he so determined for me to come home? I look down at Brian one last time. Jonathan is whispering in his ear. Both of them are staring at the screen and nodding almost exactly in unison. Whatever Jonathan's saying is deflating Brian's anger. I can see his jaw start to relax.

Suddenly, everyone stands up. Their eyes are glued to Pioneer. They start to speak in unison.

We are strong when we are whole.
We are one mind.
One body.
One spirit.
Always.

I look at Will. I want him to look unsure of himself as he chants, but as they repeat the chant again and again, his expression becomes more and more confident. Our chants have power. I've always known that. I can feel that power now, rising up from the middle of the group, surrounding everyone.

When the chanting stops, Mr. Brown walks over to Will and wraps him in a giant hug. I can't see Mr. Brown's face very well, just the halo of thinning black hair on top of his head. "I know this must be hardest on you, son. Take heart, you'll have your Intended back soon." He looks at the rest of the Community.

"We must be stronger than we imagine we can be. Continue to follow the path Pioneer's set out for us now even if he can't physically show us the way."

The hairs on the back of my neck and arms are standing on end. I feel like I might throw up. I may have left the Community, but I'm not free of them. I won't ever be free. They will never stop trying to make me come home.

Pioneer starts talking again, but I can't listen to any more of it. Suddenly the big double doors at the front of the barn swing open and my parents rush in.

"Lyla left our counseling session. We can't find her. She could be anywhere." My mom gives Mr. Brown a pointed look, and they both start scanning the room. Everyone begins talking at once and getting up from their blankets. I have to get out of here. Now. In a few minutes they'll all be scouring the entire property for me. I wasn't supposed to hear Pioneer's message—that much is clear. If they find me, what will they do? I crawl as fast as I can across the loft to the ladder. There's no one outside yet, but it won't be long until there is. I almost fall when my feet touch the ground; I feel all loose-limbed and unstable. Breaking into a run as soon as I've got my balance, I head straight for the woods. I don't stop until I am way past the trailers and almost to the main road.

I check my watch. It's been almost two hours since Cody dropped me off. He should be on his way by now. I have to head farther up the road, stop him before he heads into the trailer park. After what I've just seen and heard, I want him as far away from this place as possible. I run harder, pumping my arms and legs to gain momentum.

The ground is hard, a solid thing beneath my pounding feet, but in my head it's becoming a quicksand of grasping hands. My mom's, my dad's, Pioneer's, Mr. Brown's, Will's, Brian's. If I don't move away from here fast enough, I might never get free.

I get about a mile down the road when I'm lit up from behind, my shadow suddenly appearing on the road in front of me. I turn around. There's a car coming from the direction of the trailer park. It's too far away for me to tell if it's one I recognize, one of theirs. There's nothing between here and town except fields and trees. Even if I keep running, there's no way that I'll stay ahead of it long enough to get away. The car gets closer, slows. I stare into the headlights and then squint out into the trees to my left, consider making a break for them while I still have time. I start to step off the road and into the grass when the car's door opens. Will's head appears over the top of the car door.

"Lyla, it's just me," he says.

After what I saw in the barn, this doesn't make me feel better.

"Leave me alone, Will." I back farther into the grass.

He looks down at the road and kicks a rock. "I'm not trying to bother you, Lyla. But you ran out on your parents. They're worried. We just want to make sure you're okay."

"I'm fine," I snap. "So you can go back now."

He looks up quickly and I can see that I've hurt him. "Why are you mad at me? I just wanted to make sure you were safe."

"You broke into Cody's car," I say because I don't want him to know I was just in the barn eavesdropping on him and everyone else. "Why would you give me something like that?" I'm talking about the owl, but I can't bring myself to come right out and say the word. Just thinking it puts Pioneer's voice in my head.

Will looks at the trees, to the spot I was planning to head for when he pulled up. "I knew you wouldn't like it, but Mr. Brown thought . . . I just wanted you to remember who you are, where you come from. You're forgetting, Lyla, becoming someone else when you're with them." He lets out a long, deliberate breath like he's trying to keep from getting upset. "I don't want to lose you. Can you honestly say that you don't miss me . . . us?"

I do, but not the way he misses us.

"Will, you need to let me go," I say instead. "I'm not going back to the Community. Not ever." I hope that he goes back and tells them this. I want them to finally get it, to leave me alone.

Will stares at me. "You don't really mean that."

"The thing is, I do," I say.

Will takes a step away from the car and closer to me. "No, you don't. He's got you so fooled. They all do. . . ." I back up. "Why can't you see it, Lyla?" He moves faster, bridging the gap between us, and I stumble a little. My heart cartwheels in my chest. I've never been scared of Will before, but now . . .

Headlights shoot up over the road, illuminating Will's face. He looks wild, desperate under the bright light.

I turn away from him and run toward the car with my arms over my head. "Hey, stop, please!" I say.

The car slows to a stop beside me and I recognize it. I rest my hand on the roof and try to catch my breath as Cody gets out.

"Lyla?" He looks from me to Will and his face goes hard. He rushes headlong at Will.

"What did you do now?"

Will doesn't back down. "Nothing. She left her counseling session early. I just came looking for her." He looks over at me, waiting to see if I'll add anything.

"She doesn't need you to look after her." Cody is right in Will's face now. "She's got me. So leave her alone. And if you ever break into my car again . . ."

"What? What're you gonna do?" Will's taunting him. They're going to start fighting if I don't do something. Behind Will another pair of headlights appear on the road. More people from the Community looking for me.

"Cody, come on, let's just go. We should go." I pull on his arm. He resists at first, but then I step between him and Will. "Please don't do this."

He looks disappointed, like I've picked sides and picked wrong. I look over at Will and his mouth turns up in a half smile. He thinks I'm defending him too. I frown at him and then pull Cody away.

The white van that Will and the others came to school in pulls to a stop next to Will. No one gets out of the car, but I can see the outline of whoever it is behind the wheel. Will puts a hand up to lessen the glare from the headlights and shakes his head at the driver before he gets back into his own car. I scramble into Cody's car and wait for him to get in. He sits down hard and without a word speeds toward town. I turn around in my seat and look at the other two cars. They're still just sitting in the middle of the road, watching.

"You're not going back there again. Ever," Cody says, his eyes on the road, his hands clenched around the wheel.

I lean back on the seat and look out the window at the moon. Even it seems to be watching us.

"Agreed," I say, but even as I do I have this sinking feeling, like somehow I may not have a choice.

I've sacrificed my life for them. Is it too much
to ask them to do the same for me?
—Pioneer

TEN

Pioneer is sitting on my chest. I can barely breathe. I can't move. My arms are pinned to my sides. He's smiling down at me, the same gentle smile he had when I first met him, which directly contradicts the insistent, panicky howl of the Community's alarm. In his hand is a black-handled knife. Light flashes across the blade, blinding me.

I am dreaming. On some level I know this and yet I can't wake up, can't make it stop. *Wake up!*

"Little Owl," he says, and there's something eager in his voice, something needy.

Pioneer's knife comes down across my throat. I can taste my blood. I feel like I'm drowning. I open my mouth, but I can't pull in air, not around the blood bubbling in my throat. I can hear it, a horrid gurgling that echoes in my ears. My neck and chest are wet and warm, but my fingers and toes are tingly and cold, quickly going numb.

I'm dying.

Just like Marie.

"Everything will be okay," Pioneer says. His voice is dreamy. He brings the knife up to his own neck.

Pioneer drags the blade across his throat. A long red line grows in its wake. His eyes never leave mine, even as the color drains from his face.

I scream. The sound rushes through my ruined throat like it's coming from the center of my being and not from my mouth at all. It sounds like a thousand people shouting in unison.

And I'm awake in Taylor's bedroom—facedown, panting into the floor. I must have fallen out of bed. My hands are on my neck, which feels sore even though none of what just happened was real. The skin there is warm and dry and blessedly intact. I knew it would be, but I still had to check. I'm so tired of this nightmare. Pioneer's in jail. I'm safe.

"Holy crap, Lyla!" Taylor is sitting up in her bed. Her eyes are puffy with sleep and her hair's a mess. "I almost peed my pants that time. Do you have to scream like that *every single night?*"

Cody bursts through the door, followed by both his parents. His mom is rubbing her thigh vigorously with one hand. "Charlie horse," she says when Cody gives her a questioning look. "Jumped out of bed too quick."

I press my forehead into the carpet. I'm actually injuring people now with my craziness. "Sorry!" I mumble without looking at her. I'm crying. I can't help it. I hate that I'm disrupting them each night. It's taking a toll.

There are dark hollows under everyone's eyes, and I'm to blame.

I use the bed to pull myself up to standing, wiping my tears as quickly as possible on the way up, praying that they don't notice.

"Same dream?" Cody asks.

"Yeah."

"What else would it be?" Taylor groans. She picks up her alarm clock. "Great. Three in the morning. I'll be lucky to fall back to sleep before it's time to get up." She rolls off the bed and takes her pillow with her. "I'm crashing on the sofa," she grumbles. Her mom yawns, gives me a pitying look, and limps after her.

The sheriff scratches the back of his head and then runs one hand across the top. It's what he always does when he's frustrated. He's done it every time he's come to check on me in the middle of the night. "So what'd Mrs. Rosen say about these dreams? You've told her they haven't stopped, right?"

I shake my head. I was going to yesterday at our session, but now . . .

"I'm so, so sorry, you guys," I say.

The sheriff pats my arm. It's his version of a hug. Then he clears his throat. "You want us to stay? Until you calm down some?"

I shake my head. I'm not okay, but I doubt that I'll figure out a way to be tonight. "I'm fine. I'm just gonna try to go back to sleep." I pick my pillow up off the floor and force a yawn.

"Okay, time to tuck back in. Let's go, Cody." The sheriff motions him to the door.

Cody walks over to me first and pulls me into a quick hug and kisses the top of my head. The sheriff turns away and clears his throat. I'm not sure who feels more awkward about Cody's little display of affection—the sheriff or me. I'm still not used to Cody kissing me in any way shape or form in front of his family, especially his dad.

"Okay, son," the sheriff says, tapping the doorframe for emphasis. "You'll see her in the morning."

Cody grins at me and rolls his eyes.

"Think you can get back to sleep?" he asks from the doorway.

"I always do eventually."

The sheriff drags him out into the hallway. He doesn't like us to be alone together in any of the bedrooms, especially in the middle of the night. More than one time I've come out of the bathroom at night to find him in the hallway, checking on us. I don't think he's entirely comfortable with our relationship, especially since we all live under one roof. And the fact that I'm from the Community probably doesn't help either. I know he likes me, but I can't be his dream choice for Cody's girlfriend.

Cody closes the door and I climb back into bed and pull the covers up around me. I stare at the ceiling. After a few minutes, when my heart finally stops pounding, I try to close my eyes and make myself fall asleep, but it's no use. I am one hundred percent wide awake. I turn on the little lamp beside the bed and fish my new library book out of my backpack. It's thick and every page is stuffed with words. *Perfect.* I need a nice long distraction.

Just as I'm starting to get drawn in by the story, the door cracks open. Cody's face appears briefly. He winks and then shoves something black and square across the floor before shutting the door again. I stare at it for a second, then scramble out of bed and pick it up. There's a little piece of masking tape across the side of it. The words "switch me on" are written on it in black marker—a walkie-talkie, not unlike the ones we used to use in the development. I slide back into bed and switch it on. It crackles to life immediately. The sound does strange things to my stomach. The sense of déjà vu is overwhelming. I half expect to find myself inside the guardhouse again, watching Brian as he rearranges his playing cards.

I adjust the volume button so it's quieter, just as Cody's voice floats out of the speaker. "Fuzzy-Headed Mama, are you there? Over." I catch my reflection in the mirror and laugh. My hair is a wild halo around my head. It could definitely be described as fuzzy.

I press the talk button. "This is Fuzzyheaded Mama. What's up?" I hesitate and rack my brains for an equally clever handle for him, but I can't come up with anything. "Cody? Over," I say lamely.

"Really? 'Cody'? That's the best you can do? My own name?" *Click.*

"Nothing else fits." *Click.*

"Come on, I've gotta remind you of something." *Click.*

"Um . . ." I chew on my bottom lip and think. "Maybe . . . Ferris?" *Click.*

"Too easy," he answers back. "Try harder." *Click.*

I lean against my pillow. "I'm really, really bad at this." *Click.*

"You can do it," he urges.

I try to, but it's like my brain is a permanently blank page. "I got nothin', really," I say, but when he doesn't answer, I keep working on it and try again. "Oh! I know, FX," I say.

"What?" Cody says, and I laugh.

"FX—special effects. Clever, right?" I feel a little silly now that I've said it out loud.

"FX . . . ," he says slowly. I can almost picture his face as he considers it. "It's okay—for now. Your handle, however, is absolutely perfect."

"In more ways than one," I say dryly, and even though I can't see him, I know he's smiling. We talk until I'm practically slurring my words I'm so tired. I fall asleep with the walkie-talkie still crackling beside me on the pillow. I want to feel like Cody's still with me in case Pioneer shows up in my dreams again.

How far would you go to keep your loved ones from destroying themselves? Giving up is not an option. I won't let it be.

—Pioneer

ELEVEN

I don't get out of bed when Taylor's alarm clock starts blaring music. Instead, I pull the covers up over my head and squish my eyes shut. School isn't what I thought it would be and today feels like it's even more up for grabs than yesterday. Will we spend the whole day isolated in the library again? I don't think I could stand it, to be trapped with Brian, Will, and the others, not after last night.

"Hurry up, slacker, you've only got about thirty minutes."

Taylor's up already. I uncover my head slowly.

"And I'm not helping you do your hair today. Too tired. So good luck with that." I pull the covers down and watch as she storms through the room, her wet hair raining on her dresser and the carpet as she yanks on a pair of rumpled jeans. "I overslept after last night." She gives me a pointed look, but she's not angry, not really. She's looking at me the same way she looks at Cody when he irritates her—tender and bothered at the same time. For a split second she reminds me of Marie, but it doesn't make me sad. It's kind of nice.

"I'll be lucky to pull *myself* together, let alone you." She's exaggerating; even soaking wet she's beautiful, but she'll never admit it.

I stretch and my book and the walkie-talkie fall off the bed. I pick them up immediately and shove them into my book bag. This room is Taylor's. The only part of it that I allow myself to take up space in is the corner where my bed is. She says that she doesn't mind sharing it with me, but I am constantly worried that she'll change her mind, so I try to keep my clothes and all other personal items under the bed or in my backpack.

"Sorry about last night," I say.

She stops rubbing and shrugs. "You can't help it. I get it. I just hope it doesn't last forever, you know? I'm exhausted."

Her understanding always surprises me. I keep expecting her to get angry, to yell at me for keeping her up and for taking away her privacy, but she never does. It is both wonderful and unsettling—so different from how Pioneer said Outsiders would be.

"Thanks, Taylor," I say, grinning.

She looks up at me, at my silly grin, and rolls her eyes. "Go get ready already. You'll be late."

I sigh and head for the showers. No matter how many

mornings I've been here, I still feel weird taking my shower in their bathroom or maneuvering through their halls in my pajamas.

It only takes me fifteen minutes to shower and get ready. At the last minute I decide to put on a little blush and lip gloss. Somehow it feels like I should now that no one's telling me that I can't. Besides, Marie would want me to, and to be honest, I'm sort of starting to like makeup.

I pull on a sweatshirt and jeans. When I left the Community, I thought that I'd run out and buy all kinds of clothes—stuff I've never worn before—anything other than the jeans/T-shirt/sweatshirt combo that I always had to wear before. But every time Taylor or Cody's mom has taken me into a clothing store, I end up wandering around. Taylor picked out a few things for me, but all of them are too snug, tight in all the places I'm self-conscious about, so I've defaulted back to my old clothes.

When I go back to Taylor's room, it's empty. I walk over to the window. The blinds are still shut. Taylor never remembers to open them, so I always do. I can't stand for the room to stay dark all day. It makes me feel like it's underground or something. I can't be in a place that feels that way . . . not ever again.

There's something sitting on the sill. A bird. *Will's wooden owl,* I realize with a growing sense of horror, meticulously glued back together.

My whole body goes cold. I stare hard at it, but I don't touch it. It's on the inside of the window. Will climbed up the tree outside and was in this room. While I was sleeping. I feel like I might throw up. How could he do this, scare me like this? What happened to the boy I danced with that night by the river?

I press my lips tightly together to keep from screaming. I put my hand on the window latch, lock it tight. I look outside quickly, terrified that I'll see Will or one of the others staring back at me from the tree right next to the house before I pull the blinds back down. Then I grab the owl. I hate the way it feels in my hand, the strange heavy weight of it. I shove it into the front pocket of my backpack and head downstairs. I need to talk to the sheriff, to show him the owl and tell him what happened last night in the barn. I head for his office, but he isn't there.

"He's already at the station," Cody says from behind me. "What is it?"

I must look as shaken up as I feel. I glance down at my backpack. I can't tell him about the owl, not before I talk to the sheriff. He'll go after Will as soon as we get to school, and this time I won't be able to get him to back down. If he hurts Will, there's no telling what Mr. Brown and the others might do to retaliate. If Will managed to get inside this house, they'll find a way in too. I don't want Cody hurt because of me. Besides, it's my problem. If anyone should have to deal with it, it should be me.

"Nothing. I . . . just wanted to ask him about Pioneer—make sure he's still in jail. After my nightmare . . ." I don't like lying to him, but I tell myself that it's only a temporary one. As soon as I get a chance, I'll talk to the sheriff and then both of us can talk to Cody once we've dealt with things.

"He's not getting out," Cody says, and puts an arm around me. "You're perfectly safe with us."

Man, how I wish that were true.

"Better get a move on or you'll be late," Cody's mom shouts from the kitchen.

I follow Cody into the kitchen. His mom smiles at us before sipping on her coffee. "I've got to go meet with the ladies about the Winter Festival again. Confirm our rental order for porta-potties." She makes a face. "I will be so glad to get on the other side of this event." She waves as she collects her coat and purse and then she's out the garage door and gone. For a moment I wonder if I should go after her, tell her what's happened at least since she could probably call the sheriff, but it's too late, I can hear the garage door rumbling open.

"I talked to Dad about last night," Cody says, and for a moment I'm sure that he knows what I found, but then I realize he means what happened at the trailer park.

"He said he's going to talk to Mrs. Rosen about stopping the counseling sessions with your family for a while, especially now with Pioneer's first court dates coming up. He thinks that they're trying to scare you into not testifying."

I swallow hard. I'd almost forgotten about the trial. That on top of the owl and school and Will and the others—it's almost too much to take. I rub my temple with my fingers.

"Hey, we'll get through this," Cody says. "You're not alone. You have us."

This should make me feel better, but it doesn't. Instead it ups the constant hum of terror I've felt since I found the owl. How long before Mr. Brown and the others try to take Cody and his family away from me too?

The road up to the school is almost empty. The news vans and reporters from yesterday have thinned out considerably. With Pioneer's first court appearance coming up, there are a lot of other angles to our stories and not enough time to stick to any one of them for too long. Principal Geddy and Mrs. Ward are waiting for Will and the others by the front entrance again when we walk up. I try not to laugh when I see the principal. If it's possible, his pants are even tighter today, cutting his chubby middle in two, making it seem like his stomach has lips.

"So, Ms. Lyla, how are you?" Principal Geddy looks anxious, like the path his day will take is tied to my well-being or lack of it.

"Not too bad," I lie.

Mrs. Ward joins us. She's got on a bright orange coat and a denim skirt that just reaches her knees. I stare at the patterned tights on her legs and the same black boots she wore yesterday. Cody said that on the weekends she sings with a nineties cover band in town. It makes sense. That she works at a school counseling kids? Doesn't. I smile at her.

"How's the book? Did you get a chance to crack it open yet?" she asks.

"Um, yeah. It was . . . not really my thing."

I managed to read the first few chapters last night before bed. It was interesting, but not the easiest book for me to tackle. The characters were all either succumbing to a hideous plague or trying to survive it while battling this guy with supernatural powers named Randall Flagg who had gathered a group of followers in Las Vegas. It hit a little too close to home. I brought it back to school with me so that I could turn it back in. No more apocalypses for me. I want rainbows and unicorns and happy endings for the rest of my life.

"What book?" Cody looks at me. I unzip my backpack and hand it to him.

"Stephen King's *The Stand*? A great book, but probably the worst choice of books *ever* for you."

Mrs. Ward looks defensive. She'd read the title out loud yesterday, so she knew what I was getting myself into. "I thought it might be a good parallel for her to explore, you know, to see how the characters stood up against a powerfully evil force. How they forged their own path."

"She's already lived that." Cody smiles at me proudly. I feel myself blush.

Mrs. Ward clears her throat. "I'm sorry if the book

didn't work out, Lyla." She looks a little embarrassed and I feel sort of bad for her. I actually do believe that she wanted to help . . . she just has no idea how to go about it. "Well, why don't you two go back to the library now and pick something else? We'll meet you in there once the others show up. And Cody, make sure you head to class well before the bell." She smiles slightly before turning to talk to Geddy again.

"Okay," Cody says once we're inside the library. "So what do you want out of a book? Fantasy? Lots of action? Kissing?" He raises one eyebrow at me. "Can I read over your shoulder if there's kissing?"

"Somehow I doubt you'll be trying to read," I say, and elbow him in the ribs. Sometimes his jokes remind me of Will's, but instead of making me feel uncomfortable, they thrill me. I can never quite meet his eyes when he talks like this.

"I don't know what I want," I say. I'm not trying to be difficult. I don't even know where to begin.

"We have about ten minutes before Mrs. Ward gets here and shoos me out. How about you pick one at random and go with it? Read a little tonight, and if you don't like it, try a new one tomorrow. Now we just have to pick which kind—fiction or nonfiction?" He waits for me to decide.

I shuffle from foot to foot. "Fiction for sure." Where else am I going to find those rainbows, unicorns, and happy endings?

"All right, so we're in the right section then. Now pick out a book, any book." He gestures at the shelves.

I go for the shelf by my feet. Might as well start at the bottom and work my way up. I pull out a book and inspect the cover. I read the title out loud to Cody: *"Lord of the Flies."*

He groans. "You're like a magnet for the wrong kind of book. Pick again."

I put the first book back and move over a few feet and pick from the middle shelf. *"The Forest of Hands and Teeth."* I turn the book over and read the description out loud.

Cody snatches it out of my hands. "Seriously? That's what you managed to end up with?"

It gives me the giggles. "Should I pick again?" I ask.

"Absolutely not," he says. He's laughing too. He walks back to where I found *Lord of the Flies* and picks another book from the same shelf. *"The Princess Bride,"* he says, his mouth curving up on one side as he reads. "Perfect. You'll love this." He flips it over. "I mean, *I* haven't read it, but the movie is epic. It's a fairy tale."

"I think we have a winner," I say, and we take it up to the counter and check it out.

By the time the others start filing in, I'm alone at one of the tables with my book and Cody's on his way to class. I'd stopped thinking about the owl and everything else and immersed myself in Buttercup's story . . . that is, until

Will walks in. My stomach drops into my shoes. I have the overwhelming urge to either hit him or go hide.

He collapses into the seat beside me and rests his head on the table. His face is turned toward mine and his eyes are red and bloodshot. He looks horrible.

Good. I hope he does. After what he did last night, he should feel bad. It was disturbing and terrifying and twisted.

"Sorry. For last night," he says in a low voice. "I only followed you to make sure you were okay, I swear. I shouldn't have let him get to me."

"What?" Is he talking about out on the road? That was bad, but the owl . . . was so much worse. I open up my bag and, without a word, place the owl in the center of the table. "Why would you do that?" My voice cracks and my eyes well up.

Will looks at the owl and then at me. He picks it up and inspects it. "It broke?"

"Don't do that!" I yell, and everyone looks in my direction. I hadn't noticed that the rest of the kids were there. I lower my voice. "Don't pretend like you don't know what I'm talking about. I never thought . . . I never thought you'd want to scare me into coming back. Not you."

Will shakes his head back and forth. He looks totally confused. "I don't. I swear."

"Cody threw that owl out of his car yesterday after we found it. You came back to the school to get it, glued it back together, and left it *inside* my bedroom last night like some kind of warning. Admit it."

His eyes widen. He doesn't say anything at first and then he turns in his chair to face the others. "Who?"

They don't take their eyes off me. If it wasn't Will, then who was it? Brian? Julie? Mr. Brown? My mom? It could have been anyone in the Community, I realize. One of them is watching me all the time, taking pictures. The photo album at my parents' trailer is proof of that.

"I'm not going back. No matter what any of you do."

Brian leans back in his chair and smirks. "That's not what Pioneer says."

Julie stands up, walks over to me. "We're not trying to scare you, Lyla. But, I mean, what do you want us to do? The Outsiders are around you all the time, keeping us away, threatening to take us from our families again if we try to talk to you. We have no other choice but to sneak around. We just want you to remember who you are. Where you belong. I know what you think you saw in the Silo has you scared, but it wasn't real. You had a concussion, and being down in the dark in the cell . . . it made you hallucinate."

"Pioneer killed Marie! I saw him do it. How else could she have gotten her throat cut?"

Julie shakes her head. "She killed herself, Lyla. You had her convinced that the sheriff and the others were going to get in, that you were going to help them and she would go to jail. She shot one of the deputies out on the wall. Did you know that?"

I blink and try to focus. "What? No, that's a lie."

"I was out there with her. I saw her do it."

"No, no, I don't believe you. I . . . she would've told me."

"She knew you were falling for Cody. She was afraid you would hate her for hurting one of his friends, your precious Outsiders."

I look over at Brian. He looks away, his hands clenched into fists.

I think back to our last few moments in the Silo, how I begged Marie to let me out. I can't remember it clearly. There are only bits and pieces of memories swirling in my head. I was so sure Pioneer killed her. He killed her. I saw him. I couldn't have made that up and yet . . .

"Will?" I look at him, hope that he'll argue with Julie, come to my defense. If he didn't put the owl in my room, there's a chance . . .

Will looks away from me.

"You had a concussion, Lyla, and you were isolated for days . . . ," he says softly. "Jonathan, one of the Freedom Rangers, is ex-military. He says everyone hallucinates if they're left alone in the dark too long. . . ."

"SHE DIDN'T KILL HERSELF!" I bang the table with my fist. "PIONEER KILLED HER! I KNOW IT!" I stop yelling, swallow hard. No one was in that room but

Pioneer, Marie, and me. Her autopsy hasn't been released to the public yet. I can't prove to them that it happened the way I said it did. I don't want to doubt myself . . . but I was pretty confused, falling in and out of consciousness. Could they be right?

But no. NO, there's no way! They're trying to make me crazy. I have to get out of here. I need to clear my head. I need to . . . I need to . . .

I launch myself out of my chair, knocking it over in the process. I head for the door just as Principal Geddy opens it on his way inside. He looks up at me, startled, but I don't stop. I just keep moving past him, through the door and straight into Mrs. Ward.

"Lyla!" Geddy comes back out of the library, letting the door shut behind him. Both he and Mrs. Ward stare at me.

"I can't stay in there with them," I say loudly. My voice echoes in the empty hallway.

"What happened?" Mrs. Ward puts a hand on my shoulder, but I shrug it away.

"Can we just get to our classes already? Please?" I snap. My voice is hard and borderline disrespectful—enough that I cringe. Back in the library I'd *almost* doubted myself. Part of me still believes in what went on at Mandrodage Meadows, still believes that Pioneer's right and I'm all wrong.

"You're mine, Little Owl."

But I don't want to be.

If God cannot trust his own angels . . . how much less will he trust those made of clay? Their foundation is dust, and they are crushed as easily as moths.

—Job 4:18–19

TWELVE

I have nowhere to go but back into the library with Principal Geddy and Mrs. Ward. They've promised me that they are just about to send us off to our classes. I'll only have to endure the others for a few more minutes.

I can do this. *Don't fall apart, Lyla.*

I follow them into the library and move to a table in the back of the room, away from Will and everyone else. I can feel everyone's eyes on me, but I don't look up. I can't. My whole body feels hot and uncomfortable. Principal Geddy's talking. I make an effort to concentrate on what he's saying and block out everything else, but mostly I just stare at the fake wood grain on the table in front of me, tracing the patterns it makes with my finger.

Five students file through the library door a few minutes later. They gape at us. A few of them seem to have forgotten how to close their mouths entirely. One or two are smiling. It's these smiling students that make me the most nervous. I feel like they'd take a look under our skin if they could to see if we're different from them on the inside somehow. I guess maybe it would make them feel better if we were.

Jack, the girl I met in the bathroom yesterday, is one of the five. She smiles when she sees me and waves. I wave back. Will turns around to frown at me. I wave a little harder at her and fake a smile. I'll be friends with whoever I want now.

All in all, there are three girls and two guys. The guys don't look friendly at all, but then again, the Community guys aren't looking all that friendly either.

Principal Geddy steps forward and claps his hands to get our attention. It's like he's never sure anyone's ever really listening to him.

"I've arranged for a few of our students to give you a proper tour of your lockers and show you to your classes today. I'd like to get you acclimated to the regular school day as quickly as possible so that you can start getting to know the other students and catching up on the curriculum." He lifts a stack of papers into the air. "Mrs. Ward and I spent several hours last night going over yesterday's test results and placing you in classes accordingly. You'll find that your classes . . . will vary greatly, but should cover all of the current gaps in your education."

Brain shoots a glance at Heather and Julie and all three cross their arms and frown. I know what they're thinking: *What gaps?*

"Next to me are Jack, Sam, Phoebe, Alex, and Alicia. We've enlisted some of our student council members as well as some of our athletes to give you a sense of what the student body is like here." The students nod or wave at us. Jack does this little salute thing. I think most of us are staring only at her. It's hard not to with that glittered hair and chest of hers.

"Okay, people at this table in front of me, take your things and follow Alex. This table, follow Phoebe. Table three—Alicia. Table four—Sam. And table five, follow Jack—you too, Ms. Hamilton. Enjoy your tour. Mrs. Ward and I will be checking in with you throughout the day." Everyone starts to move all at once. No one looks too excited about leaving the library.

"And if you need anything at all in the meantime, please come by the office and we will do what we can to assist you." I can't help thinking that Principal Geddy added this last comment after we got up to follow our tour guides because he was hoping that we wouldn't hear him and take him up on his offer. The sooner he can have us safely and invisibly integrated into the school, the easier he'll breathe. I follow Will toward Jack, but I stay far enough away from them both that there's no chance that he'll try to talk to me.

"S'up, newbies." She looks us over. "So, do you guys coordinate your outfits ahead of time or what?" she asks, one eyebrow raised. I look at everyone else. They're wearing basically the same thing—jeans and T-shirts. I promise myself that I will make Taylor take me shopping again. This afternoon. Brian glares at her. When no one else answers, she shrugs and starts walking backward so that she can still see us. "Okaaaay. Ready to brave the halls and find your lockers?" She takes off for the door and we follow her.

"All right. This is the main lobby area. To your right is the office and to the left are the guidance offices. We're gonna start this tour at your lockers and then I'll walk you by all of the classrooms you'll need to find." She pulls out several sheets of folded paper from her pocket. "I have all of your schedules right here and for the most part you're in the same classes, so this shouldn't take too long." She hands out the schedules to each of us. It's a bunch of squares with times and classes written on it. It reminds me of the assignments board back at the clubhouse in Mandrodage Meadows.

"So, I'm a junior like most of you guys," Jack says. We stare at her. "You know, I'm in eleventh grade." When we still just stare, she shrugs. "Basically, I'll be in the same classes as some of you. Haunting the same hallways. If you have questions, I'm supposed to be at your disposal." She does a little curtsy as she walks. Somehow I'd thought that she'd be all graceful and light-footed, maybe because of the glitter in her hair and her fine-featured fairy-like face, but she walks with a plodding purpose.

"Hey, I'm glad you got put in my group. I was hoping

to get a chance to talk to you again," she says, her head close to mine and her voice low. I smile. It seems like she really wants to be my friend. I look back at Will. I could really use a new friend about now, especially since Cody's already said he probably won't be in most of my classes. He's taking advanced classes, and from the way Principal Geddy said the word "gaps," I'm sure that I won't be in any of them.

"So, it looks like you're the only one remotely interested in being here, am I right?"

I nod. "They have to come. Their caseworkers made it a condition of their moving back in with their parents. I mean, I have to too, but I'd come anyway."

"It's because you guys aren't supposed to be around people who aren't like you, right?" She leans in a little closer. Behind me Will clears his throat. I don't have to look back to know that he wants me to stop talking to her. "Pretty much, yeah," I say loudly enough for Will to hear. I'm not going to do what he wants ever again.

Jack looks back at Will and then at me. "You're consorting with the enemy. Good for you." She gives me an admiring look. "Rebel."

I chuckle a little. I hope I'm worrying them back there. They deserve it. Now that Jack's here and I'm not alone with them, I'm one hundred percent positive that what they're trying to make me believe about Marie isn't true. I don't know why I let them get to me before.

"Okay, I can't stand it—I have to ask. If I'm overstepping, just tell me to shut up and back off. Is it true that you shot that Pioneer guy? I mean . . . during the raid?"

I hesitate. I can hear Will suck in a breath. Brian's at the back of the group, which is a good thing, because if he'd been close enough to hear her, he would probably be freaking out on her right now.

"Yes, I shot him," I say quietly. I put my hands in my pockets and fight the urge to turn around to see their reactions.

"That's so tough! Escaping that shelter and shooting the guy who locked you in there. Your story is completely awesome." She looks at me and grins. "It all sounds very *Resident Evil* . . . just without the zombies . . . or the corporate conspiracy."

I shrug and she laughs. "You have no idea what I'm talking about, do you?"

I nod. "You're talking about that movie with the Umbrella Corporation and the creepy little girl." I affect a British accent and quote her: "You're all going to die down here."

Her eyes widen. "Wow, so you haven't been as sheltered as I've heard." She does this little head tip that makes me feel like she's impressed by this.

"Uh, no, I was every bit as sheltered as you heard . . . Cody's shown me a bunch of movies every night so I can catch up—especially the ones with monsters and special-effects stuff in them. I've been kind of holing up at his house avoiding reporters and them." I tip my head back slightly at the others. "If it's a horror or science fiction movie, chances are I've seen it now. Just don't ask me anything about real life, because I'm at a loss there."

"So where are we going?" Will asks Jack loudly. His voice is sharp. He doesn't like her.

"To all the best places, honey. Lockers and classrooms and cafeterias, oh my." This last reference to *The Wizard of Oz* makes me like her even more. She picks up the pace and we have to hustle to keep up.

We spend the next hour locating all of our lockers and practicing the combinations (2-9-5, pull), walking past the classrooms that we'll be in, and figuring out where the gym and cafeteria are. The cafeteria is the biggest surprise. There are vending machines on one end with every kind of junk food in them. Cokes and Cheetos! I smile a little. Jack explains in detail how to grab a tray and how much lunch costs, but it's lost on everyone but me. They've all brought their lunches because Pioneer said that most Outsider food is preservative-filled and horrible. I wonder how they're managing to eat now that our gardens and livestock aren't available anymore.

During the tour, the bell rings and classes let out. The hallway floods with students. I hate how they stare at us, elbowing each other and whispering. Their laughter bruises. They think that we're some kind of joke. Most of them don't seem very nice at all. For an instant I swear I see every last one of them the way I used to when I was little—when I was convinced that every Outsider I saw was wearing a person mask that hid sharp teeth and green skin.

"So, this tour is supposed to be over now, but I think there's one more thing that you might be interested in seeing." She turns down a shadowy hallway that's close enough to the gym that I can hear the squeak of sneakers from where I'm standing. It seems to lead to a fire exit and nothing else, but near the end of it are a set of narrow double doors. There's a heavy metal chain woven around them that's secured with a padlock. Jack glances at the hallway behind us, then works her fingers into the crack where one of the doors meets the doorframe. The door isn't hanging right, I can see it now. It's leaning in a little and there aren't any hinges. She muscles it open, begins to squeeze into the space beyond, and motions us to follow. I look over at Will and he shakes his head. Heather and Julie look at me too and cross their arms. I have a choice: either stay here with them and wait for her to come back or follow. It's an easy choice. I take a step forward and shove myself into the space Jack disappeared through. Just beyond the door is a set of steps that lead down.

"Look, barely anyone knows about this place. I mean, my dad and an assorted other few, but no students, see? I figured maybe you guys might need an escape hatch to sometimes dive into if your day gets too, you know . . . rough." She looks at me and grins. "I mean, being the center of everyone's attention can wear on you, trust me. Before you came along, I was the one to avoid."

She jumps from the third-to-last step into the dark room below. I can see the silhouettes of at least a hundred desks stacked on top of one another. There are old movable chalkboards and stacks of books too. It smells musty and a lot like the supply room in the Silo. It unsettles me, but I don't want her to know it, so I go down the last few steps and lean against the wall. My throat closes up. I can't breathe very well. My heart races. *Don't panic. It's just a room.*

Jack wanders farther in and flicks a light switch on the far wall. There's a low-wattage bulb above us set inside a wire cage. It only adds to the feeling that we're underground. A thundering sound above us makes me look up at the ceiling. I can almost see the walls starting to close in. I start breathing in shorter, shallower bursts. Telling myself to be calm isn't working. I'm going to need to get out of here very soon.

Jack hasn't noticed that I'm freaking out. I'm regretting following her now. I watch as she settles onto the top of one of the desks that isn't stacked and leans against the cinderblock wall behind her. There are three long bulletin boards flanking her, two on one side, one on the other, with photos and Post-its and index cards tacked to them. I can't make them out very well from where I stand. Beside her is an old typewriter situated on another desk with a pile of notepads and stacks of clean white paper, and next to that a laptop. Up above there's the faint sound of squeaking shoes. We must be under the gym.

"I've sort of claimed this place. All this stuff's mine. The typewriter's crazy, right? I found it down here. I write stuff sometimes, and I love the sound it makes when you hit the keys. Totally old-school, but awesome." Jack lets her legs dangle every which way. "I moved up here last year when my mom got remarried. Needless to say, Dad is not the coolest. And being the principal's kid isn't exactly a pass to popularity. Add to that the fact that this school has seen maybe three new students in the past six years—and that I'm not exactly 4-H material—and you can probably guess how much of a freak they all think that I am. That is, until you guys came along." She grins. "This is a good place to get away from it all and think."

I'm staring at her very sharp shoes—they're covered in spikes around the ankle cuffs. She lifts one up in front of my face. "Like 'em? I got 'em on eBay. Next to impossible to get cool shoes around here." She laughs at my wide-eyed expression and gives my outfit a once-over. "I'll help you order a few pairs if you want. 'Cause, wow, you could so use my help."

I find myself nodding. I wouldn't mind a pair of shoes like hers. It might be a little like wearing armor, like the acceptable alternative to wearing one of Cody's monster masks to hide behind. It seems to be working for her.

"So, this is the school's basement. They keep all of the

extra desks and stuff here, obviously, but the important thing to remember is that no one comes down here regularly and it makes a great place to eavesdrop on the stuff going on up there." She points to a vent in the ceiling, and when I listen I can hear people talking. "But since you look like you're waiting for the boogeyman to show up at any moment or something, I'm gonna assume that you probably won't be interested in hanging out with me here . . . right?"

I nod.

"It's because of what happened?" She looks me over closely. I can't help wondering why she would think bringing me down here was such a good idea if she's that familiar with my story.

"You know, I'm a pretty good listener if you ever want to talk to somebody." She says this casually, but even so, I'm starting to feel like the only thing she wants to talk about is what happened in the Silo. She keeps bringing it up. I was hoping we'd talk about other stuff entirely.

"I'm not much of a talker," I say as I head for the stairs.

"I'm figuring that out. But hey, you gotta know that not asking you about your past is like next to impossible, right? I mean the biggest news around here other than you guys is whether or not the Winter Festival will have sleigh rides this year. You can't fault a girl for being curious." She stands up and wipes off her butt with her hands before craning her neck around to check to see that it's free of dust. "And if you don't put your story out there, someone else is liable to make one up for you, one that isn't anywhere near the truth. Just sayin'."

She comes closer. "Look, I write for the school paper. I could help you let everyone know what you guys are really like. . . ."

I don't let her finish the sentence. I step past her to get a closer look at the bulletin boards. The notes and pictures . . . they're all about us. I feel as if I've been slapped. She doesn't want to be my friend at all. She's just trying to get me to tell her my story so she can scoop all the other reporters out there. Without a word I turn and run back up the stairs and squirm back through the broken door.

Will and the others are sitting on the floor with their backs on the opposite wall, waiting for us. Will stands up when I come through and opens his mouth to say something, but I walk right past him and hurry out into the hallway still teeming with students. He's only going to say that this serves me right, that I shouldn't trust Outsiders. But when it comes down to it, I can't trust him either. So where does that leave me?

The Outsiders claim to have rescued us. Liars!
They've condemned us to a living hell. That's the real truth.
—Mr. Brown, member of the Community

THIRTEEN

We start our classes five minutes later. Jack walks us there. She keeps apologizing and trying to make conversation, but I refuse to even look at her. My first class is with Will, Heather, Julie, and Brian. *So much for getting away from them.*

The other students watch us walk in. I can feel their eyes on us as I lead the way to the last few empty desks. We have to work to avoid backpacks and a dozen or so pairs of legs that stick out into the aisle, tripping more times than actually taking steps, because no one bothers to make room for us. I can hear giggles behind me and my face burns as I finally make my way to the back.

Brian is the last of us to reach the seats. The only one left is the one right next to me. *Perfect.* I perch on the edge of my seat, attempting to make the space between my desk and his appear wider. I can feel him glaring at me. I'm tired of trying to pretend like I don't see it.

"What?" I say. "If you've got something that you want to say to me, just say it already."

He shakes his head. "So you're gonna be one of them now, huh?"

"I'm trying to figure that out," I say in a low voice.

"Trying? You either are or you're not. If you're going to wreck everything for the rest of us, shouldn't you be sure?"

His words sting. I turn around, away from him and the others, and take out a notebook and pencil to give myself something to do. It isn't fair. Everyone wants something from me. Will wants me to be his Intended again, Jack wants my story, Pioneer wants my soul, my parents want my obedience. Brian wants my repentance. They all expect me to know what I'm supposed to do and I don't. I wish I did.

The boy in front of me turns around and holds out his hand. He's cute in a disheveled kind of way. "Hey, I'm Vince, one of Cody's friends."

I hold my hand out and let him shake it. "Hi."

He grins and moves so that he's almost the whole way around in his chair. I can see Will and Brian tensing in my periphery, and for a second I start to get nervous that they'll do something to stop me from talking to Vince—something *to him*, to be precise.

"So, how's your first couple of days going?" he asks. I make a face and he laughs. He leans over my desk and I lean into the back of my chair to keep the space between us the same. I want to talk to him, but right now, in front of them, it isn't a good idea.

"After class I'll introduce you to my girlfriend, Michelle. Maybe you guys can hang out a little." He taps his fingers on the top of my desk and cuts his eyes toward Will. "So, those guys basically hate me right now, don't they?"

I nod slightly.

"For talking to you?"

I nod again.

"Wow, they're definitely . . . protective."

"That's an understatement," I mutter. I try to imagine what Will and Brian look like to him, and the first word that comes to mind is "crazy." *Does he think that about me too?* I don't want him to. I roll my eyes and shrug, hoping to suggest that I think they're crazy too, then immediately feel bad about it.

"Okay, class, settle down and let's get right to it, shall we?" A very large woman with wiry black hair appears in the classroom doorway, and Vince winks at me before he turns back around. The woman is carrying a stack of books under one arm and is looking over the class, especially those of us in the back row. She walks over to her desk, drops the books on one corner, and grabs a giant coffee mug with the words "History is the version of past events that people have decided to agree upon" written on it. She takes a dainty sip and then leans against the back of the desk. She's breathing heavily after carrying in the books, so it takes a moment before she starts talking again.

"Okay, so as you can see, we have some new students today." She gestures at us. Heads swivel in our direction. I squirm a little in my seat. Out of the corner of my eye, I see Heather reach for Will's hand. Julie does the same on his other side. The rest of the class sees. I can hear muffled laughter. Heather doesn't reach out for my hand and neither does Brian. I've effectively broken their support chain by sitting in the midst of them. *Good.*

"I expect that you will treat our new students with kindness and understanding considering the ordeal that they've been through. And I know that I can count on at least some of you to help them get up to speed in the next several weeks." She picks up a piece of paper from her desk and pulls a pair of glasses from the nest of hair on her head, props them on her nose, and begins to read it. "Will Richardson, Heather Miller, Julie Sturdges, Lyla Hamilton, and Brian Wallace, correct?"

I nod, but the others just stare at her blankly. The staring seems like their default response to everything so far. It's starting to annoy me.

"Okay, well, I'm Mrs. Cykes, your American History teacher. We've been studying the Cuban Missile Crisis this week. If you aren't familiar with this particular incident, I'd recommend that tonight you go home and read chapter ten in your book to catch yourself up to speed and then complete the questions on pages 272 and 273." She looks at us over her glasses. "You should be writing this down in your notebooks."

I lean over my desk and start writing. Pages 272 and 273. *Got it.* She waits for the others to do the same, but when they don't her expression goes from stern to slightly unsettled. She eyeballs Brian one more time, takes another measured sip from her mug, then holds up a remote and points it at the television on the wall just above the whiteboard behind her desk. The class starts clapping.

The way the screen goes blue before the program she wants to play comes on makes my stomach flip. It's like when Pioneer showed us his cobbled-together news footage of a bunch of disasters to convince us that we needed to go into the Silo for good. For a second I can almost smell the cool, slightly musty smell of our meeting room back in Mandrodage Meadows.

"Okay, settle down, settle down, everyone. I expect you to be taking notes during this presentation. There'll be a quiz directly after it's over." She flips the light switch on the wall and plunges the room into darkness. The television screen fills with black-and-white news footage about the Cuban Missile Crisis. I've never heard of it before. She turns the volume up and everyone slumps down in their seats. Vince plops his backpack onto his desk and then pulls out a phone and starts running his fingers across it. He's playing a game, I think. Cody does that with his phone sometimes.

About halfway through class a piece of crumpled-up paper bounces off my desk and lands on Heather's. She flattens it out and looks at it and then her face goes all red.

She hands it to Brian. I crane my neck to see what it says. There's just one word scrawled large enough for all of us to see.

Freaks.

I look around. Most of the class is turned around in their seats watching us, snickering. Brian starts to get out of his seat, but Will holds him back, shakes his head, then bends over the paper on his own desk and writes something, rips it out of his notebook, and hands it to Brian. Brian's jaw tenses as he reads, but he doesn't try to get up again. I turn back around, prop my head on my hand, and try to concentrate on the TV. The hour lasts forever.

Eventually, I get caught up in the story unfolding on the screen, how close America came to a possible nuclear war. I watch as they show students in schools like this one, crouched under desks with their hands over their heads as a siren goes off in the background. One a lot like the one we had. I recognize the fear that I see on their faces—it's the same fear I felt when we had our drills. It's so much like what my life has been like for the past ten years that it brings tears to my eyes. And yet this happened more than fifty years ago. And there wasn't any nuclear bomb, and the world didn't end. I wonder where those people are now and how long it took before they finally realized that they were safe. *How long will it take us?*

The bell rings. Mrs. Cykes looks up from the open book at her desk and slowly struggles to get her bulk out of her chair and over to the light switch. Kids start leaving immediately. Vince stands up and makes like he might wait for me, but then Will glares at him and he rethinks it.

Cody's waiting outside the door for me. I take his arm and hurry us down the hall. I'm not really sure that we're headed in the right direction, but I want to get away from Will before he can try to start something with Cody again. I can't get away fast enough.

"Ready for some lunch?" Cody asks. I've been so caught up in trying to navigate the school, avoiding the other Community kids, and figuring out the other students and classes that I completely forgot about eating.

"I guess so," I say. He reaches for my hand.

Will walks by us, but doesn't say anything to Cody or me. He looks back once and the look on his face . . . it isn't full of anger at all now, just sadness. I can't keep up with his mood swings today. Five minutes ago he looked ready to throw me over his shoulder and haul me out of here. He hurries past with Heather, Julie, and Brian in tow. Brian's saying something to him in a voice low enough that Will has to lean over to hear it. They've got their schedule papers in their hands and are looking down the hallway at the entrance to the cafeteria. The way they're walking—side by side—reminds me of the way Will, Marie, Brian, and I used to in Mandrodage Meadows, each of us flanking the other like bookends. My heart aches a little in spite of my anger at them. I miss that.

"Is it pretty terrible so far?" Cody asks softly.

I shrug and start to shake my head no, but then think better of it. "Yep, pretty much, but it's starting to improve."

Together we follow the others to the cafeteria. There are so many students and so much noise that for the first several minutes I'm completely overwhelmed. I keep a tight hold on Cody's hand and let him lead me through the various lines. He pushes our trays through the line and I halfheartedly grab stuff. I'm not sure that I'll be able to eat anything. My stomach's too knotted up to be hungry. I let my gaze travel the rest of the cafeteria to try to calm myself down. All along the walls are posters for that festival Cody's mom is working on. I helped her draw them over the Thanksgiving holiday. They look good and they're attracting a lot of attention. At least one thing I've done recently turned out okay.

"There you are! I've been looking all over for you." Jack sidles up to me and grabs my arm. I glower at her, but she doesn't seem to notice or is determined to talk to me in spite of it.

"I just want to borrow your girlfriend for a second, won't be long," she says to Cody as she drags me from the line and out the side door of the cafeteria. I'm too shocked that she's taking me away—and that she called me Cody's girlfriend—to resist. It's quieter here, but only marginally. I pull my arm out of hers and cross my arms over my chest. I don't really want to talk to her. I'm afraid that she'll use whatever comes out of my mouth to concoct her article for the school paper.

"Listen, I know you think I'm kind of a jerk for taking you down in the supply room and practically forcing an interview on you. And I get it, I'm sorry. I'm not exactly skilled at being subtle. It's just I get so laser focused sometimes, you know?"

I shake my head. I'm not going to make this easy on her. I overrode my ingrained distrust of Outsiders in order to give her a chance earlier, and she's made me feel stupid for it.

"Look, as much as I want to interview you, I'm not going to harass you about it. Before, I was just thinking about my college applications and how cool an exclusive interview with you would probably look on them. You know—well, actually you probably don't—it's kind of tough to get into a good school without something solidly awesome to make you stand out in your transcripts, and of course this type of exclusive would so be that kind of thing for me. . . ."

I cross my arms and interrupt her. "This is your idea of not harassing me?"

She winces. "Right, sorry. Did I mention that I have diarrhea of the mouth, especially when I'm trying to say I'm sorry?"

I smile in spite of myself. As soon as I do, she relaxes a little.

"It's fine. I'm not mad. Not really, not if you mean what you're saying about not harassing me," I say. I mean it too—mostly. I came here hoping to find my place, some friends. It wouldn't really make sense if I turn away the first one who seems to be trying . . . even if she did go about things all wrong at first.

"Good." She lets out a breath. "So I guess I should let you get back in there." She turns to head down the hallway and away from the cafeteria. She's got an apple and a bottle of water poking out of the top of her book bag. I hadn't noticed them before.

"Wait, where are you going? Don't you have lunch now too?" I call after her.

She turns around. "Yeah, but I never eat in there. I've got an article to finish for this week's paper and it's way too loud. Can't hear myself think. Besides, my dad is always there this time of day. I see him enough at home already." She grins at me and walks backward for a second before she spins on her heel and lopes away, her boots squeaking as she goes. She turns down the hallway that leads to the supply room she showed me earlier and disappears. *She eats her lunch down there?*

"Hey, what was that all about?" Cody's leaning against the door to the cafeteria, balancing a tray in each hand.

"I'm not entirely sure," I say, "but I think that she's trying to be friendly."

Cody grins at me. "Look at you getting all social. Nice." He waits for me to walk back into the cafeteria and then together we head to the lunch table in the corner, where Vince is sitting with his arm around a fair-haired girl I can only assume is Michelle. I look for Will and the others, but I can't see them anywhere. I'm not overly surprised. They're probably huddled together somewhere as far from everyone else as they can get. Good. I can use a break from their constant stares. I settle down at the table and wave at Michelle when Vince introduces us. He launches into a story from when he and Cody were little kids and they tried to wash the inside of the sheriff's car . . . with bleach. It isn't long before both boys are telling story after story, each trying to embarrass the other. I spend most of the next half hour laughing so hard that my stomach aches. Finally, finally, things seem to be looking up.

"So, after school today I kind of have a surprise for you," Cody says when things quiet down and Vince and Michelle get up to throw out their trash.

"Like what?" I ask, dipping a piece of celery into some salad dressing. The celery is dry on the ends and sort of overly pliable. I make a face and Cody laughs.

"You know the food's bad when they can't even get the celery right," he says. "So, we've been hanging around my house for way too long. I was thinking that it's time I took you out. On a date."

I look over at him, my celery wilting in my fingers. Some of the salad dressing drips on the table. A date? I grin, a big, silly, over-the-top one. Things really are finally starting to look up.

"Yes, please!" I say eagerly. I think I'm supposed to play it cool . . . but I just can't. "So when? Today?"

Cody laughs. "Yes, today. Well, I mean tonight."

I've got homework tonight already—after only one class—and chances are I'll get more before the day's out. None of it will probably be easy and I'll probably have to stay up late now to do it, but I don't care. Even that sounds awesome, so much like what I've heard Outsider life is like that it makes me want to jump up and down. "Okay! Let's do it," I tell Cody. I drop the celery back on my tray and abandon the idea of eating anything more. I feel like I could float right out of my seat.

Cody exhales. "I was weirdly nervous just now," he admits, and I put my hand over his and squeeze it. He leans over and gives me a quick peck on the cheek, right there in front of everyone. I fight the urge to look over my shoulder for Will and the others. This would be the moment that they would choose to reenter the cafeteria. It's almost enough to make me put some distance between Cody and me like I usually do, but no, I won't let the Community or Pioneer ruin this. Right now, this moment, I choose to be a normal girl—one with friends, a date, and maybe even a boyfriend. They can't keep me from any of it, not anymore. I lean up and kiss Cody right back.

Lust will turn her head, but fear will bring her home.
—Pioneer

FOURTEEN

I have no idea what people do on a date. My only frame of reference is the dates in the movies that Pioneer showed us. I wonder what Cody and I will do, how I'm supposed to look, what we'll talk about. You'd think it wouldn't seem like a big deal, since I've lived with him for a couple of months now, but something about the formality of it, the scheduling, makes me jittery.

I'm sitting on the edge of the sofa in the Crowleys' family room, freshly showered and primped and stuffed into Taylor's idea of the perfect date outfit: tight jeans, high-heeled boots, and a V-necked top that she said "showed off my assets." Cody's still in his room getting ready. Taylor went in to help him a little while ago. I can't help wondering what kind of primping she's putting him through and I start to laugh, but then feel weird because there's no one nearby to laugh with. I can hear Cody's mom in the other room chatting with the ladies on her festival committee. They're busy making wreaths to put up on all the lampposts downtown. The waiting is driving me nuts. If I get any more nervous, I think I might explode when Cody finally comes downstairs, so I wander into the dining room to join them.

"Lyla, honey, you look so pretty!" Cody's mom says when I walk in. The other ladies look up.

I smile at them and most of them smile back, but there's one who just purses her lips and pointedly looks away, rummages through the pile of bows at the center of the table. It takes me a minute to recognize her. She was one of the parents with Mrs. Dickerson at school on my first day. I didn't realize that Cody's mom was friends with her, but Culver Creek isn't exactly a huge town, so maybe it's not that out of the ordinary. Does she know how this woman feels about me?

I start to back out of the room, but then Cody's mom puts her arm around me. "Want to help out while you wait? We could use an extra pair of hands. Knowing Taylor, Cody could be stuck upstairs for a while."

I want to say no, but I don't get the chance. One of the other ladies pushes a wreath into my hands and another slides a set of ornaments and wire across the table until they're directly in front of me. I watch them for a moment and then pick up an ornament and start securing it to the wreath with the wire. The room smells like cinnamon sticks and fake evergreen, but still, it feels festive and after a few minutes I've almost forgotten to be nervous about my upcoming date. I start humming along with the Christmas music.

"You know the song?" one of the ladies asks. She sounds surprised.

"'White Christmas'? Yeah, we play it every year." It's only after I say this that I realize that this year we won't. This year I will spend Christmas outside of the Community. My stomach sinks a little. "Christmas is my favorite time of year. Pioneer . . ." I trail off for a second when his name flies out of my mouth, but when Cody's mom gives me an encouraging look I continue. "We would each get a special gift and sit around the fireplace singing carols and toasting marshmallows." For a moment the memory is so strong that if I close my eyes I might almost believe that I'm there. Every person in the Community had a stocking hung at the clubhouse and we would spend the whole month of December making sure that each one was filled to the top before Christmas Day. We'd make most of the stuffers—things like hand-knitted scarves and carved wooden keepsake boxes. I've always looked forward to seeing what Will or Marie or my parents put in my stocking. As much as I want to be free of the Community, there are all these little things that keep popping into my head when I least expect it, reminding me of all that I'm giving up. As bad as the last few months were, most of my time in Mandrodage Meadows was good.

"I thought you believed in aliens, not Jesus," Pursed-Lips Lady says. "Christmas is a Christian holiday.

"Really, Kate, that's not necessary," one of the other ladies says under her breath.

Kate ignores her, looks at me. "Well? Do you believe in aliens or not?"

I'm so shocked by how angry she seems with me over the idea that I—that we—celebrate Christmas that I don't know what to say. I guess I don't believe in the Brethren, but when I try to say this it feels wrong. I left Pioneer, and by default the Brethren too, but this doesn't mean that I've figured out for sure how I feel about them. How do you suddenly stop believing something you've believed your whole life?

Kate looks at Cody's mom when I don't answer. "You see, she's still one of them. I can't believe you took her into your home, Nora. For all you know, she's spying on you and Stan both. Gathering information for that Pioneer for his trial . . . or worse. Those people don't just decide one day to leave. I saw a show once. They need years of counseling to get free, and even then most of them return to their cults. She's brainwashed, mark my words, and you're putting your whole family in danger by taking her in."

"Enough!" Cody's mom snaps. "Kate, if you can't keep this nonsense to yourself, *you'll* be the one I kick out."

Kate reels backward as if Cody's mom just slapped her. "Well, I was hoping I could make you see clearly, but obviously when it comes to this girl you're as foolish as your son. Did you know that he won't even hang out with Brent and my Nathan anymore? They've been friends since they were four, but this girl comes along and the both of you take up with her, no questions asked, and the rest of us are supposed to what? Just go along with it?"

Cody was friends with Brent, the boy who pulled the fire alarm at school? He never mentioned it in all the times we talked about his friends. My stomach turns over. I've been so wrapped up in how much I've been through, how much I lost to be here with Cody, that I never stopped to think about what our relationship has cost him.

"The boys say that they walk around school humming and holding hands. One of them almost attacked Brent during a fire drill."

"No, that's not true," I say. But she talks right over me.

"They're dangerous. All of them. Have you forgotten already that Robert and Lyle almost died when her people shot them during the raid? How can you take her in, knowing that she was part of that?" She doesn't wait for an answer before she starts gathering up her coat and purse. She heads for the door, but then stops, turns around, and points her finger at me.

"You don't fool me, girl. If it was up to me and a lot of other people, you and your whole bunch would be banned from this town."

"What's going on?" The sheriff is leaning against the doorframe, frowning at Kate. She pushes past him without answering and throws open the door, letting a cold blast of air inside. Bows and ornaments skitter across the table and fall onto the floor.

"We're watching you," Kate says to me. "You tell your people that. We won't let any of you hurt this town."

In spite of how upsetting her speech just was, I almost let out a hysterical laugh. Here we were afraid of them all that time, and now it looks as if they're just as afraid of us!

The sheriff shuts the door behind Kate, and the other ladies get busy gathering the fallen ornaments and bows.

"Don't let her bother you, honey," the lady closest to me says as she sits back down. "She doesn't speak for all of us. *We're* glad you're here. We know you don't belong to that group anymore."

I smile at her, but I can't help wondering how many other people she does speak for and if her understanding is only reserved for me, not the Community.

"Ahem." Taylor clears her throat dramatically. "Lyla? Ready for your date?"

Cody edges into the room and comes to stand next to Taylor. His hands are tucked behind him and his face is beet red.

"What're you hiding back there?" I ask.

Cody sighs heavily and brings his hand up. He's holding the strangest bouquet that I have ever seen. It's made out of socks. They're rolled up and taped into rosettes and attached to green pipe-cleaner stems. There's a giant red velvety bow tied around them to keep it together. Cody pushes them at me. He looks ready to run from the room.

"Taylor's idea," he mumbles.

"Heck yes, it was my idea! I even Googled how to make

it for you." Taylor steps into the room and holds her phone out, takes a picture. "Ha! They turned out better than I thought they would."

I look from her to Cody to the sock bouquet. I don't get it and apparently none of the other ladies do either. We're all just staring, openmouthed.

"The socks are a clue to where my little bro's taking you," Taylor says impatiently. "Oh, for the love of—you're going bowling." She takes a step backward and pulls her arm behind her, then swings it forward.

I nod and pretend to know what she's doing, but it still doesn't make any sense. The other women start grinning so wide that I have to fight not to laugh.

"You have to borrow special shoes there, so you need socks." Taylor shakes her head sadly. "My best ideas are always wasted on people who can't possibly appreciate them. I would *die* if a guy did something creative like this for me."

"Seriously. You'd die for a sock bouquet?" the sheriff asks, one eyebrow arched.

"Maybe," Taylor says, and then she's blushing as hard as Cody is. After a moment she starts to crack up laughing. "Okay, maybe it's a little weird."

I smile at her and then at Cody. "It's a very cool idea, you guys, thanks."

How long have they been planning this? At lunch Cody made it seem like a casual thing, spur of the moment. But he must have had the socks before today. I'm a little surprised that Taylor helped him, but then again, she did something similar when Cody and I first met. She arranged a special meeting for us at the hospital while I was there before the raid. I guess technically that could be considered our actual first date, which would make this one a second date, but I'm still counting this date as the first. I was part of the Community back then.

Taylor, her mom, and the other ladies in the room all have their phones out now. They hold them up in near-perfect unison and start snapping our picture, and despite what happened with Kate just a few minutes before, I start to feel excited, nervous all over again.

I'm about to go on a date. For real.

"Ready?" Cody asks. He puts his hand on my back and starts pushing me toward the door.

"As I'll ever be," I say.

The bowling alley is a rambling one-story building completely covered in neon signs. The biggest one says BALLS AND PINS over the front door, glowing a sickly green. It's noisy and dark inside and smells of frying oil and beer. Cody gets us these really awful shoes and then shows me how to toss a heavy ball down this long aisle so I can try to knock down a bunch of pins. It takes a few tries before I get the hang of it, but once I do, I like it. A lot. And I'm good at it too, which is a total surprise.

"How can you be better than me in less than half an

hour?" Cody shakes his head as he looks at the scoreboard above us. Music blares in the background. He's shouting so I can hear him.

"Because I'm awesome. But you knew that already," I joke as I bring the ball up by my face and take the three steps forward to the edge of the lane. I throw the ball and it rockets down the lane, straight through the center. All but two pins fall down. I look over my shoulder at Cody and grin. All at once I feel strange.

Light.

Confident.

Blissed out.

I can't remember feeling this way before, even in Mandrodage Meadows. My happiness there seems muted compared to this. This is happy times ten. Pioneer's not watching and neither is the Community. I feel free.

"You are definitely awesome." Cody comes up behind me and pulls me into his arms, kisses the top of my head before he leans over and grabs his bowling ball. "But the game's not over yet."

He throws the ball. It rolls down the lane, lists to the left halfway down, and drops into the gutter half a second before it reaches the pins. He hangs his head and groans.

"Ha! I think it might be now," I giggle. I do a silly little dance, so unlike me, but then again so is being better at something than the person I'm with.

Cody takes his ball and faces the lane one last time. He has no chance of winning now. I have one more turn, but he doesn't. He looks up at me just as he reaches the edge of the lane. "I'm not going to win, but I say we place a bet on this throw."

"What are the stakes?" I ask, grinning.

"If I get a spare, you have to go with me to the Winter Festival."

"And if you don't?"

"You have to go with me to the Winter Festival," he says, his lips curling up on one side in the most adorable way.

"Um, sounds like you win either way." I don't mention that really I'm the one who's winning. I've wanted him to officially ask me ever since his mom mentioned it the first time. Manning the skating rink together didn't count. I wanted it to be a date the way tonight is. And now it will be.

Cody chuckles. "Hey, I have to win *something* tonight."

"Okay, you have yourself a bet."

Cody doesn't get a spare. I take my last turn and end up guttering the ball twice because Cody keeps trying to distract me by jumping up behind me and tickling my waist.

"Hungry?" Cody asks when the game's over. He puts his arm around my shoulders and steers me away from our lane. "I hope so, 'cause I'm starving."

"I could eat," I say casually—just as my stomach lets out an enormous growl.

"Sounds like it." Cody laughs and I do too. I've decided dates are awesome.

There's a restaurant attached to the bowling alley at the far end. We turn in our bowling shoes, then head over there, Cody's arm still around me and my head resting on his shoulder. The school day and the unpleasantness with Kate feel very far away now, like it all happened weeks ago. There are other students here, ones I recognize from the hallways or some of my classes, but it's like they don't realize who I am now that I'm not with the others.

"This place—Bo's—is my all-time favorite." Cody looks at the double doors ahead of us. I can't see inside because the doors have curtains on them—blue ones with a pattern made out of keyhole silhouettes. "Last summer I worked here part-time . . . that is, until my dad decided he wanted me to work at the station instead." He doesn't sound angry exactly, just frustrated. "A few more years and it won't matter; I'll be in California and there's no way I can answer his phones then."

Cody has always said that he's heading off to California when he's done with high school. It's still a long way off, but this kind of talk makes me wonder where I'll be when he does. Will I be heading to California too—off to some art school there? Or will I still be living in Culver Creek? I still can't seem to dream more than a few weeks into the future, because I'm not used to the idea that there'll be more time than that for me.

When we walk through the door, I understand why Cody likes the restaurant so much. The entire place is wallpapered in movie memorabilia. The booths are oversized, cut into strange shapes, and covered in giant stripes.

"Bo is a huge Tim Burton fan," Cody says like this explains it. The restaurant seems to be straight out of a dream, or a nightmare, or maybe both. I try to imagine the rest of the Community here and can't. Anything this different they would definitely see as evil.

"Interesting," I manage to say. We slide into a booth by the window facing the parking lot. Cody passes me a menu. I've never actually eaten at a restaurant, at least not since I was very small. I've been staying close to Cody's house since I moved in, keeping a low profile, so to speak. The sheriff's gone a lot at dinnertime and the rest of the family seems content with takeout and TV trays on the nights that Cody's mom doesn't make dinner. So far I've had pizza and pork fried rice and sub sandwiches, but I've never ordered anything by myself. Cody's mom or Cody has done it for me. There are way too many choices here and all of them have weird names. In the end I close my eyes and poke my finger at the middle of the menu where the entrees are listed. I order the one closest to where it lands and then Cody laughs and orders the same thing—a *Big Fish* sandwich with a side of Oompa Loompa onion rings.

"Bo—the guy who runs this place—was the first person around here to really get what I want to do with my life." Cody leans over the table and grabs my hand after we've ordered. "He let me hang out here a lot on weekends the past few years so I could work on my creature stuff in his back rooms before my mom convinced my dad to let me use the basement. You see that over there? I made that one." It's a life-sized model of a pale-looking guy with wild black hair and fingers made of knives, but instead of looking frightening, he looks sad . . . lonely. He looks the way I felt back in Mandrodage Meadows toward the end, how I feel sometimes even now.

"It's Edward Scissorhands, one of Burton's best characters. He kind of reminds me of you, actually," Cody says like he's somehow reading my mind. "I mean, you don't look like him or anything." His cheeks flush. "What I mean is that he was hidden away from the world for a long time too. And when he finally gets out and discovers it, there's this great wondering, happy look that he gets sometimes when he discovers something that he loves . . . and you get it too, like just now when you were bowling."

"Really?" It's weird to hear him talk about me this way. And the way he's looking at me makes me fidget. "So does he ever get used to everything?" I ask, mostly because I feel this overwhelming need to keep the conversation going so I don't start giggling out of embarrassment. "Edward, I mean?"

"Kind of—I'm not sure if I should tell you—in case we watch it. I'll spoil it."

"No, tell me, you won't spoil it, promise. I'm curious,"

I say. I look over at the Edward statue, at his hands. From the looks of him, he had a much rougher road to go than I do.

"Well, at first he does okay and starts using his scissors to prune people's bushes and then he starts cutting their hair. But then he makes a couple of mistakes and accidentally hurts someone and people run him out of town and he ends up . . ." His voice trails off. "Maybe this isn't a movie you should watch."

The moment goes from light and fun to serious.

"Is it true that you were friends with Brent before? Before I came along, I mean?" I ask.

Cody's eyes widen. "Where did you hear that?"

"A woman from your mom's festival committee said that you and Brent and her son Nathan were friends before I showed up. Is that true?"

He lets out a sigh. "We hung out, but mostly during baseball season. We've been on the same teams since elementary school. But I wouldn't call them my best friends or anything. They can be real tools sometimes. I knew that even before you came along . . . you just gave me a good excuse to distance myself."

I pick at my napkin, rip tiny pieces from one corner. "Still, I don't want my being around to cause problems for you."

Cody moves from his side of the booth to mine and takes my face in his hands. "Let me worry about that stuff, okay? I like having you around."

"Maybe, but what happens if more people start to feel the way that Brent and his mom and the others feel? Do you really want a girlfriend who has nightmares all the time and has to go to counseling once a week? Sometimes I miss it—the Community. Because I still don't belong here, Cody. Not yet, not completely . . . and maybe not ever. What if I can't be normal?"

Cody puts his hand under my chin, guides it up gently until I'm looking into his eyes. "I happen to think being normal is highly overrated." He rubs his thumb along my bottom lip before he bends his head to mine and starts to kiss me—right there in the restaurant in front of all the other customers, as if to prove what he's just said is true.

We've kissed before—lots actually—but no matter how many times we do, my stomach always seems to do somersaults and every nerve in my body goes on high alert. I bring my hand up to his face and pull him closer.

"All right, you two, here's your check." Our waiter is standing over us. He drops the check on the table and shoots us a "time to leave" look.

Cody lets me go and the waiter rolls his eyes and heads for the table next to ours. I look out the window while Cody gets his money out and pays. Most of the parking lot is shrouded in shadows, all but the first few cars, which are directly under the neon signs outside. I lean in closer to the glass. My heart stutters. There's a white van parked in the spot facing the restaurant. There are two people sitting inside. Watching me watch them. Were they there the whole time we've been in the restaurant? Taking pictures for my parents' creepy photo album? They saw us kissing just now. I back up into Cody, practically knocking him out of the booth.

The van pulls out of its parking space and slowly drives by the window, close enough that I can see Mr. Brown in the passenger seat. Jonathan is driving. Both men stare at me, their eyes hard and accusing.

"The Brethren expect you to be pure. They are watching always." Pioneer's words fill my head as if the two men have somehow managed to put them there just by staring at me. This shouldn't matter to me anymore, I'm out of the Community now, but somehow it does, somehow the words still steal away the moment, begin to make it feel wrong.

And just like that, my first date is officially over.

I was brought up in your world. I know very well how depraved it is.

—Pioneer

FIFTEEN

When we open the door to Cody's house, the first thing I hear is Pioneer's voice—for real this time. The sheriff and Cody's mom are sitting on the sofa in front of the TV, and Pioneer is on the screen. I suck in a breath. He's completely bald. His head is shiny and pale—smooth. He looks old and harder than before. He's sitting at a table, his wrists shackled and his arms stretched out in front of him. I can't help noticing that his hands are pressed together palm to palm like he's getting ready to pray. Across from him is a man in a suit. I recognize him. He's the same person that interviewed Julie at the hospital.

"Lyla, Cody." Cody's mom attempts to get up from the sofa. The wreath she was working on starts to slide off her lap and she has to sit back down to keep it from falling. "Stan, shut it off."

"No, it's okay, leave it," I say. I look back at the screen and we all go quiet so we can hear what Pioneer will say next.

"Mr. Cross. Thank you for agreeing to speak with us today," the interviewer begins.

Pioneer's lips curl into his warmest smile, but now that he's so thin, it's not nearly as endearing as it used to be. His skin stretches over his cheekbones, sinks in underneath them, and his teeth seem much too big for his mouth. "I'd prefer it if you'd call me Pioneer. I don't go by that other name anymore."

"Okay, *Pioneer,* then." The interviewer gives him an indulgent half smile. "If we could, I'd like to start by having you tell us what the Community is all about." He leans forward until his elbows rest on the table, steeples his fingers beneath his chin, and stares at Pioneer. It makes him look concerned. I wonder if he really does care, or if he's watching the clock while Pioneer talks. *Are Outsiders immune to Pioneer in a way that everyone in the Community isn't?*

"Well, first off, let me say that I am grateful that you gave me an opportunity to tell my side of things. Up until now the police and the government have done all the talking, and I think folks have giant misconceptions about me and my family," Pioneer says with more country twang to his voice than usual . . . than ever.

"We built Mandrodage Meadows just after 9/11. I met a fine group of people around that time who were as fearful about the direction that the world seemed to be heading in as I was. Every single one of us was concerned about bringing up our children in a place so rife with violence and destruction. We wanted to feel safe again. It wasn't long before we figured out that if we pooled our resources we could make our dreams come true. We could build a place where we could depend on one another, grow our own food, bring our children up in the sort of wholesome atmosphere that didn't exist at that time—or in this one, for that matter. It's that simple. I think most people fantasize about doing something similar, but for whatever reason never follow through. I was just lucky enough to find others as committed as I was. I have always felt blessed to have them."

"But isn't it true that you yourself don't have a family? You were an only child." The interviewer peers at a stack of cards in front of him. "Born to a mom, one Annabelle Cross, who neglected you enough that the authorities were called on multiple occasions? She was a dancer in a gentlemen's club and left you alone at night? Your father wasn't around?" He asks his questions in a pleasant, curious voice that contradicts their bluntness.

I didn't know Pioneer's mom was like that. Weirdly, I've never even considered that he had parents, though obviously he did. He never, ever talked about them, but I never saw it as strange, because none of us talked about the people we left behind when we moved to Mandrodage Meadows. If you weren't part of the Community, you didn't exist.

Pioneer tilts his head a bit. He stares at the man for a full minute without answering. He's smiling, but it's forced. I know that look. It's the one he always got whenever one of us stepped out of line and needed to be punished. I lean forward and hold my breath.

"I don't have blood relations in the Community, that's true, but friends can become one's family over time, can't they? The people of Mandrodage Meadows are my family, blood or not. Our shared destinies bind us together." He doesn't respond to the bit about his mom.

"And did your *family* know that you had a criminal record when they moved out west with you?"

Pioneer's smile is frozen. He had to know that the interviewer would bring it up. Isn't it a reporter's job to get the whole story? But it doesn't look like he did. It looks like he expected this interview to go in an entirely different direction.

"My record is irrelevant. The truth is we wanted to be alone. We were *content* to be alone. We impacted the towns nearby as little as possible with our presence. Not once in all the years that we lived in Mandrodage Meadows did we take government assistance or sponge off of anyone else. So to have the government, and everyone else for that matter, target us—me—in the manner they have is just . . . well, terrifying." He hangs his head a bit, his mouth drooping downward. When he looks up again, his eyes are shimmering with tears.

"But if you are so peaceful, why all the guns? The police report says that following the raid they recovered over eighty rifles and the materials needed to convert at least a third of those rifles into fully automatic weapons."

Pioneer's sad look slips just a little. "The rifles were used mainly for hunting. We were never going to convert them to automatics. We had the necessary permits. You have to understand that twenty families lived out there. Most of those made up of at least four people. We wanted to have at least one gun for every person. This way everyone learns to protect themselves from wild animals and such . . . and to provide for each other equally. There's a measure of security that being comfortable handling guns can give a person."

"So having all of those guns made all of you feel safer?" the interviewer prompts.

Pioneer glares at him. "Every family out there was touched by tragedy in some way. Tragedy perpetrated by someone else, tragedy that could have been avoided if they'd only known how to defend themselves. So yes, feeling safer was part of it. And it should be obvious after what the police and ATF did—taking our children for a time, raiding our homes—that their fears for their safety weren't unwarranted."

"And being led by a man with a criminal record for assault helped them to feel safer too?" the interviewer asks.

"That was a long time ago. I am *not* that man anymore. I found my purpose, to care for these people, and it changed me." He leans forward and I can actually hear his chains scrape across the small table.

"And the additional parts for the fully automatic weapons? Where did they fit in?"

"Several of the men in the Community attended gun shows from time to time, and one of the ways we made a living was buying used gun components, fixing them up, and reselling them online." He moves closer to the camera until his face takes up most of the screen. "We had nothing to hide. We still don't. Lots of people make a living that way."

"But that wasn't the only charge against you. There were the allegations of child endangerment and abuse. Can you speak to that?"

The sheriff looks over at me, but I keep my eyes glued to the TV. I don't want to miss what they say by trying to reassure the sheriff that I'm holding up okay.

Pioneer scooches back in his chair again and runs a hand across his heart. "There wasn't any child endangerment."

"Really?"

"No. There was just one very confused girl and an extremely inept sheriff who didn't like us and who was looking for any excuse to get rid of us. Do you know that he made several trips to our development before that raid ever took place? There were only two visits from deputies to our Community over the first seven years that we lived out there, before the current sheriff was elected into office. Two. After he was elected, there was at least one every year. The last two occurring within the same year. He brought his son out on that last one—whom he has been grooming to become a deputy himself and who is about the same age as every kid in our Community. It's odd that after his son came around, one of our girls suddenly started to doubt our way of life. If the sheriff truly thought we were dangerous, why on earth would he bring his son anywhere near us? Does that sound like good parenting to you?"

I look over at the sheriff. His jaw is clenched, and the muscles in his neck are taut. If he could attack the television and somehow hurt Pioneer, I think he would.

"Then, at just about that same time our girl goes into town, the sheriff's son shows up again to follow her around and—here's where it really gets suspicious—she's hit by a car just after he finds her and ends up in the hospital overnight, where both the sheriff and his boy visit her several times. I believe that they used that moment, when she was vulnerable and scared and away from home, to convince her that somehow her own family was out to harm her. I had my family do a little digging and have found out that the woman that hit our girl was the grandmother of one of the sheriff's most loyal deputies. Now, don't that just seem like the *mother* of all coincidences?"

The sheriff practically leaps out of his chair. "You sorry sack of—" Cody's mom puts a hand on his arm and he remembers where he is. "Dog crap. Everyone's related to someone else around here. No way to avoid it in a town this small," he finishes irritably, and Cody's mom relaxes. She's big on keeping everyone's language toned down because she knows I'm not used to hearing it. This is usually most challenging for Cody's dad.

The lady that hit me was related to one of his deputies? No one told me this. Is Pioneer lying?

"Is what he said—about the lady that hit me—true?" I ask. They turn to look at me, their faces somehow guilty, and I regret asking, because it's obvious Pioneer is telling the truth. Why didn't they tell me this? I thought that bad language was the extent of what they hid from me, but now I'm not so sure.

"He questions our poor girl in spite of her concussion," Pioneer says. "Then he asks her mother to leave them alone to talk. Doesn't take a genius to see what he was up to."

"I see. So why did he decide to target you, do you think?"

"Because he doesn't understand us or our way of life, and like a lot of people in this country, he wants to control what he doesn't understand. Freedom of speech and religion are fine as long as it's a speech and religion that everybody's okay with. We know that the way we choose to live is not the way most of you out there would commit to living. We aren't asking for your blessing, just your tolerance. Isn't that what this country's supposed to be about? Tolerating a variety of ideas and beliefs? I don't keep you from sending your children to public school or going to the church of your choice. But I'm supposed to just lie down and let the sheriff and people like him decide that I am a threat with evidence so flimsy that no person in their right mind would believe it? I'm supposed to watch these men march on my home and my family with guns in hand and not feel the need to defend them? I'm supposed to believe that my family will be safe in their custody when the actual act of *entering into their custody* means that we'll be separated from each other by people we don't even recognize as having any authority over us?"

A man's hand appears on-screen next to Pioneer and taps his shoulder. Pioneer looks up at him, his eyes wild. I can hear the man murmur something but can't make it out. Pioneer takes a measured breath.

"That's all I'll say about that." I think he looks like he'd love to say much, much more. His lips are pressed so tight that they turn white.

The interviewer looks at his notes once more. "You just mentioned your beliefs. Is it true that you and your family—as you call them—felt that the end of the world was near? And that you were planning to seal yourselves underground around the time that the raid occurred, with the hope that an alien race you call the Brethren would be coming to help you rebuild the earth after they destroyed it?"

Pioneer looks off-camera a minute, then answers. "Along with many, many other people around the world, yes, we felt—and continue to feel—that the end of the world is at hand."

"But the date you gave your people wasn't correct, was it?"

"On the contrary, it signaled the end of peaceful times for us and the beginning of a period of extreme persecution that will precede the genuine end. And as you can see, that is indeed taking place."

"Very convenient, don't you think?" the interviewer asks half under his breath.

Pioneer's glare is deadly. "No, I don't. I think our version of time is very different from the kind of time that the Brethren experience."

"Well then, have your Brethren given you a new date?"

Pioneer's smile stretches the way an alligator's does right before it clamps down on its prey. "It won't matter if you know the date. You won't survive it. Not if you don't repent and believe me."

"But you believe that your Community will?"

"Of course."

"You've lost a member since the raid, right? The girl that helped capture you? What about her? Is she still Chosen, or is she in danger like the rest of us?"

"She's in danger," Pioneer says directly to the camera, to me. "I don't want her to be, but when she left, she forfeited her safety. The Brethren will only spare believers. The truth is that I'm hoping that she'll be watching this interview. In fact, it's the only reason I decided to do it. I want her to know that she can still come home. I want her to come home." His eyes seem to bore into mine. It makes my skin crawl. "Before it's too late." He hums the song the others sang to me at the hospital. I can hear it plain as day. My heart beats faster. My brain supplies the words, sung in Julie's cheerily empty voice.

Come back to the fold. Come back to the fold,
There's not much time before your body goes cold. . . .

The interviewer is silent for a moment; he seems to be surprised by the humming. "And what do you say to your Community about the murder you're being charged with? Of the girl found in the shelter?"

He ignores this question. "This time is meant to be a season of purification for *my family*." He leans closer to the camera so that his face is large on the screen. "Brothers and sisters, be strong. Don't let them turn each of us against the other. Cling together. This is your chance to prove your worthiness for what's to come. You've seen your sister fall. Do you see how easy it is to lose your faith? Little Owl lost it in a matter of weeks. Don't be deceived and think that you aren't in danger as well. You live among them now. Your children go to their schools. In the coming months your faith will be under constant attack. If you falter even just a little, you will be lost. For now, you are still under the Brethren's protection, but it's time to mark yourselves so the whole world will know that you won't be misled. The Brethren demand it, and so do I."

He puts his hands up to his face and then slowly,

meaningfully rubs them across his scalp. "Show these Outsiders where your loyalties lie. Show them that we aren't afraid of their sheriff and their government and their laws and all of their lies. We are beyond their rules. They do not govern us; *I* do. Give them a visible sign."

He wants everyone to shave their heads like he has. My hand goes into my own hair. *The women too?* I can't imagine it. Maybe I'm vain, but the thought of getting rid of my hair makes me sick to my stomach. I wonder if the rest of the Community is watching this interview right now. He obviously thinks they are. Will they do it? My parents? Will? Heather and Julie, who each carried brushes with them around the compound to make sure their hair was always silky? Will they give up their hair for him?

Pioneer's voice is getting louder now and it interrupts my thoughts, snaps me back to the interview.

"You need to make it plain where your loyalties lie, because bad things are coming. Keep yourselves pure, family! Remember who you are! Show them. Show me that you believe."

"They won't do it. They can't," Cody says softly.

"Can you imagine them around town like that? Kate and the others will have a field day. And the trial . . . ," Cody's mom says, her voice trailing off.

"Will become a circus," the sheriff grumbles. He stands up. "We have just one more day to prepare for this mess, and after this, I'll need to call in some extra guys to back us up." He starts to walk from the room, but hesitates when he gets close to me. "We didn't tell you about the lady that hit you and her connection to the office because it didn't seem like a big deal at the time. It's a small town. Practically everyone can claim some distant relation to everyone else around here. There was never any plan to have you hit. We don't work like that, Lyla. I hope you can see that." And then he does something unexpected. He hugs me. "All of this is going to get worse before it gets better, but you're not alone. Don't let him rattle you. You know who he is, and after you testify, everyone else will too."

Everyone except the Community, I want to add. They won't believe a word I say. And after what happened with Kate earlier, I'm not sure any other Outsiders will either. But I hug him back anyway and nod because I know he wants me to. He looks so tired. The last thing he needs on top of everything else is to be worried about me.

The normal life I was so sure was mine feels like it's quickly slipping from my fingers. It's as if there is an invisible chain still tethering me to Pioneer and the Community. If I don't figure out a way to escape it soon, I might never be able to.

If you're going to do something, do it well.
And leave something witchy.
—Charles Manson, leader of the Manson Family

SIXTEEN

Cody's walkie-talkie is lying on my pillow when I wake up the next morning. I don't remember fishing it out from under the bed, but I do remember having the same nightmare about Pioneer again and screaming into my pillow just loud enough to wake Taylor and not the others. I look over at her empty bed. She moved down to the sofa again without saying a word. I'm not even sure she was all the way awake when she left. I stretch and hold the walkie-talkie up in front of me. Cody probably isn't up yet—it's too early still—but I switch it on anyway, hoping I'll be wrong.

The static sound is still disconcerting. I press the button down. "FX? Are you there?" I hold it close to my ear. Wait. After a minute of silence, I try again. "Cody?" I take my finger off the button and the static softens, stops. I smile. He's up.

Someone starts to sing. And it isn't Cody.

Come back to the fold. Come back to the fold.
There's not much time before your body goes cold.
The end is here, and I want my sheep home.
There's no safe place for you to roam. . . .

A whimper escapes my mouth before I clamp my lips shut. Pioneer is on the other walkie-talkie, but how? It can't be him unless . . . he escaped somehow?

I scramble out of bed. If he's using the walkie-talkie, he's somewhere close by. The others got into the house before, when they left the owl. They could be helping Pioneer do it again. Somebody made sure that the walkie-talkie was on my pillow. I walk over to the door and peer out into the hallway. It's dark and quiet. I can't tell if it's because everyone's still sleeping or because Pioneer's already inside. I run over to the window, slowly lift the curtain and look outside. I almost scream when I see someone staring back at me before I realize that it's just my reflection. I press my face to the glass. It's still dark, but not so dark that I can't see the yard below. No one's there.

A sudden movement in the tree outside the window catches my eye. Someone is crouched in it, nestled into the shadows so completely that I didn't notice him at first. I can't see who it is for sure, because he's wearing a ski hat pulled low over his head and a scarf is wound around his face so that only his eyes are showing. They're intense and blue like Pioneer's, though. The walkie-talkie is next to him, wedged between two branches. I can hear the static from it through the closed window. He stares at me and holds up one finger to make a shushing gesture. I am rooted to where I stand, unable to move, unable to breathe fully. All I can do is stare. This is it. He's come for me.

He turns a bit and pulls a sack of some sort from behind him. Something inside it is moving. He dips one thickly gloved hand into the sack and pulls whatever it is out—a tan and speckled owl with a face that's all white and heart-shaped. The owl struggles to get free—its body twisting from side to side, its beak snapping at the gloved hand that holds it. Suddenly Pioneer swings it from its feet and slams it into a thick tree branch beside him. Then he rears back and does it again and again until the owl goes limp. I'm screaming by the time he's done, calling for Cody and the sheriff. I back away from the window and Pioneer puts the walkie-talkie up to his scarfed mouth. He sings the song again, but this time his voice doesn't sound right. It's too low, gravelly. Maybe because it's muffled by the scarf. Out in the hall I hear Cody calling my name. I back out of the room so I can keep my eyes on Pioneer. He's climbing down from the tree now. Is he coming inside, ready to do to me what he did to the owl? I turn and run into the hall, collide with Cody.

"What is it?"

I pull on his hand. "Pioneer's here. He's outside. We have to get your dad. Now!" I move toward his parents' room just as his mom comes out.

"Another dream . . . ," she starts to ask, but I stop her.

"He's here. Pioneer's here!" I scream, and she goes from squinty-eyed to fully awake.

"Your dad's at the station," she says to Cody. She runs back into her room and picks up the phone. She yells orders at us as she dials. "Wake up your sister. Now!"

"He's going to get in," I say desperately, then remember the walkie-talkie. "He's already been inside!" Taylor's downstairs on the sofa. He could have her.

Cody heads for the stairs. "Stay up here with my mom. Lock yourselves in," he says.

"No!" The last time we got separated when Pioneer was around, Cody got hurt. "I'm coming with you."

He looks like he's about to argue, but I move past him and rush down the stairs before he can. I can see the family room from here. It looks empty. My heart is a hammer in my chest, beating against my rib cage. I tiptoe into the hall, turn to check the front door. It's locked. The little security chain is still engaged. I make my way over to the sofa. Opposite it is the small hallway that leads out to the garage. Pioneer could be hiding there. Waiting.

I stop.

Listen.

I can hear someone breathing. It's low and measured. Taylor still asleep on the couch? From where I'm standing, I can't see over the cushions to be sure. I back up, go into the kitchen, and grab a knife from the block on the counter. Cody is next to me now. Without a word he grabs one too.

Together we rush into the family room. It's empty.

"What are you two doing?" Taylor asks from behind us, her voice sleep-hoarse and barely audible. We wheel around, and as she looks at the knives in our hands, her eyes go wide.

Outside I can hear the first faint sounds of a police siren.

We go through the whole house, the three of us huddled together so close that it's hard to walk. Cody's mother joins us a few seconds later, the phone still in her hand. Every door and window is shut. Pioneer isn't inside. Outside the sun is almost up. It makes the frost covering the yard glisten. Cody's backyard is wide open, but beyond it is a strip of woods that runs for miles in both directions. Pioneer could be there now, hiding. Watching with the others.

The sheriff gets to the house first. He doesn't come inside right away, but spends a long time walking the yard, looking up into the tree by Taylor's window. When he comes inside, he's holding Cody's walkie-talkie. It's wet from the frost. I don't want to be anywhere near it ever again.

"No one's out there now, but there's footprints by the tree and . . . some blood," the sheriff says. "Someone was in the tree, but it wasn't Pioneer. I called the jail. He's in his cell right now."

"But it was his voice singing," I say. "I'm sure of it."

"They could've used a recording to make you think it

was him. He's sung that song on camera a few times during interviews. It wouldn't take much to record it off of the TV and replay it for you. They're trying to scare you." He rubs his jaw. "I'm going to have several of my men watch the house from now on. I want you to stay home from school today, and I don't think you should go to the courthouse tomorrow either."

But this is the furthest thing from what I want. Last night when I went out with Cody, I got a small taste of what it means to be a normal teenager, and it was better than I thought it could be. If I don't go to school, then the Community wins. I'm just trapped inside a house instead of the Silo. "No. They'll think what they're doing is working. I don't want them to think I'm scared. Please. Don't let them take this from me too."

The sheriff looks at me, considers. "Fine, but I'm taking you three to school . . . and picking you up. Nobody goes out alone until I say different. And I'm increasing our deputy count at the school as well."

School seems too loud and too crowded after this morning. Every locker that bangs shut makes me jump. I keep searching the halls expecting to see the man in the mask, holding up the owl by its feet and staring at me.

Who was it if it wasn't Pioneer? I rack my brains. The only guys in the Community that I know for sure who have blue eyes are Will, my dad, and Mr. Brown. But none of them are the right size to be him. Come to think of it, neither was Pioneer. Whoever it was was stocky, muscular. Will's way too lanky and so is Pioneer. My dad and Mr. Brown are closer height-wise, but neither is anywhere near as stocky. If I had to pick someone who fits the body type, I'd pick Brian, but it can't be him either. His eyes are brown.

I gather my books from my locker. If I'm not sure who it could have been, how will the sheriff ever be able to narrow it down? I slam my locker shut. But even if somehow I could, what can he really do anyway? He can't arrest one of them without any real evidence. The person was wearing gloves and took the owl with him when he ran. Sure, there's some blood, but without anything else to go on but my word, it's not enough. I've lived with Cody's family and heard the sheriff talk about cases enough to know that.

I follow Cody and Taylor through the building. Someone bumps into me by accident and I let out a yelp. As determined as I was to come to school today, I can't shake the feeling that I am constantly being watched. Probably because I am. Pioneer may be in prison, but I'm the one who isn't free. No matter what I do, how much I fight to be.

"So, do you think they'll go through with it?" Taylor asks Cody in a voice so low that I barely hear.

Cody looks over his shoulder at me and then frowns at her. "You had to bring that up? After this morning?"

"She's going to see them in a few minutes. What does

it matter if I talk about it?" Taylor huffs. "Hey, Chad, back it up a little. You're practically stepping on my heels."

Chad—the deputy that the sheriff assigned to us for today and the foreseeable future—backs up a little, but not enough for Taylor and she sighs.

At first I'm still so wrapped up in figuring out who was at their house this morning that I have no idea what she's asking Cody about . . . and then I remember Pioneer's interview from last night. His hair. He wanted everyone to shave their heads. The others could actually come to school today bald.

The fear I've been keeping tamped down since this morning turns into dread. I'm not sure how much more I can handle, but I don't seem to have a choice. Everything is so complicated and I'm so tired of trying to figure it all out. I thought life outside the Silo would be easier than this. I feel like everything I thought I understood about my family and friends and what they're capable of is wrong. I'm constantly surprised at how far they'll go to stay faithful to Pioneer.

Cody stops next to my first class and kisses my forehead. "It'll be okay, Lyla. Whatever happens, whatever they did or did not do to themselves . . . has nothing to do with you anymore." But even he seems weirded out today.

"You'll be here after class?" I ask. I want to grab his hand and make him sit in *my* class with *me*, but I know I can't. Still, I don't want to be without him when I see Will and the others.

"Definitely. And Chad's staying with you." He gives Chad a meaningful look, and the deputy nods. I give Cody a hug, allow myself to lay my head on his chest for just a moment. I close my eyes and try to imagine us back at the bowling alley instead of waiting in the halls for the Community kids to show up.

"Bye," I say, and duck into the classroom just as the warning bell rings. Chad follows me. He takes an empty seat up front. He's not in his uniform, but still he's much older than the rest of the class. Besides, like the sheriff said last night, it's a small town. Most of them know who he is. They start to whisper and shoot looks in my direction.

"How come you're in here?" Brent, Mrs. Dickerson's son, taps Chad on the back with his pencil. I almost groan out loud. Once he tells his mother Chad was here and if Will and the others show up the way I'm worried that they might, she'll get us all thrown out of school.

I find my seat in the back. I look out the window and watch a little gray bird dart in and out of a tree as I wait for Will and the rest of them to show up. It makes me think about the owl and my stomach roils all over again. I will never get the image of it dying out of my head.

My stomach seems to be tying itself into tighter and tighter knots every minute. I squirm in my seat. *Are they going to skip school today?*

All at once there's a commotion out in the hall. I hear shouts and whistles and laughter and even before I see them I know that they've done it. *Please no.* But there's no point in hoping for a different outcome now. It's too late.

Brian appears in the doorway first, followed by Heather, Julie, and finally Will. Brian's the only one looking up, meeting everyone's wide-eyed looks with his jaw clenched and his eyes flashing. His lack of hair probably doesn't bother him nearly as much as the others. He'd buzzed it down to match Jonathan's a few days ago. What's another inch? He marches in and the others follow, but much slower.

Each and every one of them has a shiny head, completely free of hair and so pale and smooth that it shines under the overhead lights. They didn't try to disguise it at all. Will looks up and his eyes meet mine and I watch him deflate a little. It takes me a moment to realize that he was hoping that my head would be shaved too. Heather and Julie won't look at me at all. They just keep their eyes on the floor. They're holding hands, their shoulders pressed tightly together. Seeing them without hair makes me want to cry. All around me the other students are gasping and laughing and pointing. Some look disturbed, but most just look entertained, like this is some kind of joke.

"Whoa, what have you freaks gone and done?" Brent shouts out.

"Cut it out," Chad says, glaring at Brent. He pulls out his two-way radio and starts talking into it. I can't stop myself from thinking about the walkie-talkies earlier. I want to be angry with all of them, to confront them about this morning, but then I remember how upset Will was after Pioneer and the other men killed all our horses just before we went into the Silo. He doesn't have the stomach for something like that—even if he's angry with me, he'd never be okay with what happened to that owl.

The other students start to laugh, a series of staccato bursts that make Will and the rest of them wince. They aren't making fun of them so much as laughing because the baldness makes them nervous. I get that—it makes me nervous too.

Julie lifts her chin and smiles. It's a wobbly, unsure sort of smile, but as soon as Heather joins her, it becomes stronger, more sure. They stand shoulder to shoulder and face the classroom. It's almost like a curtain goes down inside of their eyes or something. They seem to look right through everyone. Will moves closer to them and so does Brian. They start to chant.

The Brethren will save us.
Pioneer guides and protects us.
We will look to them alone
In all that we do
In all that we say
In all that we believe.

Watching them makes my heart feel as if it's going to break in two. I can't tell if they really believe what they're saying anymore or if they just can't face the possibility that they don't, not after all that's happened and all they've done.

Even Brent goes quiet as they start the chant all over again. It's so disturbing to watch, even he can't find something funny about it.

Chad moves down the aisle toward Will and the others. "Okay, okay, that's enough. Time to go." He puts a hand on Brian's arm and Brian jerks away, chants louder, right in Chad's face. The classroom door opens and Mr. Geddy and the other deputies assigned to the school rush in.

Will and Brian hold tight to the girls and chant even louder. They're shouting now. Heather and Julie look less scared all the time and more and more excited. You can feel their fervor in the air. It's electric. Will glances down at me. I can see the unspoken plea in his eyes and it's heartbreakingly desperate. He knows I won't join them and yet he wants me to.

The deputies begin to surround them and corral them out the door. They don't fight, but they don't stop chanting either. The whole class watches as they move through the door single file. No one talks at first, we just listen to the chanting as it grows softer and finally dies out.

Once they're gone, every student turns to stare at me. I may not have gotten up to chant, but even now they still see me as one of them. I feel bruised and fragile, ready to break. I don't know how to be here right now, after what just happened.

Before I know it, I'm turning and rushing out the door,

down the two hallways I'm most familiar with to the supply room Jack showed me, the only place in the entire school where I'll be able to take a moment to breathe. I don't even care that it reminds me of the Silo. All I care about is getting five minutes of peace.

I push my way through the door and rush headlong into the musty space. It's dark and quiet and still, which only serves to emphasize the storm raging inside me. I run into one of the desks in my hurry and bang my shin. Crying out, I growl in the desk's direction and kick the desk leg and it feels so good that I don't stop, I just keep kicking it over and over. The desk scoots backward with every kick, scraping against the dingy linoleum. The sound is grating and awful, but satisfying.

"Bad day?" someone calls out from the back corner of the room. I peer into the darkness and can just make out the scuffed tips of Jack's boots. She leans forward so I can see her face. Jack grins, her mouth curving open enough so that I notice the gap between her two front teeth. "I was just listening to the vice principal's meeting with the PTA ladies. From the sound of it, they're still trying to boot your group out of school." She points at the vent. The voices coming out of it are loud and angry-sounding.

I'm breathing hard enough that it takes me a minute to answer. "I thought I was alone." I'm hoping she'll hear the edge in my voice and take what I've said as a hint for her to leave, but she seems to miss it completely.

"What happened?" Jack looks at my face, studies it like the answer to her question will write itself across my face.

"Why do you want to know? So you can put it in your paper?" I know that she apologized for trying to interview me before. I'm out of line, but I can't help myself. I need to lash out at someone. She just happens to be the only one here.

She slides off the desk she's been perched on and walks closer to me. "I swear I'd only write an article if it was okay with you—which, truthfully, is sort of out of character for me, but I guess I'm turning over a new leaf and all of that. If you need to talk, talk. I'm a pretty good listener."

"Okay," I say, arms crossed around my chest. "Please be someone I can trust." I hadn't exactly meant to say that last part out loud, but I did and now it's too late to take it back. It's just that I really do need someone to talk to, someone who isn't Cody, someone who can just be my friend. Cody's a great listener and I feel like I can tell him a lot, but he's a guy and I like him and sometimes this muddles my thoughts instead of clarifying them.

Jack's face goes serious. "Okay. I will be. I mean, I am." She says this formally, like an oath or something, and I feel the knots in my stomach start to loosen. She holds out a hand and we shake on it.

"Okay," I say again. I look around for somewhere to settle. I have a feeling that once I start talking I might not be able to stop.

"Look, we don't have to do this here. I know it's not comfortable for you. We could take off . . . maybe get a coffee or something?" Jack pulls me toward the stairs. "You seem like you have a *lot* to get off your chest." She looks down at my boobs. "No pun intended," she says. I surprise myself and laugh.

"Won't we get in trouble for ditching?" I ask as she pulls me up the steps.

"Only if we get caught." Jack leads us down a maze of hallways so fast that I don't have time to pay attention to which ones they are or how to retrace our steps, and suddenly we're outside, the wind whipping our hair into our faces, our school bags slapping our thighs as we trot to her car. I'm not sure if it's the crispness of the air or the sure pull of Jack's hand, but I feel better, even though I haven't told her anything yet. And maybe that's wrong after this morning and what happened just now with Will and the others. If Cody realizes that I'm gone, he'll worry, and the sheriff . . . will go ballistic. Sneaking off is completely out of character for me. It's impulsive and reckless and utterly thoughtless and somehow the only thing that's managing to make me not want to kick something. As scary as this morning was, I don't want to tell Jack I can't go. Besides, we'll be in the middle of town somewhere, surrounded by lots of people. So far they've gone to a lot of trouble to make sure that I'm the only one who sees their threats. This might be the best possible way to keep myself safe.

Nothing good can come of flirting with Outsiders. How can you keep company with death and not expect it to rub off on you?

—Mr. Brown

SEVENTEEN

Jack heads into town, the main drag to be exact. She's got the radio turned up extra loud and music I've never heard before shakes the car. She taps the steering wheel as she drives and sings along, her voice high-pitched, clear, and . . . well, bad. But she doesn't seem to care at all.

"This is why in public I'm a writer, not a singer," she explains with a grin.

I smile and she gestures at me like she wants me to sing too.

"I've never heard this song before."

I've been listening to some of Cody's and Taylor's music, but I still don't feel like I recognize more than a handful of songs. But even if I did know the words, I'm not sure I could let go and sing them as unselfconsciously as Jack is right now. Back home I'd almost always mouth the words instead of really singing them. I have no idea why. I'm not really even sure if I'm all that bad a singer . . . I guess I'm just a really, really private one. I lean back against the seat and look out the window. I try to work up the desire to start singing too, but I can't, so I just listen to Jack and tap my fingers on my leg to the beat. I feel like an idiot.

Jack parks in front of the diner on Main Street, in the heart of downtown. She leads me inside and we pick out a booth in the back corner, away from the front door—at my request. If they're still watching me, I don't want to make it easy.

"We might as well add lunch to that coffee, since we won't make it back to school in time to eat . . . if we make it back at all." Jack shoots me a mischievous look, her eyebrows raised.

I don't want to go back, but I also know that it's only a matter of time before someone realizes that I'm gone. When Chad returns to my classroom, he'll figure things out and tell the sheriff.

"I can't stay gone. Cody and his family will be looking for me soon, especially after what happened this morning," I tell her.

Jack puts her menu down without opening it. "Which was what exactly?"

I start with Pioneer's interview from the night before. Turns out she saw it too—probably most of the people in town did—and she guesses where I'm going with the story even before I actually get there. I purposely leave out what happened at Cody's house this morning. I am positive it'll scare her away.

"Wow. Do you think they wanted to cut their hair or did their parents make them?" Jack asks. Her tone is measured—careful—like she doesn't want to upset me by saying the wrong thing.

"They decided." I was sure that they had . . . until the words come out of my mouth. "I mean, I think. Maybe not. I . . . I don't know." I try to imagine Heather volunteering to lose her hair and I can't, even after seeing her chanting earlier. Could her parents have forced her?

"Aren't you two supposed to be in school?" Mrs. Rosen is standing over us. My heart nearly drops to my shoes. I start to stammer and can't answer.

"The other cult kids shaved their heads," Jack says like this makes any sense to Mrs. Rosen at all.

Mrs. Rosen motions Jack to slide over and sits beside her. They seem to know each other. I look at Jack and she blushes a little.

"I see Mrs. Rosen sometimes too."

And it is in that moment that I understand why she keeps trying to be my friend. In some ways we really are alike.

"Girls, leaving the school without permission is not okay, no matter what's occurred." She's not reprimanding us so much as stating a fact. She sighs and pulls out her phone. "I'm going to call the school and let them know that you're with me. Lyla, we need to talk anyway about what happened the other night at your session. Your parents were worried sick and so was I. I was hoping you'd call to explain, but since you haven't, now seems like as good a time as any to address it."

I don't even know where to begin. So much has happened since then.

Mrs. Rosen makes her call to the school and then folds her hands and waits for me to start talking. She sends Jack over to the long counter by the cash register to order a coffee and wait for her to give the okay to come back.

I tell Mrs. Rosen everything. I know that the sheriff will fill her in anyway even if I don't. And it feels good to get it off my chest. I start with the day I got the owl from Will and came to the trailers for our counseling session. I describe the circles and the photo album in my room and about finding the shattered owl on Taylor's windowsill all glued back together. She pulls out her phone at one point and asks if I'll let her record what I'm saying and I agree. After seeing Will and the others today, I feel like I have to. I was afraid of having them get mad at me before because I know how much they don't want to leave the Community, but now I'm starting to see that what's happening to them is wrong and someone needs to stand up and say so.

Mrs. Rosen looks sick by the time I stop talking. Her face is white and there are tears in her eyes. She reaches across the table and takes my hand in hers. "You are a very brave girl."

I pull my hand from hers and pick up the salt shaker,

make a big deal about wiping off the smudges from the silver top. "Um, thanks," I say.

"I know that telling me all of this wasn't easy, Lyla, but you have to see that it isn't a betrayal of your friends and family. They need help, and because of your honesty, we're going to make sure that they get it. I'll start working on this today. Right now, in fact." She gets up from the table and motions Jack back over.

"Can I count on you girls to head right back to school?" She eyeballs Jack when she says this.

"Yeah, yeah. But can we eat first? We missed lunch." Jack makes sad puppy-dog eyes at her and Mrs. Rosen laughs a little in spite of herself.

"You have thirty minutes to return to the school. If you order now, you should have time to eat and get back before I call to check up on you."

"Deal, thanks, Mrs. R." Jack smiles at her and flags down our waitress.

Twenty minutes later we're back out on Main Street, making a beeline for Jack's car. I'm not watching where I'm going because we're in such a hurry, and my feet hit an uneven spot in the pavement.

My arms shoot out in front of me and I grab the closest person on the sidewalk—and it's not Jack. I clamp my hands down on both the person's arms to keep from falling. Too late I notice the way one of his sleeves is rolled up and the wide white bandage covering his left forearm and hand. He sucks in a breath.

"Watch it!" he shouts, and I let go immediately, but it's too late. I can see that I've hurt him. He pulls his arm into his chest and shudders.

"I'm so sorry," I say. "I didn't mean to do that. Are you okay?" I look up—right into Jonathan's face. It's him. The Freedom Ranger.

He stoops to pick up the bags that he must have been holding before, but dropped when I ran into him. I kneel down to help him and introduce myself. "I've seen you over, um, with my family . . . at the trailers. You're Jonathan, right?"

He stares at me. "You didn't see me by the trailers. It was the barn."

I stand up fast and step a little closer to Jack. He saw me that night? But he never let on to the others. Why? It can't be because he was trying to protect me. He doesn't even know me. But then I think about Pioneer's video and Mr. Brown's talk and realize that he probably knows me pretty well—at least their version of me.

"Um, yeah," I say, because there doesn't seem to be any point in denying it.

"I'm Jonathan." He nods at me. I can't help noticing that he still has his hair. I'm sort of surprised. I thought he was becoming part of the Community.

"What happened?" I ask, my eyes on the pink skin peeking out from underneath the bandage.

He hesitates long enough that I almost ask him again. "I was carrying a pot of boiling water and bumped into the counter. My potholder slipped and I grabbed the pot with my bare hand to keep it from falling. Stupid trailer kitchens don't leave much space to move around in." He frowns at me like he doesn't like me asking him questions.

Jack grimaces. "Not good."

Jonathan mumbles, "No, it wasn't."

"Did you go buy some analgesic cream?" I ask, gesturing to the bag, which he holds a little closer to his chest. "It'll help relieve the stinging." I know something about this. I worked in the clinic at Mandrodage Meadows at least once a week. You'd be surprised how often people burned themselves, and it wasn't like Pioneer would let us go to the hospital unless it was something pretty serious.

I don't know why I'm trying to help him. I guess because I'm hoping if I'm nice he'll let his guard down and I can ask him why he's joining the Community, why he's decided to believe in Pioneer.

Jonathan looks down at the bag and then at me. "Yeah, I just got some."

I look at the bag, which is gaping open; only one of its handles is in his grasp. There are a couple of bags filled with nails, nuts and bolts, and several rolls of duct tape, but no cream.

He sees me looking and pulls the bag closed.

I shrug and try to act like he doesn't unnerve me, but he does, especially the way he's barely answering my questions. I start to turn away.

"So, are you happy now?" he asks.

The question is almost an accusation, and seems to come out of nowhere since I'm still thinking about his injured hand. "What?"

"Are you happy now? Now that you're with the sheriff and his family?"

I don't know what to say.

He inches a little closer and I take a step back. "You've put your trust into people who don't deserve it," he says.

Here we go.

He steps even closer to me until he's right above me, staring me down, his bright blue eyes laser-focused on mine. "Your family has given you chance after chance to come home. They shouldn't. You're a fool."

He has blue eyes.

I watch openmouthed as he brushes past us and hurries down the sidewalk and past the diner. Was it him this morning with the owl? Is that how he hurt his hand? Did the owl scratch him or something, and he's trying to cover it up with the boiling-water story? My blood seems to rush from my head to my feet and I feel a little faint. But he doesn't even know me. Why would he do that? It makes more sense that it was Mr. Brown . . . and yet his body, the size and shape . . . it could be him.

I almost ask him right there in the middle of the street just to see the expression on his face when I do, but he's already too far away, and I'm not sure I want the whole town to know I'm curious about anything remotely linked to the Community.

Beside me, Jack's bent over furiously writing something down on a small pad of paper she's balancing on her knee.

"What are you doing?"

"I need to write this down before I forget what I'm thinking right now. It's going to make such an awesome article."

I stop walking. "I thought you weren't going to write about me."

"I'm not, I'm writing about *him*." She points her pencil at Jonathan, who's halfway down the street now, headed for the van that he uses to pick Will and the others up from school. "He's an angle I need to explore. What was up with the purchases? Random, right? And he couldn't have been more creeptastic about it."

"You know him?" I ask.

Jack smiles a little. "Um, not exactly. Did the basic digging already, but I don't have much yet. Just that he's ex-military and a recent convert to your Community. But give me a few days to dig around some more and I will."

"Will you tell me what you find out?" I ask.

"Absolutely. Whatever you want to know."

Jack and I get back to school in time for our last two classes. Will and the others are supposed to be in them with me, but their seats are empty. My eyes keep drifting to their spots, and I have trouble concentrating on the teacher as he drones on and on about proofs and postulates. I wonder how long it'll be before Mrs. Rosen shows up at the trailers to take them to foster homes. About halfway through the class period, a girl seated near me tugs at my shirt and leans over to whisper into my ear.

"They were sent home. The superintendent got called down here because of what they did to their hair. He suspended them from school." Things seem to be unraveling so quickly now. I wonder if Pioneer will regret asking them to shave their heads once he hears, once they're taken away.

As soon as the final school bell rings, I'm up and out of my seat and in the hall, looking for Cody. It doesn't take me long to find him.

"I heard," he says before I can open my mouth. He takes my book bag from my shoulder and puts his hand on my back. "Dad said things would get worse the closer we got to the trial. Still sure you want to be there tomorrow?"

"I have to," I say. I have to hear what Pioneer says when the judge asks whether he's guilty of the charges against him. When he opens his mouth to lie, I want him to see me in the crowd and know that whoever he sent to the house this morning failed to scare me away.

I feel a lot of relief and, um, joy that the end of this world is still coming. We all do.

—Julie Sturdges

EIGHTEEN

When we pull up to the courthouse, I can see why the sheriff tried to convince me to stay home. The crowd standing outside is enormous. It's like a bigger, scarier version of the one that surrounded the hospital at Pioneer's transfer, and my palms start sweating as we search for a place to park. I'm squished in between Taylor and Cody, so I can't get a clear picture of exactly how many people are outside, but I can hear them—people shouting, lots of bodies rushing past the car and toward the courthouse.

We have to park several blocks away. On the walk to the courthouse, Cody's dad keeps his arm on mine and the rest of the family walks in front of or behind us. It feels like they're trying to build a human wall around me.

The sidewalk is jammed with people. Their eyes are focused straight ahead on the people just past the stairs leading up to the building. My Community. Every single one of them is bald, their heads gleaming softly in the weak sunlight, their faces pale but smiling. It's both scary and weirdly comical. At first I can't find my parents in the group. The absence of hair has made everyone look the same. They're all in a line, holding hands and chanting. It sends a ripple of disquiet through the crowd. Everyone falls silent as the members of the Community get louder and louder, their voices sure and clear and strong. My insides feel like they're literally shaking apart.

I finally find my parents. They're at the center of the line, between Mr. and Mrs. Brown. Will is beside my father, along with his parents. None of them have seen me; in fact I'm not sure what they see, if they're looking at anything at all. Their eyes have that weirdly blank detachment in them, what I realize now is their way of insulating themselves from the Outsiders. The sheriff tightens his grip on my arm and moves me away from the spectacle.

Off to one side of the Community are the Rangers. They aren't chanting. Their arms are folded across their chests. They stare out at the crowd, and when I look to see what's got their attention, I notice Mrs. Dickerson and a large crowd of other townspeople. She looks angrier than the last time I saw her, fired up by what happened at school the other day. Now that Will and the others are suspended, she'll probably start working on kicking the whole Community out of town.

The sheriff and I begin weaving our way closer to the steps that lead up to the courthouse itself.

"Lyla! Lyla!" I turn in time to see that my parents are

looking right at me, calling for me, their arms outstretched. Will's calling me too. And Heather. And Julie. Every one of them pleading for me to turn and join them. Their eyes aren't as blank now, but they are needy and desperate-looking. For a moment I can't move. It's like they've got hold of one part of me and the sheriff and Cody have the other part and no one's letting go.

Several of the reporters close in. Out of the corner of my eye, I see Taylor stand up a little straighter and position her body into the pose she's forever practicing in the mirror, the one movie stars do when they're on a red carpet. The sheriff frowns and nudges her forward.

We slip inside the courthouse before the reporters are able to catch up with us. A couple of minutes later and we're through security, down a long hallway, and through a set of double doors into a large room filled with wooden benches all facing where the judge is supposed to sit. It reminds me of a church or the meeting room in the clubhouse back at Mandrodage Meadows. We settle into the benches behind what Cody explains is the prosecution's side. The lawyers are already at the long table set up for them, whispering to one another and riffling through thick stacks of paper. On the other side of the room, Pioneer's lawyer is busy setting his briefcase on another table. I watch his movements, his hands, his face. He seems calm, sure of himself. I wonder if this means he feels certain of Pioneer's innocence or just confident in his ability to convince people of it.

The seats around us start to fill up as people trickle in. There's still nearly half an hour before Pioneer's scheduled to appear. I study every person as they walk inside, trying desperately to get my mind on something other than what's about to happen. Cody sits on one side of me, his mom on my other side, and Taylor sits next to her. The sheriff's not with us. He went out to talk with several people in the hallway, all of them in suits and important-looking. Cody's mom has saved him a seat. I'll breathe better, I think, once he's in it.

Cody's hand is cool in mine. My palms are clammy. It's embarrassing, but I don't let go. We don't talk. I can't think of anything to say, and even if I could, I'm not sure the words would come out.

"Hey." Jack taps me on the shoulder before she slides into the seat behind me. "Did some digging on our friend. Turns out our Mr. Jonathan served two tours in Iraq with the army. He was honorably discharged a few years ago. He lived with his parents for a while after that and hasn't held down a regular job for more than three months at a time. I found his Facebook account and he has lots of pictures up of him with the Rangers and a bunch of articles about Pioneer. He wrote a few about freedom of religion and how the raid on the Community was unconstitutional. He's huge into the Second Amendment and goes to rallies supporting it pretty regularly."

"Jeez, you found all that out on the computer?"

"Yep, scary how much you can find out about a person,

right? Hey, have you talked to Mrs. R at all since the diner?"

"No, why?"

"She just missed our appointment last night." Jack settles back into her seat. "She's usually on my case about forgetting, but this time I showed and she wasn't there."

My stomach does a barrel roll. *Is she already working on getting Will and the others away from the Community?*

My parents and the others show up a few minutes later with Jonathan and two of the other Rangers. They take up the entire back row—both sides. Still, not all of the Community members are there. I don't see Brian or his mom, Marie's parents, or several others. I wonder if they chose to stay behind or if Mr. Brown ordered them to because he didn't want them to hear the charges being read, to hear Marie's name mentioned.

A door near the front of the room opens up and a woman hurries in, settling herself at a low desk just to the side of the judge's seat. Just as she gets situated, Pioneer appears in the doorway, his hands shackled in front of him. He's dressed in black pants and a white shirt with a thickly knotted blue tie lying down the length of his chest that matches the color of his eyes. It makes them seem even more icy and intense. The top of his head is covered in a fine fuzz of hair. He must not be able to keep it cleanly shaved. He shuffles forward slowly, his eyes roaming the room, growing brighter when he sees our Community, brighter still when he sees me.

He stares me down. Winks. He's trying to unsettle me. I force myself not to look away, even though I really, really want to.

"Did you like my present yesterday, Little *Owl?*" he asks, before his lawyer nudges him to be quiet. Cody's hand tightens on mine. Pioneer turns his attention forward just long enough to find his chair and sit down before he swivels around to look at me again.

"I wanted you to understand how much I still care," he says.

I don't want to be scared, but I am. My ears ring with the echoes of the shots I fired at him back in the stable on the day of the raid. For a second I'm almost positive that I can smell the burnt gunpowder in the air—like dirt and metal and a blown-out match.

He leans toward me, almost over the wooden barrier that separates him from the spectator benches. He waits half a beat before he grins, starts humming the song I heard him sing on the walkie-talkie. His lawyer leans over and pulls at his shoulder, tries to make him stop.

"You're still mine, Little Owl," he says without turning around.

I feel as if those five stupid words connect us, are fingers that burrow deep inside my chest just above my heart and squeeze. They have the power to stop my breath. I look back at my parents. They're staring at me, small, almost tender smiles on their faces. They don't seem to notice what Pioneer's doing. I look at the others. The only person who seems to have the faintest flicker of understanding is Mr. Brown, who looks pleased by what's happening. He might not have killed the owl, but I'll bet anything he knows who did.

I feel like the room is getting smaller, like the walls are moving in. My breaths are coming fast and shallow and my lungs feel tight. I grip Cody's hand so hard that he makes a little sucking-in sound through his teeth. Still I can't make myself stop squeezing. He doesn't try to pull away even though I know he's uncomfortable. Instead he puts his other hand on top of mine and gently strokes it. My fingers slowly start to relax.

"All rise . . ." A man in uniform begins to speak, and everyone in the room stands as a woman in a long black robe strides to the front of the room and takes her seat behind the judge's bench. She's talking and then the lawyers are, but I can't concentrate on any of it. At one point Pioneer is asked to stand up and the judge reads over a list of charges. *First-degree murder . . . attempted second-degree murder . . .* The words come to me in bits and pieces as if from a long distance, as if I'm underwater listening for them.

The judge looks at Pioneer. "Do you understand the charges that have been brought against you today?"

"I understand that I'm here today because the truth is something none of you want to face. Your own wickedness—"

"Mr. Cross! Answer yes or no only," the judge says loudly.

"The truth will flow from my mouth until I am too weak to speak or dead. Punishment is coming to all of you—"

"Mr. Cross!" the judge practically shouts as the bailiffs begin to close in on Pioneer, their hands on their guns. He turns toward the rest of us.

"Pray and fast with me, brothers and sisters! Don't poison yourself with their food and drink and lies! The end is near. Signs and wonders are coming. Keep your bodies pure and your minds clear."

"Get him out of my courtroom. Now!" the judge bellows.

The bailiffs grab Pioneer. He struggles as they begin to pull him out of the room and yells at the judge. "You've had your chance to see the way. There will be consequences now. Wait and see! For all of you." Pioneer's face is manic, bright red from the struggling. The bailiffs hoist him toward the door. He gives me one last look and then he's gone.

The people around us start whispering. Pioneer's outburst was more excitement than they dared hope for, and now they're celebrating it by rehashing it with one another. I look at the back row, where my parents and the others have bent their heads close together. Their mouths are moving, but so quietly that I can't hear. I know what they're doing, though. They're praying. But is the prayer directed at Pioneer now or the Brethren?

The judge asks to see the lawyers in her chambers and

just like that it's over and we're filing out of the courtroom. The whole thing lasted less than fifteen minutes. I follow the others out, Pioneer's words still ringing in my ears. He said bad things were coming. I know I shouldn't believe him. That he can't know that . . . and yet I feel as if somehow he's going to make sure his words come true. But he's only one man. A jailed man at that. *What can he possibly do?*

Your jail won't hold him. He will go free.
Then you will realize who he is and you will be sorry.
—Mr. Brown

NINETEEN

I leave the courthouse in a daze, stumbling down the steps, my eyes focused on the crowd still lingering outside—Brian and his mom, Marie's parents, and the Rangers, as well as Mrs. Dickerson and her group, who are holding up protest signs now with LEAVE CULVER CREEK at the top. They think the Community's evil. The Community thinks that they're evil. Both sides are convinced that they're the good ones. *So then why do I see such hate and anger on both sides?*

"Lyla!" From behind me my mom's voice rings out high and clear. It's hard not to shudder all over again at her appearance. She rushes down the stairs, my dad's hand on her arm, barely able to hold her back. She throws herself at me headlong. I haven't seen her since our counseling session. Her hug is too tight. I struggle inside of it, feeling an almost violent urge to flee. I can feel her tears sliding down my neck and into my shirt. "I've been so worried about you. You ran out on us and then wouldn't take my calls." This outpouring of emotion is so intense . . . so unlike her. My feeling of impending doom intensifies.

I don't know what to say to this; I can't make sense of this woman who loves me and yet wants nothing to do with me if I don't believe the same things that she does—who blames me for my sister's death and yet clings to me like she's afraid I'll disappear too.

Cody and Taylor stand silently next to me. I look at them over my mom's shoulder, easier to do than it should be because her hair isn't blocking the way. They make no moves to rescue me. They're as frozen as I am. I'm starting to believe that without hair the members of the Community wield a strange sort of power. No one wants to get too close to them. It's like they're contagious. Almost in spite of myself, I reach up and put a hand on the back of my mom's head, run it down along the skin there. It's smooth and naked—vulnerable.

"Come home, Lyla. There's no time for rebellion anymore. You belong with your family and the people who love you. Bad things are coming soon. You heard Pioneer. I don't want you to be punished with them. Please, honey!"

My mom pulls away a little so that we can look straight at each other. Eye to eye. Her face is red, tear-streaked, and panicked. Her hands still cling onto my arms, hard enough to be painful. "You aren't one of them. Deep down you know your place."

I try to see past the hairless dome of her head, past the

sunken cheeks and wild fear. But there's nothing left when I do. This woman in front of me is not the mom I want—the one that I wish for so much that sometimes there's nothing in the world but the ache of it. She is damaged and desperate and too afraid to ever see who Pioneer really is. My mom is nothing more than a stranger and I want her to stop touching me.

Now.

I pull away a little too violently and almost fall. My mom's face crumples for a moment, her hands falling to her sides like they're too heavy for her to hold up any longer. "I can't watch you be destroyed. Honey, don't you see? If you aren't with us, then you are opening yourself up to the punishment that's coming." Her eyes travel over to Cody, and her hands, limp just seconds ago, ball into fists. "Why can't you leave my daughter alone? You've managed to fool her, but don't think for one minute you can fool me, Outsider! You'll pay for what you've done to my family. And it won't be long now." Her face goes a little slack before a slow, purposeful smile stretches across it. "It won't be very long at all."

"Stop it!" I yell, but she ignores me. Her eyes bore into Cody's and she laughs, a harsh, angry sound that feels like it's slicing me in two. I look at my dad, hoping that he'll start to pull her away because he's always been the buffer between us, but he just stands there looking old and tired, his hand rubbing at his temple, his face expressionless. He won't even look at me.

Taylor stands in front of Cody as if to deflect my mom's words. Behind them is a growing crowd of reporters. I hadn't noticed them before, but now they are inches away, microphones pushed out in front of them so that they catch every word. They haven't called out a question. I think they're reluctant to interrupt my mom, who seems to be on some sort of lunatic roll.

Mom looks up at the crowd. "All of you. Not just him. Mark my words. Dark days are coming. No world that lets men take children from their very front doors to murder them and turns daughters against mothers and allows rapes and beatings and poverty and ignorance will be allowed to go on forever. There is a reckoning on its way. When it comes, you will remember what I've said. You will see that our Pioneer really is a prophet, but it'll be too late. You've had your chance to repent and you threw it away."

By the end she's looking directly at me—still hoping I'll somehow come with her—and I have to fight the fear that slithers along my spine. *Pioneer's using her and the others to make something bad happen somehow. I can feel it, but how?*

Behind her the rest of the Community begins to gather. I can't move. I can't see. The world is narrowing to a tunnel with my mom's face at the end of it. When I finally begin to back away, it isn't under my own power: the sheriff has found us and is pulling us away from the mob to his car. My mom gets smaller behind me, but I can still see her staring after us, my dad's hand in hers. There are dark clouds behind them, spreading out across the sky. All at once it starts to rain.

The sheriff leads us past the place where we parked and down one more block to a restaurant. None of us have said a word since we left the courtroom. All I know is that I won't be the one to break the silence. There's no way to explain my mom or Pioneer or the rest of the Community, not even to myself. The whole experience was like getting served one giant slice of crazy pie.

The restaurant is old and nestled at the base of one of the taller downtown buildings, one of the only places to eat that's remotely close to the courthouse. We settle into a table with a crisp red-and-white-checked tablecloth. There aren't any menus. Instead there is an elaborate buffet stretched out across the center of the restaurant. Around us the other tables are filling up with people I recognize from the courthouse. Before long the entire place is packed. The sheriff waves to the lawyers prosecuting Pioneer's case as they walk past—each with phones glued to their ears. Farther over I recognize several of the reporters eyeing us as they pick at the salads on their plates.

"All right, let's get something to eat." The sheriff heads for the buffet and we follow, but I'm not hungry. I trail behind the others, grabbing a plate from the stack by the buffet. There are dozens of home-style dishes, most of which are casseroles—all of which remind me of the communal meals we used to eat. I make myself take a roll and a few packs of saltine crackers. Just the smell of everything else is making my stomach turn. Cody and the sheriff load up their plates, though, their faces grim but determined like it's their duty to fill up since we're here. Taylor and her mom follow my lead and build a small pile of crackers on their plate, then add apples almost as an afterthought.

"Your mom is . . . intense," Taylor says on our way back to our table. "She really believes all that stuff, doesn't she?"

I nod. "That may be the understatement of the century. Yeah, she does. Wholeheartedly." The bitterness in my voice shocks both of us into an awkward silence.

We settle into our seats and start eating just as a handful of Community members show up with the Rangers. They occupy three tables on the opposite side of the restaurant, far away from the prosecuting attorneys and assorted deputies eyeing them carefully. My parents are with them. I slide down in my chair and will them not to see me.

"I thought Pioneer ordered them to fast and pray," Cody says between bites, his eyes on my parents.

I steal a furtive glance in their direction. None of them look at us at first; they seem to be in deep conversation with one another and the Rangers. I can see Pioneer's lawyer in the middle of the group and realize that he's brought them here to go over what happened after Pioneer was dragged away. From the looks on their faces, whatever happened wasn't good. They sit stiffly in their chairs. I can see Mr. Brown and Brian at one end of the table. Both are staring over at me—until I catch their eye and they look away. I look at the others too, but no one meets my eyes. They ignore our table completely, skipping over it as if it isn't there. Are they trying to shun me as some kind of punishment for not changing my mind when my mom asked me to? Does it mean that they'll stop trying to threaten me into coming home? I try not to get my hopes up. What happened with the owl yesterday morning feels more like the beginning of something than the end.

Brian, Jonathan, and Mr. Brown get up from the table together and head for the buffet. They're really going to eat? Has Pioneer's outburst before backfired?

The sheriff watches them walk past us and tension rises off all the men just as thick as the steam coming off the food trays. He puts his fork down and turns in his chair a little so he can keep his eyes on them. They don't acknowledge him and he doesn't say anything either, but I can tell the sheriff really wants to. He may not have evidence enough to confront them about the owl, but he's sure that they're behind it.

Our whole table stares at the three of them as they go through the line. Jonathan stands by the salad section, lingers near the salad dressings and pointedly ignores us. Still, I'm sure that he feels us watching, because he keeps fidgeting, picking up salad dressing ladles and then setting them down again. At one point he drops one, sloshing dressing onto the counter. He glances up at us, then moves to the other side of the buffet where we can't see him clearly. I almost feel sorry for him. He seems so nervous and out of place. I wonder if he's starting to regret being a part of the Community. He didn't grow up in it like I did. Can he really be completely committed in such a short period of time?

Brian and Mr. Brown go back and sit down, their plates heavy with every kind of dish on the buffet line. Jonathan follows a moment later. The lawyer has a plate of food too, but the rest of the tables are completely food-free. My parents are sitting with Julie's and Heather's parents, sipping ice waters and listening as Pioneer's lawyer talks between bites of food. I can't help wondering if the smell of fried chicken and onions is hard for them to take. If it is, they don't show it. I watch them take in Mr. Brown's and Brian's full plates, then do nothing. No one seems put out that they're eating. I stare at them, stunned by their disobedience. They move their food around their plates with their forks, but I never see them actually take a bite. Maybe they aren't eating after all? But then why go through the charade of getting food in the first place?

Cody and the sheriff go up to the buffet several times and end up eating three plates of food apiece. The rest of us nibble halfheartedly on our crackers and fruit. I'm itching to leave. Being in the same room as the others and their bald heads is too much. Eventually the sheriff notices and starts looking for our waiter so he can ask for the bill.

The Community starts to leave before us. I watch as they mill around the front door and pull on their coats. Jonathan walks over to the cash register and grabs a mint from the bowl beside it. His hand is still thickly wrapped. The bandage is brown in spots and wet in others. I can't tell if they're food stains or seepage from his wounds. Either way it's gross. If the owl scratched him or bit him somehow and it isn't a burn, could it be infected? I wish I could find a way to get close enough to him to pull the bandage down and check the skin underneath. Then I think about him up at the buffet, his injured hand grazing spoons and food, spreading germs, and I almost gag.

"You should change those," I call out as he heads for the door. I watch his face to see if my noticing his wounds again rattles him at all. I need to know for sure if he's the one who hurt the owl. Maybe if I can be certain I won't be so scared, won't keep feeling like it could still be Pioneer.

He raises an eyebrow at me. He's sweating. A lot. I can see beads of it on his upper lip and forehead. He's either sick or nervous or both.

The sheriff looks at Jonathan, who shudders visibly. "You should get that checked out, son." The sheriff has the same look on his face that he had the day he questioned me in the hospital. Jonathan has just earned a larger spot on his radar.

Mr. Brown puts his hand on Jonathan's shoulder and

glares at the sheriff. "You want him to go to one of your hospitals so you can try to wheedle information out of him like you did her? I don't think so. This time there's nothing you can do to prevent what's coming." He pushes Jonathan toward the door.

The sheriff's jaw clenches, but he keeps his cool. I've never seen him lose control, especially when he's working things out about something or someone in his head, but I can see it in his eyes: he has the same fear that I do. Bad things really are headed our way.

Our fears are confirmed just a few hours later when he and Cody get violently ill.

That's what attracts people. He's completely happy. Gentle. He dances, he sings, he looks beautiful . . . this draws a lot of people just like people are drawn to little babies.

—Sandra Good, member of the Manson Family, speaking about Charles Manson

TWENTY

The sounds of Cody and his dad throwing up are awful. It's almost like they're screaming into the toilet. I feel like the whole house shudders every time. They're in two different bathrooms, curled up across the throw rugs in painful comma shapes, hands clutching their stomachs.

Cody's mom, Taylor, and I run from bathroom to bathroom, handing them wet cloths to wipe their mouths with. I hold my nose and try not to gag, but the smell is awful. It's like the worst case of flu that I've ever seen times ten. It has them moaning and writhing and glassy-eyed. The worst of it was when Cody didn't make it to the bathroom in time and we had to mop up the sick while he yelled at me not to look. At least now they're both sequestered close to a toilet.

It goes on for hours until both Cody and his dad are retching up bile and nothing else. Their eyes are sunken in and they've started running for the sink to guzzle water straight from the faucet, only to lunge for the toilet and start throwing it back up again. There's desperation in their eyes now and their skin . . . it's so, so pale. I feel panicked, every bit as much as and maybe even more so than on the night of the false alarm at Mandrodage Meadows.

"They're dehydrating—we have to get them over to the hospital." Cody's mom starts throwing blankets at us. "Wrap them in these and I'll get some buckets to take in the car."

The ride to the hospital is terrible. I can barely look at Cody. His face is gray and there's a sheen of perspiration on it. Every time I try to look at him, I have to bite my lip to keep from crying. I force myself to stare straight ahead, at the triangles of road that the headlights illuminate, and try to hold the bucket steady so he can dry-heave into it. Every time he spits weakly into the bucket after another bout, I wince. Taylor sits between her parents doing the same thing for her dad, but she's crying loudly the entire time.

"What's wrong with them?" she wails.

Her mom's head bobs slightly. "I . . . I'm not sure," she answers, her voice tight. She presses the gas pedal down a little harder and we rocket forward in spite of the wet roads and swirls of snow curling in front of the headlights.

I stay perfectly still in the backseat, holding Cody's bucket with one hand and clapping the other over my mouth so that I don't say what I'm thinking, so I don't parrot my mom's words to them. *Bad things are coming. You are all going to be punished.* If I say them out loud, I'm afraid it will make it true. And if it is true, I have no one to blame but myself. If Pioneer's been right and I've been wrong all of this time, then this is only the tip of the trouble that's about to come, and the fact that Cody and the sheriff are being targeted in particular is all my fault.

When we get to the hospital, the emergency room is full to bursting. The creepiest part? Practically every single person there was at the courtroom earlier today. All of them are pale and clutching their stomachs. Many have buckets or small trash cans lined with garbage bags in their laps. I'm afraid it'll take hours for Cody or the sheriff to be seen, but then Cody goes unconscious, slumping over so quietly and quickly that we barely have time to grab his shoulders and push him back in his seat so he doesn't fall headfirst onto the floor.

Everything happens very quickly then. Nurses rush over with a gurney and hoist him on it so fast that I can only stand back and watch, horrified. They're talking to themselves and to the doctor who's barreled through the double doors and into the waiting room to help them.

"The mother confirmed that he was at that restaurant. They all were," one of the nurses says, her lips pursed. "Dr. Harris saw the first few patients. He seemed to think that it might be a salmonella outbreak. Widespread too. Happened just after that Pioneer guy had his arraignment."

She looks at the doctor meaningfully. He shakes his head and shushes her, eyeballing Taylor and me as he does. She goes quiet and they practically run Cody back through the doors that they just came through.

"What was she talking about?" I ask out loud.

A man sitting close to us leans forward in his chair and grimaces a bit, places his hand on his stomach like he's trying to hold it in place. "People are getting sick all over town. You heard the nurse. They're pretty sure it's salmonella poisoning. Someone put it in the food at the restaurant close to the courthouse. We all ate there."

The sliding doors that lead out to the parking lot whir open and one of the reporters that sat at the table next to us shuffles in, her face wiped free of makeup, except for a swipe of black mascara under one eye. She goes right to the nurses' station to check in, then collapses into a chair nearby. The man who was talking before waves a hand at her to get her attention. "Hey, have you heard anything about what's going on?"

The reporter shifts in the seat sideways as if sitting straight is unbearable. "Nothing concrete. Yet. But I'd bet that this was some kind of bioterrorist act. When someone's determined for Armageddon to happen, nine times out of ten they take it upon themselves to help it along, know what I mean?"

The hair on my arm goes up on end and I can feel my scalp tingling. Pioneer couldn't have done this. He's locked up . . . it's impossible . . . but the Community . . . could have. My parents, Brian, Mr. Brown, Jonathan were all there. And they didn't eat a thing.

That's why Mr. Brown, Brian, and Jonathan went up for food. That's why Jonathan looked so nervous. They put something in the food. And the others knew. That's why they wouldn't look at me. My own parents sat there and watched us all eat and never tried to warn me. They were willing to let me get sick. If I'd actually eaten anything other than crackers . . . if Taylor or her mom had . . . would we all still be at the house, too weak to get to the hospital? I go cold when I think of just how much worse tonight might have been, of how little I really know about anyone in the Community anymore and what they're capable of.

I walk over to Taylor, try to find the right words to tell her how sorry I am that this happened, but she holds a hand up between us, blocking my face from hers. The amount of anger in that one gesture surprises me.

"Don't, okay? Just don't." Taylor's face crumples up and tears start to roll down her cheeks. "Dad and Cody are in danger because of you. Again. Maybe they're okay with putting your safety before theirs all the time, but I'm not, not anymore. I don't want to lose them. I just . . . I wish you'd never come to live with us." The way the words come out, in a rush like they've been pent up inside her for a long time, is a crushing blow, and I sway as if they actually have the power to knock me off my feet. I thought Taylor and I were getting close, close like Marie and I were. Tears gather in my eyes.

The emergency room doors slide open again and Taylor stops talking. We both look to see who else has gotten sick. But instead of another victim, Mrs. Dickerson appears in the doorway with a crowd of other townspeople close at her heels. She walks into the center of the waiting room, her eyes wild. "You see? I told you this would happen. I knew. *I knew,* but no one listened and now Melody and Brad's son is upstairs in intensive care. All because of them." She's speaking to everyone, her voice loud and angry, the tone of it the same as Taylor's a moment ago, only stronger.

I try to move away from Taylor and her mom and hide behind one of the columns, but I'm not fast enough and she sees me. "You. *You* don't look sick. Why? Why aren't you sick? If you're not one of them, how could you be there and not get sick? Why isn't she sick?" She's not asking me anymore. She's asking the crowd. "She's still one of them. Has to be. She knew what they were going to do."

Without warning, she lunges at me, tries to grab hold of my sleeve. The people behind her begin to surround me. I look over at Cody's mom for help, but she's turned away, holding the sheriff's shoulders to keep him steady while he heaves into the bucket in his lap. Mrs. Dickerson's hands slide over my coat, almost grab hold of my arm. What is she going to do with me once she has me? I don't want to wait around and find out, so I back up, slip through the narrow space behind the column and the wall, and then run down the hospital hallway.

I barely avoid knocking over a doctor as I pound down one corridor after the other until I finally find another exit. I burst through the door and rush headlong into the parking lot beyond, toward the road that leads away from the hospital.

My breath steams into the cold night air. I have to get away. They think I'm still with the Community, and I have no idea how to convince them that I'm not, and I'm scared of what they'll do if they catch up to me.

I'm not sure where I'm headed, I'm just moving until I can't run anymore. They think it's my fault that this happened. Even Taylor. What if Cody and the sheriff decide to blame me too? If not for the poisoning, then for putting them in danger? They've done nothing but try to help me the past few months, and now they're in the hospital because of it. In my head I keep seeing Cody being wheeled away by the doctor, his face almost gray. *What if he dies? What if* all *the sick people do?*

A few cars rush past on the street, kicking up a slushy mix of sleet and snow as they pass. I can't go back to Cody's house after tonight. I can't face Taylor and her mom when they come home. I can't keep putting them in danger. Besides, Taylor wants me gone. I don't want her to have to tell me so again. Once was enough.

I stare up at the sky—still spitting snow down on

me—before pushing my hands deep into my coat pockets and walking on. I'm on Main Street, right next to the diner Jack took me to just the other day. The sidewalk is empty and the diner's lights are off, the CLOSED sign up in the window.

I look around at all of the darkened shops. Despite all of the Christmas decorations and white lights, every building downtown still feels creepy, deserted. I haven't seen a car drive by once. What if Mrs. Dickerson and the others come looking for me? There won't be anyone to help me. I feel a growing sense of panic grip me and I start walking again . . . but the farther I walk, the more I realize that I'm heading toward darker streets, out of the most populated section of town. *What do I do now?* Even if I make it through the next few hours without a problem, there's always tomorrow night and the next and the next. I can't stay out here indefinitely.

There's only one place for me to go.

Back to the Community.

Pioneer told them to take me in no matter what. They want me back home. If I go, they won't have to break into Cody's house anymore to scare me. They'll leave Cody and his family alone. And maybe once I'm there, I can find proof that they poisoned the food at the restaurant before they have a chance to get rid of it. The more I think about it, the more I'm sure that this is what I have to do. Besides, Pioneer said that more than one bad thing was coming. He said signs and wonders. Plural. Whatever happened at the restaurant was just the start. I need to figure out what's happening next and stop it if I can before it's too late. With the sheriff and most of his other deputies sick, I might be the only one who can. I can't just hide away at Cody's and hope that it all goes away. I can't run from Pioneer, the Community, or my past—not anymore.

It's a few miles' walk at most to the trailer park. If I jog, I could get there in under an hour. I look at the road that leads in that direction. It's darker than most of the other roads. It's mostly fields, farmhouses, and trees the entire way. I shake my head and gather my courage. I take one step and then another away from the well-lit town and into the dark.

If this was a scary movie and I was the main character in it, this would be the point where the ominous music would start playing, where the audience would probably cringe and yell at me to stop. But even if I agree with them, that this is possibly the worst idea I've ever had, I have no choice but to go.

We are all our own prisons, we are all our own wardens, and we do our own time. Prison's in your mind. Can't you see that I'm free?
—Charles Manson

TWENTY-ONE

I stop just shy of the trailer park. It must have been later than I thought when I left the hospital, because the first fingers of daylight are clawing their way across the fields. I hesitate, unsure of what to do. Should I head straight for my parents' door and knock right now or wait a little until I'm sure that they're awake?

It'll be at least another hour before people start to emerge from their trailers. I'm so cold that I can't feel my feet or my fingers. I stare up at the barn. I could go in there to wait. It has to be at least a little warmer than outside. Nothing about this plan makes me feel good, but I go with it anyway. If I stay out here any longer, I'll get frostbite.

I go to the barn's front door. There's no lock, only a rusty latch. I slip inside. It's dark, darker than outside, but I can see patches of sky from holes in the roof and it lights things enough so that I can make my way without tripping on the few scattered folding chairs in the center of the room. There's snow on the floor, piles of it just beneath the holes. The back of the barn, underneath the hayloft, is smothered in shadows, but I head for it anyway because it's the only part of the barn that seems to be completely intact and free of drafts.

I put my hands out in front of me and feel my way to the far wall, then over to the left-hand side of the barn. I get a splinter lodged in my finger from the rough wood and have to lean my shoulder against the wall and use it to guide me instead.

There are a few horse stalls back here; I can't see them, but I can feel where the wall disappears above my chest. Every time it happens, I panic. I have this awful feeling that Pioneer's hiding inside one of them the way he did the day of the raid, grinning into the darkness, reaching out to grab me as I pass by. I move as quickly as I can, almost falling twice in the process.

My nerves are thrumming, like live electrical wires traveling through every inch of me. When I finally reach a door, I'm so unnerved that I can barely manage to grasp the knob and open it. The room beyond it is lit up because the back wall is missing several planks of wood. Something rushes out of the scattered hay in front of me, something furry and small. It pushes its way through one of the gaps in the wall and I clap a hand over my mouth to muffle my scream. I sag against the wall, my breath ripping in and out of me hard enough to make my chest hurt.

The room is empty. There's not much in it except for an old workbench topped with pipe lengths, nails, duct tape, bolts, and a hot plate, its cord twisted out across the ground like a snake. I notice some rusted tools hanging on the far wall, which is blackened in places as if there was a fire—recently, since it still smells faintly like a campfire. Jonathan's bandaged hand flashes through my mind. Was he trying to put out a fire? Is that how he hurt his hand, and not with the owl? But what are all the materials on the bench for? What was he doing in here that required such random stuff? I need to find a way to ask my parents about this room and what might have happened here . . . in a subtle way so that I don't make it obvious that I came back to snoop. I shudder when I think of how happy my mom will be when she thinks I'm home for good.

I walk over to the scorched wall and the tools—run a finger over one—a long scissors-type tool. Sheep shears, maybe? They're rusty but clean. For some reason touching them reminds me of Cody's monster model at Bo's restaurant in the bowling alley—the one that had something similar to these for hands.

"Edward Scissorhands," I say out loud to myself. Thinking about the movie, about my date with Cody makes me feel calmer. I take the shears off the nail they're hanging from and carry them with me out of the room and back into the dark. I imagine that the shears are an extension of my arm. I don't want to *use* them, but it does make me feel better to *have* them.

There's only one more door along the wall and it's closed . . . and locked. There's a large padlock threaded through the door's latch. I yank on it, but it doesn't budge. They're hiding something inside. In Mandrodage Meadows the only locks we had were on the armory, the Silo, and Pioneer's quarters. If the Community had some kind of poison that they were able to put in the food at those restaurants, this is where they would keep it.

I press my face to the crack between the door and the frame, try to see inside. I can just make out the edge of a table and some loose wire sticking out along its edge, but that's it. I can hear the whir of a generator, though. I need to find a way into this room, but not now, not this close to morning. If they find me here trying to bust the lock, they'll know right away that I'm not back here because I've had a change of heart, and I'll be punished. I grip the shears a little tighter.

There's some noise outside, a revving sound. Someone is starting up one of the vans that the Rangers have been using to transport everyone into town. It's almost dawn. I make my way back to the room where I found the rusty shears and debate about whether to keep them with me or not. In the end, I hang them back on the wall. The lighter it gets, the more ridiculous I feel with them in my hands. Foot-long shears aren't exactly easy to hide unless I don't take off my coat—ever. Still, it's hard to leave them behind.

I squeeze through one of the larger gaps in the wall and walk along the back of the barn. If I'm lucky, I can make my way to my parents' trailer without being seen. I try to think of what to tell everyone. What words will make them believe that I've changed my mind? I still don't have it figured out by the time I'm outside my parents' place. Turns out I don't need to. Just as I'm about to knock, the van's horn goes off, one long uninterrupted honk that brings people to their trailer doors and out onto the path between them.

My parents' door opens and my dad practically runs right into me before he realizes that I'm there. We stare at each other and suddenly it hits me that the car horn might be going off as an alert, a temporary alarm system . . . because of me. Someone saw me leaving the barn. They've already figured out why I'm really here.

Oh, God.

I back away, or try to, but my dad scoops me up into a fierce hug. "Lyla, you're here! You've come home."

"I knew it, oh, thank the Brethren, I knew it!" my mom says as she emerges from inside the trailer to put her arms around my dad and me. I have to fight the urge to struggle away, to run. Around us I can hear voices, people walking down the path between trailers. I hear my name here and there and turn to see Will's parents smiling at us like seeing me is cause for celebration. It still unnerves me to see them without hair.

"Something's up," Dad says over my head to my mom, and they loosen their grip on me. It must occur to them too that the car horn might be a warning, because my dad leans down and looks me right in the eye. "Is this your doing?"

He looks past me, down at the road, as if he's expecting to see the sheriff or Cody behind me. I swallow. "No, sir. I mean I don't think so."

He keeps one arm around me and leads us down the stairs. My mom comes up on my other side. She's staring at me, her face shiny and happy, her hands squeezing my arm. I have to look away because I'm afraid she'll see how much she repulses me. She needs to think that I'm still a believer. I try to channel Past Me, the girl I saw with Cody on TV the day of Pioneer's transfer, but it's hard.

We follow the crowd down the path to the barn. My stomach keeps clenching and for a moment I'm almost sure that I'm about to be sick just like Cody, that somehow I've been poisoned too. The barn's front doors are wide open. From inside, I can see Mr. Brown, watching us all gather in silence. He looks excited—agitated, tapping the side of his pants leg. His eyes land on me and he raises an eyebrow, but he doesn't single me out. I exhale heavily on reflex. I didn't realize how scared I was that this call to meet was because they'd already discovered that I'm here to figure out how they poisoned Cody and the others.

My parents pull me inside and immediately I'm surrounded by the Community. Dozens of hands reach out to squeeze my arms. Dozens of fingers reach for mine.

"Lyla, welcome home," Heather says warmly.

Then suddenly there's Will, grinning softly, hopefully down at me. "Lyla." He says my name with a long, relieved sigh. It's like he's been holding that breath in since I left.

His eyes stand out, bluer than before, now that his hair isn't there. "You're here," he says, and there's such happiness in his voice. It hurts me to hear it.

"Everyone, please, if you could move in close, I have some news," Mr. Brown says loudly, his voice cutting through our huddled group. "Something's happened in town."

The room quiets and everyone looks at him expectantly. It's strange to be the only person here with hair. It feels like people keep stealing glances at my head.

"Pioneer's visions are coming true. The Outsiders have been punished."

Everyone starts talking all at once and several people clap. They all look delighted. It makes me sick. I bite my tongue and try not to show how angry their cheers make me. *How can they be happy about other people's suffering?*

Mr. Brown's mouth quirks up into a half smile. "At least fifty of them ended up in the hospital last night with a mysterious sickness." The way he says the word "mysterious" confirms what I already know. He did this, and Brian and Jonathan helped him. I know it, but I can't prove it. I need to be able to prove it.

I study the other faces around me for signs that some or all of them were in on this with them. I look extra hard at my mom, but everyone seems equally surprised. They could be acting. I can't know for sure, not yet.

"Among them were some of the very people who stormed our gates and ripped us from our home," Mr. Brown says.

A cheer goes up then, loud and clear and sure. It hurts me—every violent shout, each of them a tiny dagger piercing my skin.

"Our persecution has been difficult to endure, but our faith has not been in vain! This is proof. The Brethren have set things in motion. It won't be long now!" Mr. Brown's voice goes up in volume so that by the last word he's shouting. My mom puts her hands prayer-style against her face. Her eyes are bright and shimmering with tears.

"The end is near and now the Outsiders suffer just like Pioneer said that they would. Aren't you glad that you didn't waver? Aren't you glad that you held fast to our leader and to each other?" His voice is warm and sweet, thick with emotion and full of pride.

"Yes, oh yes!"

People nod their heads vigorously. Some are rocking in place and weeping. I turn in a circle and take it all in. It's strange to be here now, after I've been away from them for so long. I don't see them the same way that I once did. What they're doing isn't comforting or inspiring. It's creepy.

"And our Lyla's come home! Just as Pioneer said she would," my mom calls out when things wind down and the room gets quiet enough so that people can hear her. She falls on me, weeping, and I have to work to keep her upright. I want to drop her.

Just as Pioneer said she would. I shudder.

You're mine, Little Owl.

I want to yell at her to stop, for all of them to wake up

already and see how crazy this all is, but instead I do what used to come much more naturally. I smile—the blank-eyed kind that so unnerves me every time I see the rest of them do it.

Mr. Brown is walking toward us—me. I try not to tremble. "Is that right, Lyla? Are you here to stay?" He looks intently at my eyes.

I nod. "Yes, brother." My voice sounds too wobbly. I try again. "Yes, brother!" It's better the second time and the clapping starts again.

Mr. Brown hesitates for almost a full minute before he answers me—enough time for me to worry that he can see my true intentions scrolling across my forehead. He's frowning slightly too—which only adds to my uncertainty—but then suddenly his face smooths out and he pulls me into his chest. "Welcome back, sister. Thank the Brethren that you've finally seen the error of your ways."

His arm is a little too tight around me. I wasn't being paranoid—he is skeptical of me. They all probably are. I'll have to prove that I'm recommitted if I'm going to stay. They won't just let me back in and not make sure that I believe wholeheartedly again.

"Welcome home!" they all shout.

"No!" someone yells from across the room. I look up, try to see over the others, but everyone is too close. "She doesn't deserve to be here. She shouldn't be allowed to come back."

Brian. I recognize his voice now.

"Why should we let her come back? Why should we welcome her with open arms? *She's* the one who helped the Outsiders take our homes. *She's* the one who put us all in danger. *She's* to blame for my father and Marie. How can you just forgive all of it? Well, I can't. I *won't*!"

I can see him now, pushing through the people. The hate emanating from him makes me cringe. I have the overwhelming feeling that he's going to hit me. But then Will steps in between us, and several of the men nearby restrain Brian.

"She's not one of us. She was *never* one of us. Can't you see that? Let her stay and she will *ruin* everything all over again. Wait and see. She should be sick along with the rest of them. She deserves to be sick. She deserves to be *dead*!"

The men push him backward, but it's a struggle. Brian's legs keep pushing off in my direction, his whole body leaning toward me. I think he might kill me himself if they let him go. I knew he was angry, but still I'm surprised at just how much.

Mr. Brown steps closer to my dad and whispers in his ear. They look at me. I try to keep my face calm, but it's hard. I feel like Brian's words jarred everyone and now maybe they're rethinking welcoming me back. My mom sticks close to my side. She must sense it too. She's finally protecting me, but only when it serves her own needs. She wants me back in the Community.

I have to try really, really hard not to pull away.

"Lyla, I'm sure you have firsthand news of what's

happening to the Outsiders. And we'd love to know how you were able to get away and back to us."

His tone is warm and pleasant, but his eyes are sharp. Whatever I tell them right now will determine whether they really believe that I'm back for the right reasons and not to cause trouble. It's why I spent most of the last several hours rehearsing exactly what I should say.

I clear my throat and clasp my hands in front of me the way I've seen Pioneer do every time he's had something big to tell us. It always made him look humble, and I'm hoping it will do the same for me now.

"I know that I've messed up," I say. "I got confused. The sheriff and Cody . . ." I trail off because saying their names feels dangerous. *Can they sense how I feel about Cody in my voice or expression or movements?* ". . . were so nice at first and I was so curious about the world. I guess I wanted to believe that it wasn't really the end of days. I was . . . I *am* scared of facing what's coming. But when everyone started to get sick . . . it opened my eyes. The Outsiders turned on me. They blamed me for their punishment and tried to hurt me." My voice is thick with emotion now. I can't help it, not when Taylor's last words to me are still fresh in my mind. But this is good. It will help them believe.

My mom gasps.

"I've been afraid of all the wrong things. I should've been afraid of letting down the Brethren and Pioneer and all of you. I was selfish. I was confused. I see that now," I say, and tears fall down my cheeks, because as much as

I'm trying to put on a show, the words are starting to come far too easily. It feels like some part of me is relieved to be saying them. Is it possible that part of me half wants to believe this stuff still? That it always will? I hate the idea, hate myself for the possibility that it's true. If I can't be one hundred percent sure of where I stand, how do I know I'll be capable of standing at all?

"Last night after I got away from them, I fell to my knees and asked the Brethren to forgive me and I felt like they heard me and then it was like they were leading me here, leading me home."

I don't dare look down once I've stopped talking. I'm so afraid that none of what I said made sense, much less convinced them, but I keep my smile in place and my eyes on Mr. Brown.

He waits—his eyes searching mine, neither of us blinking until I am sure he is going to call me out as a liar—before he puts an arm around me and kisses the top of my head. "Pioneer always knew you would return. You belong with us. We knew you would see it in the end. We just had to have faith. And now that you know what waits for you out there, I am sure that you will never, ever consider leaving us again. You were very lucky this time. Had you not had the Brethren's protection, you would be sick too. A plant plucked from the soil won't survive. It has to stay rooted, be bathed in sunlight and nurtured always. Without those things it's doomed to wither and die."

I nod as I look up at Mr. Brown. He sounds so much like

Pioneer now. It's like he's constantly channeling him. For one terrifying moment I wonder if that's actually what's happening. If somehow Pioneer is watching me through Mr. Brown's eyes.

All the time I've been up in front of everyone, the room has been relatively silent, but now people start to speak.

"You are loved."

"You are ours."

"You are Chosen."

They come up to me one by one, welcoming me again. All the people I've played with, worked with, sung with, cried with for the last ten years, each one of them whispering a message in my ear, each one wrapping me in their arms. And as scary as it all is, it also feels good—like a cool cloth on my forehead after a bad fever or being wrapped in a blanket just out of the dryer. I have missed them in spite of everything. Crazy or not. I can't help myself.

When I've been passed through almost everyone's arms and been told I'm loved more times than I can count, the meeting begins to break up. I follow my parents back to their trailer with Will by my side. I'd forgotten how warm everyone could be. They really mean what they're saying when they say it. They missed me and wanted me home.

She just needs a little reminder of
who she is and where she belongs.
—Allison Hamilton

TWENTY-TWO

After the meeting, Will walks with my parents and me back to the trailer. Once we're inside, my parents keep smiling at me as they fight for space in the cramped kitchenette, each of them anxious to make a hot cup of tea to warm me up after my night spent outside. My mom's humming and my dad looks as relieved as I've ever seen him. I've come back; now he doesn't have to choose Mom over me anymore. He can be with us both.

I sip my tea. I don't have the slightest idea what to talk to my parents about, so I take Will to my bedroom instead, where we can hang out alone, away from their happy stares. My parents don't seem to mind, but they do ask us to leave the door open.

"So, you really mean it—what you said back there?" Will sits on my bed, his back against the wall.

"Yeah, I did." It's harder to pretend to mean it now. I don't like lying to Will. Especially when he so desperately wants what I'm saying to be true.

"You know, when you left I was so scared that you had a good reason to. I was afraid that what you thought you saw . . . you know, with Marie . . . was true. It felt like everything I ever believed in was being ripped out from under me. But then when the Rangers came and we got to stay together and Pioneer explained what really happened, it just made perfect sense. It does to you now too, right? I mean, that's really why you're back?"

This pretending is going to be so much harder than I thought. I don't want to say what he needs to hear. I can almost feel Marie's presence, weighing on me, waiting for me to make her murder be something else, something worse: her fault. My lips are dry and I bite at the spots that are chapped. "I'm back because I know where I belong now—and it wasn't with Cody or his family," I say, trying to answer without really saying anything at all. It's enough to bring a smile to Will's face, though.

"No, it wasn't," he says, his voice growing tender. "Look, I know that you see me as your friend . . . more than anything else. I've always known that, Lyla. And it's okay. I'm okay with it. I think it's enough for us to build something more on, someday, if you'll just let me try to make you happy." He pulls something out of his back pocket. It's a smaller pocket-sized version of the owl that he left in Cody's car. My stomach turns over. I look at his face, at the wistful expression on it, and I'm positive that he doesn't know that one of the others climbed up the tree outside Cody's house and killed an owl in front of me. He would never have kept this little owl with him if he did. Will might be a true believer, but he's not capable of that kind of evil.

"I kept this with me all the time you were gone. I never gave up on you, you know. Even before Pioneer said that we shouldn't give up. And I never will."

I'm starting to finally understand that Will's here for Pioneer, but it's not his only reason—it probably isn't even his main reason. He wants his old life back because it's the only way we might be together. What he believes in most is *us*—as a couple.

"Will, I . . ." My voice trails off. It hurts me, this hope he has now, but how do I make him see that we are never going to be together the way he wants and still keep everyone else convinced that I'm part of the Community again? I can't tell him yet. As much as I hate it, I have to pretend that I want to be his Intended again until I understand what happened to the sheriff and Cody and how many members of the Community are to blame.

Will gets up from the bed and moves toward me, but I take a step backward—almost on reflex. His hands were up like he was going to try to hug me. He lowers his head, and I panic. I've given too much of what I'm really feeling away and blown it, but then he just nods to himself and heads for the door. "You probably need time to clear your head and . . . let go of him." He won't say Cody's name even now. "I can do that. I'll do whatever it takes to get things back to where they were. I won't give up on our future, Lyla. Being with you is my calling."

He goes out into the hall and I'm alone in the room. I lie back on the bed and put my arm over my eyes. I'm so tired all of a sudden. The lack of sleep and everything that's happened over the last twenty-four hours are catching up with me. I'm too tired to move so that I can get under the quilt, so I just pull one side of it around me instead and stare at the wall. It isn't long before I can feel myself slipping away.

I wake up with a start. My dad's hand is on my side, gently shaking me awake. My heart's pounding and I have an indescribably bad headache. What I really need is a full, uninterrupted night's sleep—maybe an entire day. I curl into myself again and hope that he'll go away so I can go back to it, but he just keeps shaking me and saying my name. The light coming through the window is still really bright, which means that I can't have slept very long at all.

"Your lunchtime tea's ready. We let you sleep for an hour, but we should probably talk a bit, don't you think?" Dad says softly. "Come on, honey, wake up."

"No thanks," I mumble. I never finished the last cup that they gave me. The truth is that I'm not sure drinking anything with any of them is a good idea considering what happened yesterday, but I can't very well say that to him.

"You're going to need to keep hydrated. Fasting is hard on the body. If you don't drink enough, you'll start to get sick."

This makes me open my eyes. Fasting? Then I remember how Pioneer asked them all to fast and pray yesterday.

"For how long?" I ask. Since Cody and the others are already poisoned, I'm not sure why they're still doing it.

"Until Pioneer tells us to stop or the Outsiders let him out of jail," Dad says—very matter-of-fact. "Now come on, it'll get cold."

I roll out of bed and stumble after him. I'm still so tired that the room feels like it's rocking and I keep listing right and then left the whole way down the hall. I can smell cinnamon and cloves in the air.

"There you are, sleepy girl." Mom shuffles past me and ruffles my hair. The casual nature of her touch is strange. It's like she's choosing to erase all that's happened in the past few months. She moves around to the little table beside the kitchenette and settles into one of the chairs, pats the one next to hers for me. She's holding a cup of hot water with lemon.

At my spot at the table is a large mug of spiced tea. This smell more than any other reminds me of my mom both before and after we left New York to go be with Pioneer. She's been giving me this tea on cold days since before we lived in Mandrodage Meadows. Out of nowhere I get a flash of my sister, Karen, and me sitting at a table with our dolls, clinking our teacups together and giggling. What would our life have been like if she'd never disappeared? Would we be sitting at a table in our old brownstone in

New York? Would Pioneer ever have entered our lives? Would my mom be more like Cody's? These thoughts make my throat so tight that I'm not sure I'll be able to take a sip, but both my parents are watching me, looking for signs that I'm back with them the way I used to be. I can't give them any reason to doubt it, so I bring the mug up to my lips and drink.

My parents grin at one another and my mom sips at her water.

"Taste okay?" she asks.

"Mm-hmm," I say, and force a big smile.

She laughs, delighted, and runs a hand up and down my arm. "We're so glad you came home. I can't tell you how much I've worried for you. Things are going to get a lot worse for the Outsiders now before they'll get better."

"How do you know that?" I ask in a tone that I hope sounds merely curious, not accusatory.

"Because Pioneer said so. You heard him yesterday. He knew what would happen. That's why he told us to fast and pray. We just have to be strong for a little longer. But can you imagine the reward we have waiting for us afterward? A few years in the Silo while the Brethren wipe them out and we'll have our new earth. Pioneer promised that your sister will come back to us then with the Brethren. What a life she must be leading up there with them. I can't wait to be a part of it."

I look at Dad, but he won't look at either of us. I can see the same doubt about Pioneer in his face that was there that last day in the Silo when I asked him to leave with me; it's slipping in and out of his expression.

There's a knock at the door and then it opens before anyone gets up to answer it. This is the way it used to be back in Mandrodage Meadows. People weren't allowed to keep their houses locked and it was expected that any of the other Community members could enter your house without permission. There was no such thing as privacy. It seems funny that I thought that was normal before. It seems that they've brought that practice here too. Which will be good for when I want to snoop around, but bad if I want to feel safe anywhere.

Mr. Brown enters our trailer, his face flushed from the cold. He plucks a napkin from our table and blows his nose loudly and then leans against the wall and peers at our tea. "Looks good, may I have a cup?"

"We wanted to welcome Lyla home," Mom says as she gets up to pour him a mug.

"Wonderful." Mr. Brown looks at me and winks. "So good to see you here with your parents. They've missed you. The last few months have been quite hard on them. On all of us. You're our family too."

"I know, I'm sorry," I say.

"You've been gone for a while, Lyla. You've probably developed lots of bad habits, maybe gotten too used to seeing things from the wrong perspective."

Translation: he thinks I'm infected with Outsider beliefs. I knew that he would. Now I have to convince him that I've really and truly seen the light. He will be harder to convince than everyone else. My stomach quivers.

"Coming back means letting go of all of the new, wrong ideas that you've taken into your life. You have to let it all go willingly and completely if you want to be back for good."

I put my hands on my knees beneath the table and grip them tightly. After everything that's happened, I knew that I would have to convince them of my commitment. But I'm not sure what I can do. *What will they ask me to do?*

He looks over at my parents. "I'm going to have a little talk with her to get her sorted out and back on the right path. Pioneer told me what would need to be done if she returned. He left me detailed instructions on how to . . . correct her. I'd like to do it in the barn."

At the sound of Pioneer's name, I tense. *Pioneer left him instructions? For what?* I can't imagine. I look past Mr. Brown at the door and briefly consider jumping up from my seat and bolting for it. Maybe this wasn't such a good idea.

"Absolutely, we'll just let her finish her tea and head over there with her," Dad says. He pats my arm and I feel less afraid for a moment. He seems utterly calm. *Maybe I'm just being paranoid.*

"I think it would be better if I took her with me now and you both waited here. I'll have her back to you soon." Mr. Brown motions for me to stand up. "She seems ready to do what it takes to be with us again. Aren't you, Lyla?" Mr. Brown is talking in a voice that's warmer than a thick pair of mittens, all deep and soft and pleasant. Pioneer used to do that too—right before we got punished.

I get up from the table. I already know that my parents won't argue with him to keep me with them. They never did before and I'm certain that they won't start now.

I go outside with Mr. Brown and slowly follow him to the barn. On the way, I pass several of the Rangers. They're standing over at the far end of the barn in a kind of huddle, a laptop computer propped up on a log between them. I can hear someone talking on the computer. It sounds like a news report.

"Sources say that as many as two restaurants frequently visited by those at the courthouse were compromised. Some kind of salmonella poisoning is suspected, but the police have not released any statements confirming whether the poisoning was deliberate." One of the men looks up at us as he listens and frowns. It's clear from the way he watches Mr. Brown go by that he suspects the Community and that he isn't happy about it.

I have a sudden urge to call out to them, to confirm what they seem to already suspect, but I stay silent. It's too big a risk until I know how they feel for sure. I make myself keep walking with Mr. Brown—all the way to the barn and whatever he has waiting for me there.

I am the devil here to do the devil's business.

—Charles "Tex" Watson, member of the Manson Family

TWENTY-THREE

The barn is completely empty. Mr. Brown leads us to the back of it, all the way to one of the rooms I found earlier this morning, the one where the rusty shears are. For one brief moment I'm tempted to grab them off the wall and point them at Mr. Brown, but I don't. I am choosing to be here . . . sort of.

There's a chair inside, the metal folding kind, and nothing else—the workbench and all the things on it are gone. I stay close to the door, but Mr. Brown nudges me farther into the room. His wife is in the far corner. She waves at me. She's wearing the apron she always wore when she had kitchen duty in the clubhouse, the one with little cherries all over it. It's oddly cheery in comparison to the rest of the room.

"Take a seat, Lyla, no need to hover in the doorway," she says.

I don't want to sit and have them standing over me. "I'd rather stand if that's okay?" I keep the question in my voice so that hopefully they won't see this as defiance. It doesn't work.

"You see, this is the very thing that we have to address before you can truly come home," Mr. Brown says. "You used to know how to listen to your elders without question."

I steel myself as best I can, lower my head like I'm apologetic, and quickly sit down. I've been punished before. I can handle it . . . I think.

Mr. Brown crouches next to my chair and Mrs. Brown moves behind me, gathers my hair in her hands. It's all I can do not to leap out of the chair, I'm that sure that she's going to cut my hair and make me bald. I grip the edge of the chair to force myself to stay put. But instead she begins to braid it the way that my mom used to. All of the girls in the Community wore their hair in one when we were little. Maybe she's trying to make me feel like that again—little and helpless.

"They told you we were wrong. They told you Pioneer was a bad man. A criminal. Crazy." Mr. Brown smiles a sad sort of smile. "But did they ever tell you about their own pasts? Did they ever tell you all the things that they've done wrong? Or how they found out what kind of man Pioneer was before he was with us?"

"They showed me articles about his first arrest on the Internet," I say cautiously. I'm not sure what he wants me to say or where he's going with this. Behind me, Mrs.

Brown keeps working on my hair, pulling it tightly as she goes. Too tightly. I squirm a little.

"The Internet." Mr. Brown pronounces it like "enter-net." "People can post stuff on there and claim it's the truth when they know it's a lie. They don't even get in trouble for it. That's why Pioneer forbid us from having it in the first place."

There's a knock on the door and then Jonathan comes in. He's holding a laptop. He looks at me, his blue eyes bright, his head cocked to one side. "Brian said that you needed this?" He looks excited to be helping with whatever's going on. I eye him suspiciously. He's definitely in on the poisonings, I can feel it, but unlike Mr. Brown and the others, I am not sure of his motives.

"Oh, good, thanks, son." Mr. Brown rises and takes the laptop from him. "I'll get it back to you in a few minutes."

"How's your hand?" I ask him to keep him in the room and stall for time. I stare pointedly at the wall and the blackened wood.

He holds it up. The bandage is white and fresh and the skin around his fingers isn't as raw-looking as before. "Better." He is utterly calm standing there. He doesn't even look at the wall. It should make me doubt myself, but it doesn't; it only makes me more certain that I'm on the right track. He was doing something in this room, there was a fire, and that's how he burned his hands.

"I'm glad to hear it. I was worried about you yesterday."

I make my voice sweet and smile when I really want to shake him and Mr. Brown both until they admit what they've done and what they're planning next.

His mouth curves up at the corners. "I'm fine. The ones you should worry about are the sheriff and his son. They're the ones who are sick. You're very lucky that you were spared." He looks almost disappointed and a chill runs up my spine.

"When did you become one of us?" I ask, because I can't figure it out—why he's so committed to a man and cause he barely knows.

"I haven't made any final decisions about the Brethren, not yet," Jonathan says, and I can't help but gasp. So then why is he involved? "Pioneer's been talking to me about them for as long as I can remember, ever since we met at a gun show some years back. I may not be a true believer, but we do agree on one thing. This country is going to hell in a handbasket and nothing short of a serious tragedy is going to shock it into change." He rubs his hands as if the wounds are a reminder of this somehow.

Mr. Brown's jaw clenches and he looks close to saying something, but he thinks better of it and directs his focus to the laptop instead. "Son, if you don't mind, we'll need just a bit of privacy here."

Jonathan looks reluctant to leave, but after a moment he does.

"Here, I want you to watch this, Lyla," Mr. Brown says as he places the laptop across my legs.

"Is he one of us now?" I ask.

Mr. Brown looks up. "Almost. Pioneer feels that he has potential, but in order for him to have a place with us he's going to have to earn it. He has to believe all the way, not just hate the Outsiders."

"What about the other Rangers? Do they have potential?"

Mr. Brown snorts. "No, they do not."

"Then why are they here with us?" I ask. I want to make positively sure that what I suspected outside is true, that they have nothing to do with what happened last night. Then maybe I can ask them to help me figure out what's going on.

"Because we needed them to get back on our feet after the government seized our land. And Pioneer needed a lawyer, which they were more than willing to provide if we let them use Pioneer's case to further their own causes. Listen, think of them as spiders—beneficial if you're trying to keep other insects away, but repulsive nonetheless. When all is said and done, they're no better than those outside of our Community. Just because they choose to help us doesn't really change that. They don't believe in Pioneer or the Brethren. We tried to talk to them, but they won't see the truth. They're using us to make some kind of anti-government statement. So we've decided to use them to help Pioneer get out of jail and to keep this Community together. And isn't that the ultimate irony? That we can manage to use evil to keep good going?" He leans back on his heels. "Now lookee here at what I just found on your Internet."

I look down at the laptop. On the screen is a website called True News. Taking up most of the page is an article. I glance at the title. "Local Election for Sheriff of Pickens County Thought to Be Rigged." I begin to read it in earnest then. It basically says that at least two of the voting stations set up county-wide had volunteers at them who were somehow related to Sheriff Crowley and that these volunteers were being accused of throwing away votes for the sheriff's opponent. Machines at both spots malfunctioned and the ballots had to be counted by hand. I can feel Mr. Brown watching me read it. The article is accompanied by pictures of people standing in line to vote, and toward the end there's one of the sheriff holding a hand up to his face like he's trying to hide from the camera. He looks angry—and guilty.

"You see, Lyla, if you dig long enough and deep enough, nine times out of ten you'll find out something that you don't know or like about a person." Mr. Brown moves closer and pushes the arrow key to scroll down further. "And if you aren't real, real careful, you'll never even realize that it probably isn't true." At the bottom of the page, the article's author is named. And it's Mr. Brown.

"I made it up this morning—got the pictures from some local election and the one of the sheriff with his hand near his face is from the other day at the courthouse. See, unless you did a whole lot more digging, you wouldn't know that, would you? And the sheriff might never even realize that it's out there for a while, which means that anyone who ends up on this page could have an impression of him that's altogether untrue. Now, if I can do that right here, right now, to him, don't you think that he could do the same to Pioneer? You told your parents that Cody showed you something online that made Pioneer look like a criminal, right? How do you know for sure that he didn't just make it up? How do you know that he and his dad didn't purposely lead you to believe that just so you'd help them when the time came and they stormed our property? Takes less than an hour to set stuff like this up, and look how much damage it can do."

I stare at the screen and the sheriff's picture. The article looks believable, even though Mr. Brown's just made it up. I try to remember back to when Cody showed me stuff about Pioneer and the natural disasters back at the hospital. But I can't remember much about the actual web pages he showed me—probably because I had a concussion at the time. Suddenly I feel a flicker of doubt. *Could that be why he showed it to me right then? Because I wasn't going to be able to think clearly about it or ask questions?* No. Wait. Mr. Brown can't be right. I know Cody. He wouldn't lie to me. And this doesn't explain away what *I* know about Pioneer, what I saw him do to Marie. It doesn't explain away the questions the press asked Pioneer about his past.

"And take this sickness that's spreading out there. Don't get me wrong, I do think it's the Brethren's will and that it was bound to happen, but how long do you think it'll take for them to put the blame for it on us? Like we somehow found a way to poison them? Make us look bad? Think about it. We know that it's an answer to prophecy, but they'll spin it as some kind of planned attack. It won't be hard to make it look like somehow Pioneer arranged it, will it? How long do you think it'll be before the sheriff's deputies show up here to raid us again even though we don't have guns anymore or any way of producing the salmonella that they keep mentioning? You don't think that they could plant evidence to the contrary while they dig around our barn and trailers? Don't you see? They don't want there to be any Brethren. They don't want there to be a prophet like Pioneer. If they acknowledged the truth, then they'd have to admit that they've been wicked. They don't want to be doomed, so you know what they'll do? They'll spin a bunch of lies. And the other Outsiders will believe them. They see our shaved heads and our fasting and praying not as proof of our devotion to our beliefs, but as proof that we're crazy. They can't understand that Pioneer is our family and that we will support our own in times of trouble. Cancer patients' families have been known to shave their heads out of support when their loved ones go through chemotherapy and lose their hair. No one calls them crazy or mindless or dangerous because of it. Just because we do it symbolically to protest Pioneer's being in jail doesn't make us strange."

Mrs. Brown makes a noise of agreement in her throat. She's done braiding my hair and has banded it off at the bottom. It lies in a weighted line along my back. I'd forgotten how it felt when it was done up this way. There's something strangely comforting about it, familiar and calming.

"They'd rather make us disappear and destroy what we've built. They want to separate us from one another and make us weak. If they can manage to do that, then it'll be easy to convince themselves that their way is fine. A-okay. They can justify all the damage they do each and every day to one another because they'll make us look so much worse than they are. You've been to their schools. You've seen them in action. Tell me, do they treat you and the others with kindness and respect? Or do they constantly look for ways to hurt you with their words? I think if you look past the surface, you'll see that any kindness they might have showed you was calculated." Jack's face pops into my head. "Tell me, when the sheriff and the others started getting sick, did you really decide to come home all on your own or did they tell you to leave?"

Taylor. It seems impossible that he knows this, that he's guessed something I never even saw coming. She told me that she wished I'd never come to live with her family. Her mom didn't try to make her take it back or defend me when Mrs. Dickerson came after me right after that. *Were they only being nice to me because they had to for the sheriff so he could keep an eye on me or something? And what about the poisonings? Is it possible that some of the Outsiders could've done it to make us look bad, like Mr. Brown's saying? Mrs. Dickerson and her group hate the Community and want all of us out of town. Some of them were at the restaurant too. I can't remember if all of them were sick. Could some of them have done it?* Suddenly it seems possible.

"There now. You're seeing it, aren't you?" Mr. Brown beams at me, and Mrs. Brown squeezes my shoulders and kisses the top of my head. "It's a lot to take in, isn't it? They put a lot of questions in your mind and so, so many doubts, but I promise that by the time we leave this barn today, you'll be back with us all the way."

Recentering is what we call time spent focusing on the Brethren and their will for us. Pioneer always felt that the only way we could be certain of our path is if we spent time clearing our minds so that they would be emptied out of all of the worldly things that might disrupt our concentration and make hearing the Brethren's thoughts—sent through a million or more miles of space—impossible to hear. Usually we do this all together, the entire Community gathered and focused, like an antenna on what the Brethren are transmitting. Pioneer led a lot, but Mr. Brown and Mr. Whitcomb did it sometimes too. Still, I've never been asked to do it like this with just him, his wife, and me.

Mr. Brown takes the laptop and places it outside the door. He has me stand up. Mrs. Brown takes the chair and folds it up, leaning it against the far wall. She puts her hand over mine and Mr. Brown does the same with my other hand. We stand side by side. Their eyes are closed. I can't quite get myself to close my own.

Mrs. Brown peeks at me. "Close your eyes." It isn't a request. I squeeze them shut immediately. *I can do this. Just because I do what they say doesn't mean I have to believe it.*

"Breathe. In and out. Nice and slow. That's it. That's it." Mr. Brown's voice is low, rhythmic, and sure. Beside me, Mrs. Brown pulls in a long breath and gradually lets it out. The air whistles a little as it rushes out of her nose. I fight the urge to laugh. I know they won't like it if I do. Plus I don't want them to start over. Recentering has always felt a little like being stuck in a sleep that I can't totally wake up from. I lose track of time and everything goes all fuzzy, like somehow I've been underwater. It isn't painful or anything, but I've never fully liked it either.

We stand still and breathe for so long that my feet start to hurt and I have to shift from one foot to the other. One breath in. Exhale. Another breath. Exhale. Mr. Brown drones on and on and on, chanting the words Pioneer always used in our recentering sessions.

We clear our minds.
We open our hearts.
We wait to receive your message.
A blank page for you to write on.
What you tell us is the truth.
What you command we will obey.
Show us the way.

Mr. Brown nudges me and I begin to say the words with him, over and over. It isn't long before our voices blend, before the beginning of the chant becomes indistinguishable from the middle or the end, an unbroken chain of words forever circling in my head. I can't concentrate on anything other than saying the words.

It goes on and on like this. I have no idea how long we chant, but eventually my voice feels hoarse. I look up once to find that somewhere along the way Mrs. Brown was replaced by Mrs. Sturdges, Julie's mom. I never even felt Mrs. Brown's hand slip from mine.

We clear our minds.
We open our hearts.
We wait to receive your message.
A blank page for you to write on.
What you tell us is the truth.
What you command we will obey.
Show us the way.

At some point Julie's dad brings in a space heater and cranks it up to high. Soon it's hot in the tiny room. The heat seems to weigh down the air, makes breathing in and out without coughing or gasping harder and harder. I want to stop, but every time I shift in place or begin to stutter my words, the others support my elbows, and chant louder.

They begin to walk me around the room, circling so

tightly that I begin to feel dizzy and ill. Still, we chant and walk, chant and walk. I can't open my eyes at all anymore because the dizziness is overwhelming. Eventually I feel Mr. Brown's calloused palm slip away and be replaced by another. It must be later in the day now. Shadows and bursts of weak sunlight flash across the insides of my lids, making the dizziness worse. I sag against whoever's holding on to me now, stumble every few feet as we make our way around the room again. I need to stop. I'm so thirsty and I want to lie down. I need to be able to take a moment to think, but they just keep moving me around the room.

We clear our minds.
We open our hearts.
We wait to receive your message.
A blank page for you to write on.
What you tell us is the truth.
What you command we will obey.
Show us the way.

It's dark now. I open my eyes to candlelight and nothing more. I can't see much of the room at all. "Believe the words you're saying, Lyla. Don't just speak them. Let go, let go, let go." Mr. Brown is back. *Maybe he didn't leave in the first place like I thought?* I feel confused. My head is pounding.

I start the chant again, but my throat hurts so much. I need to stop. I want to stop. They won't let me. I start to beg them. "Please no more, no more. I need to sit down. I don't feel well."

"You'll feel better once you let go. That sick feeling, all the disorientation? It's the Outsiders' lies polluting your system. We need to purge it."

I'm so tired. It feels like forever since I've slept. I lick my lips, but even my tongue feels dry. I'm so thirsty. I would give just about anything to get a drink. I croak out the words and they sound brittle and whisper-soft. I try again, my face crumpling with the effort. The hands holding me up tighten on my elbows, and my arms throb. "I am a blank page. . . ." My throat closes up and hot tears roll down my cheeks. "What you tell us is the truth. What you command we will obey. Show us the way." I start to cry.

"Good. That's it, that's it!" one of my helpers yells excitedly, and I have a little hope that they'll let me stop soon. I don't know what I've done exactly to convince them that I'm recentering the right way, so I just throw myself into it, give the last of my energy up and shout the words, tears streaming down my face. "Show me the way!"

"Once more," they demand in unison, and I say it again with them.

We clear our minds.
We open our hearts.
We wait to receive your message.
A blank page for you to write on.
What you tell us is the truth.

What you command we will obey.
Show us the way!

I feel the desperation building in me. I'm so thirsty.

"Thatta girl," Mr. Brown says soothingly. "Your mind is clearing, can you feel it?"

I want to stop more than anything and the only way for that to happen is if I agree with what he says. "Yes. Yes!"

"Then I think you're ready to hear the truth and accept it," Mr. Brown says.

I have no idea what he means, but I'm so happy to be able to stop walking, to be able to stop chanting, that I don't care. I just want to rest.

They help me to the floor so that I'm sitting with my back against the barn wall. To my left the rusty shears make a clattering sound against the wall as I cross my legs and rest my head against the rough, scorched boards there.

Mr. Brown hands me a mug with some cold water in it. I guzzle it down and ask for another.

"Not just yet," he says, but not unkindly. "Let's give that a bit to settle in your system first."

He leaves the room and so do the others. For the first time in hours—maybe almost a day—I'm alone. I rest my head on the wall. I'm still so dizzy. It seems to be getting worse now instead of better. And my eyes. Every time I try to focus on something, I see a halo around it. The room seems to dip and roll under me, making me feel like I'm floating on top of the ocean. I don't like it, but I can't think of a way to make it better. Should I lie down? My brain feels sluggish. I don't feel right. It's not just the chanting, it's something else. Fatigue, maybe?

Mr. Brown comes back in and crouches down beside me. I feel his thumb press my eyelid, move it up. He studies my eyes. "It's working," he says.

"What's working?" I try to say, but I'm not sure that I actually say it. I start to laugh. Nothing's funny and yet I can't stop giggling.

"Feel better, Lyla?" Mr. Brown is smiling.

"You didn't give her too much?" Mrs. Brown looms over me. Her chin shakes as she talks and I laugh harder. I never realized how funny she looked before.

I start to drift. It's like my brain's on pause and I can see and hear, but none of it makes any sense. I don't know what's happening. They're still talking at me, making me walk. Then somehow Pioneer's there—or he's on a TV screen—I'm not sure which.

I can hear his voice. Over and over he says the same things. He talks about Marie and how she died. Over and over and over again. At first it doesn't sound right, not like how I remember, but then it's like the more times he tells me what happened, the more I can see it the way he says it happened. I thought that he killed her, but now when I try to remember I see her pulling the knife across her own neck. I see Pioneer crying over her, trying to stop the bleeding with his hand. I start to cry.

I was convinced that Pioneer was a criminal, that he killed Marie, and that the sheriff was the good guy, that Cody really loved me. But now I have no idea what to believe anymore. And I'm tired, so, so tired of trying desperately to figure it all out. I can feel myself wanting to let go of it all.

"You want to believe me because deep down you know it's true. No matter who you meet or where you roam, you are one of us. It'll never feel right anywhere else. You're mine, Little Owl. You will always be mine." Pioneer says it over and over and over again.

Things start to fade around me, go black, and still I can hear him. "Mine, you're mine. . . ."

Someone nudges me in my side with their boot and I come to. My head hurts. There's a TV in the corner of the room and Pioneer's on it. He's preaching about the Brethren. I rub my eyes.

"Come on," Mr. Brown says.

I stand up, my legs all loose and rubbery. I keep hiccupping, letting out a sob with each one. I've cried so much that my eyes feel sand-blasted and raw. Mr. Brown holds my arm to keep me from falling over. I'm so hungry and sick and thirsty. I look around, try to figure out what time it is, how long I've been in the barn, but my eyes are still so blurry and it hurts to focus. Mr. Brown leads me to another room, the one that was locked when I came into the barn before. There's nothing in it. It doesn't seem right, but I don't remember why. Jonathan's standing in the corner. He's holding a gun in his good hand. I struggle to pull free of Mr. Brown, but he holds me tight. I don't understand what's happening. Are they going to shoot me?

Mr. Brown makes me lie on the ground. I keep looking over at Jonathan and the gun. The ground is hard and cold and itchy with hay. Mrs. Brown comes in carrying two tall orange buckets. She sets them down and then goes back into the hall and gets two more. She makes trip after trip and all the time Jonathan stays in the corner, cocks and uncocks his gun.

"Wh-wh-what's happening?" I whisper.

Mr. Brown walks over to the buckets. He picks up one and then stands over me with it. Drops of water fall on my chest and neck, slide over my chin.

"You've been bad, Lyla. You betrayed us. You aren't worthy to be in the Community anymore."

I'm confused. I thought he believed me. I thought that Pioneer told him to take me back.

"But you can be. If you show that you're worthy."

"H-h-how?" I ask.

"By taking your punishment and recommitting yourself to Pioneer."

Jonathan leaves the corner and drops to his knees beside me. He holds the gun to my head, slides the end of it against my temple until it nestles into the space just above my cheekbone. I start to whimper, I can't help it.

I don't want to die. He pulls the trigger and there's an empty clicking sound. I sob and my whole body shudders.

"There are bullets in the gun, Lyla. The only reason you didn't die right then is because the Brethren jammed it. They want you to believe again. Can you do that? Can you believe?"

I'm crying so hard that I can't answer. Jonathan holds the gun up to my temple again. I let out a wail. "I believe, I believe. Please, I believe."

"It's not enough. You have to accept your punishment, to understand why it is necessary, Lyla." Mr. Brown is still looming over me, the bucket swaying slightly in his hand.

That wasn't it? I start to shake; my body is practically convulsing it's trembling so hard. "Accept it, Lyla." Mr. Brown nods at Jonathan and he cocks the gun again.

I pull in a breath. "I was wrong. I should be punished." I want to scream for help, but it won't do any good. No one's coming to save me, not this time.

Jonathan puts the gun down and grabs my head. I can feel his bandages on my cheek, soft and smelling of medicine. He holds my head straight so he can look into my eyes. "Little Owl, huh? I wonder if your neck would snap as easily as that barn owl's." Some very distant part of my brain cries out at his confession. He was the one in the tree outside Taylor's room. At least I think that's what he said. I blink hard and stare into his eyes, blue like Pioneer's and Will's. It *was* him. He killed the owl, and now he's going to kill me.

"That's enough!" Mr. Brown yells. "Hold her down." He tips the bucket. Water pours over my nose and mouth and eyes. I sputter and accidentally breathe in. I strain upward trying to get out of the bucket's path, but Jonathan is holding my head, keeping me down. Water floods my lungs and I cough, but this lets more water in. The water keeps coming and coming. I can't breathe. They're drowning me with a bucket of water. I try to stop coughing, to hold my breath, but it's hard because all my body wants to do is get rid of the water in my lungs. Then suddenly the bucket's empty. I gasp and cough and retch. Water pours from my mouth onto the floor.

Mr. Brown waits until I stop coughing and then he grabs another bucket. Over and over he makes me agree that I need punishment, all the while telling me that I deserve it, that it's the only way for me to cleanse myself of my sins. I thought I could do this, fake my way back into the Community, but I was wrong. I feel like the rational part of my brain is floating away on a current of well water that tastes like dirt and iron.

After the fifth bucket of water, I not only think that I'm going to die, I'm starting to hope for it.

Mr. Brown sits down on the floor beside me, pulls out a cell phone, and puts it to my ear.

"Little Owl," Pioneer says softly.

I can't answer. I'm crying too hard.

"Do you want me to tell them to stop?" he says.

"Yes."

"All you have to do is say the words."

I don't have to ask him what the words are. I know.

"I'm yours," I say, and I mean it. I can't fight him, not like this. It's too hard. I'm not strong enough—maybe I never was.

"Yes, you are. Don't ever forget it again."

Mr. Brown moves the phone from my ear. I close my eyes. Relief washes over me. "Thank you, thank you, thank you," I say over and over again. I can't make myself stop. I'm practically babbling, I'm so wrung out and exhausted.

"Welcome back, sister," Mr. Brown says. He scoops me up into his arms and carries me into the other room. The heater is still on high, but it feels good now that I'm wet and shivering. Clean clothes are sitting neatly folded on the metal chair, and Mrs. Brown is waiting beside it. She helps me into the chair and gives me a mug of hot tea to sip on while she towels off my face and arms. She kisses my forehead and smooths wet strands of hair away from my face. She helps me with the clothes because I'm too weak to dress myself, and then together we walk into the main part of the barn, where for the second time since I showed up, everyone in the Community is gathered. They clap and cheer when they see me. I don't know how to feel about this. I look at Mr. Brown for some clue because I want him to tell me how to feel. I don't want to be wrong and end up back in that room with him and Jonathan. He smiles and so I smile too. My parents rush forward first, gathering me to them and practically carrying me the rest of the way into the room. I'm still crying. You would think I wouldn't have any tears left, but they keep coursing down my cheeks. The folding chair from the back is brought out and placed in front of the group. My parents guide me to it. Will, Heather, and Julie surround it. They smile as I sink into the seat. My stomach flutters a little. *What's going on now?* My head sags against my chest. *No more. I can't take any more.*

Mr. Brown comes to stand beside me. In one hand he's carrying the rusty shears from the other room.

"You have to do it," Will whispers into my ear. He moves so I can see his face, touches the end of my chin with his hand.

"I don't understand," I say, but then Mr. Brown hands me the shears and all at once I do.

They want me to cut my hair. One last test and they'll leave me alone. I don't want to, but more than that I want to get out of the barn, away from Mr. Brown and the back rooms. It's hard to remember why fighting them is so important anyway. I curl my fingers around the shears.

Will pulls my braid behind my head and holds it taut. He guides my hand and the shears to it. I cut the braid. There's a sudden horrible lightness as it falls away and what's left of my hair swings forward, no longer than my chin. I drop the shears, bring my hand up to my head. I finger the uneven fringe. There's a buzzing sound then and soon Mr. Brown is shaving off the rest of my hair, mowing it off my head in rows with an electric razor. I close my eyes. It doesn't hurt. It almost feels good. My head feels so light it's almost balloon-like, empty and not mine at all anymore.

"Our Little Owl is with us again," Mr. Brown says loudly, and the room erupts into cheers.

My hair is gone, but I don't feel like crying. I don't feel anything. I'm numb and that's good. I don't want to feel. What I want to do is sleep. Maybe forever.

Everyone else is treating this moment as a celebration. Their hands keep touching me, patting my shoulders, skimming across the now smooth skin of my head. I watch as Will's parents pull mine into excited hugs. My mom looks happier than I've seen her since the night Will was picked as my Intended all those years ago.

My hair is gone. I try to concentrate on this thought, but I can't. I can't seem to do anything but stare.

"You get used to it," Heather says. She and Julie crouch down to hug me. I lean my head on Julie's shoulder. I can't seem to hold it up.

"I cried. A *lot* at first," Julie says softly as she lets me go and sits on the floor. Her fingers pick halfheartedly at the straw by her foot. "But then I thought about Pioneer and how proud he would be of me and I just knew it was something that I had to do. I'm glad I did it. I feel closer to Pioneer now even though he can't be with us. It's strange, I guess, but I feel like he knew right when I cut it. Like he was smiling."

"I feel exactly the same," Heather says.

"You must be tired, huh?" Will puts his hand on my back.

I blink, but I can't make myself answer.

"Come on, I'll walk you home. Tomorrow none of this will feel so overwhelming, I promise." Will takes my arm and I let him lead me to the door.

"Mr. Hamilton, I thought maybe I'd walk Lyla back. She's pretty tired from the recentering. If that would be all right with you, sir?" He's corralled me over to my dad.

"That'll be just fine, son." Dad nods at him and then, almost as an afterthought, leans down and kisses me, right on the top of my bald head. "I'm so proud of you, sweetie."

I make myself nod. It feels like the right thing to do. I'm not sure, though. I don't feel right. I need someone to tell me what to do. I look around for Mr. Brown, but then I seem to lose time, and suddenly Will and I are outside, the cold air slapping the top of my head and making my teeth chatter.

We head back toward the trailers. I can hear a train whistle somewhere out in the darkness. It's a long, sad sound. It makes the trailer park feel far away from the rest of town, isolated.

"I hate that you had to go through that," Will says once we're outside. I trip over something. I'm not watching where I'm going. I almost fall, but then Will catches me and puts an arm around my waist so he can help me walk. He makes a funny sound in his throat, and when I look up at him, his eyes are full of tears. "You'll be okay now. I'll take care of you," he says.

I'm not sure what happens next. One minute we're walking toward the trailers and the next I'm on my bed and Will's tucking me in. He turns the light out and I close my eyes and try not to listen when he starts to cry.

They think when they come to us threatening to take our children we will be frightened and cower. They couldn't be more wrong.

—Mr. Brown

TWENTY-FOUR

When I wake up, Will is gone. It unnerves me. I don't want to be alone. I don't know what I'm supposed to do, how I'm supposed to feel. I don't get up right away, because moving isn't easy. I'm sore and weak and spent. I stare at the ceiling, watch shadows travel across it. What's happening to me?

I remember the recentering, but only in bits and pieces. Pioneer's voice is like a thread sewn through every flash of memory, connecting all the chanting and the water and . . . the gun. I can't get him out of my head. My mind keeps going back to his words—replaying them over and over. I hold on to them, repeat them to myself. Fear sits in my stomach, rock hard and cold. I can't forget. If I forget, I'll end up back in the barn.

"Lyla?" My dad's standing in the doorway staring at me. He's got a bowl in his hand. "Feel like eating?"

Food? My stomach growls at the thought, but the fear rises up inside me until it's stronger than my hunger. Pioneer said we can't eat. Is this a test to see if the recentering took? I don't know and I'm scared that I'm not strong enough to pass it. My mind feels like it's split in two. Part of me wants nothing more than to flip the tray and run out the door, down the road and straight to town. But it's a small, weak part of me, nearly washed away by all that water, obliterated by every click of the gun. *No. Pioneer. I need to do what he wants. I'm his, I'm his, I'm his,* screams the other part of my brain, so loud that it blocks everything else out. I won't eat; I can't fail and be put back in that room with Mr. Brown. I pull the covers up closer to my chin.

"No! No food. Not until Pioneer says," I say without looking at him. I want that bowl gone so I can't see it.

"It's just broth, honey," Dad says, his voice soft, coaxing.

I shake my head. I can't fail. They need to see that I'll listen now. I can feel panic building inside me, rising up like a wave. I'm drowning in it.

Dad strokes the top of my head. The skin is sensitive without my hair there to protect it. I don't like the way it feels, but it doesn't matter. Nothing matters except staying out of the barn.

I let my dad help me out of bed and lead me to the sofa in the next room. He wraps a quilt around my shoulders and hands me a cup of hot water. I sip at it, my eyes traveling to Pioneer's picture on the wall as I do. I'm allowed the water—I understand this, but I feel the need to double-check with him to make positively sure. Unfortunately, the picture can't tell me what to do. I only manage to get half the water down. I put the cup on the table in front of me.

When the trailer's front door slams open, I almost fall to my knees and start screaming, I'm so sure it's Mr. Brown coming to get me for another session. But it isn't him, it's Will and his mom.

"Outsiders! They're coming. Four squad cars," Will's mom says. She's breathless from running. I watch as she brings her hand up. She has a gun. I shrink into the sofa. My temple starts to burn. I don't want her anywhere near me with that thing. She tucks the gun into her jeans and pulls her shirt over it to hide it from view.

"Stay calm," my dad barks, and at first I'm not sure if he means her or me. "We knew that they would. You'll make things worse by panicking."

Will's mom nods. She waits while Dad hurries to the back of the trailer.

"How are you this morning?" Will asks me. His voice is stiff, strange. He doesn't sound like himself.

"I don't know," I say, and this is true. I don't.

"I didn't know how bad it was going to be, Lyla, I swear. I never wanted you to come back that way—"

He stops talking when my dad comes back into the room with my mom. Both of my parents have guns of their own. They're everywhere. I hold my hands to my head. It's like the day of the raid all over again. I start to wail.

"Lyla, pull it together!" Mr. Brown is standing in our doorway. I stiffen and shut my mouth.

"We need you now. You have to make them leave. Show us that you're back all the way." He looks into my eyes and there's an unspoken threat in his expression. I look down at his hand. He has a gun too, it's resting on his knee and the barrel's pointed at me. I look up at my parents, but they're already moving outside with Will's mom. Will lingers by the door, watches us.

Mr. Brown looks into my eyes. "Are you back, Lyla? Or did we stop our session too early?"

My throat squeezes shut. I look down at the gun and then back up at him.

He inches closer, puts his face right up to mine until our foreheads are almost touching. "They can't take you away from us. This time we won't let them." He lets his fingers drift across the trigger. "I have people stationed all over this place, hiding, watching. If they make you go with them, they'll be dead before they can get to the main road. But that's not the Brethren's will—at least not yet. You have to make them go away, Lyla, without you, or I will send Jonathan into town and he will pay another visit to the Crowleys' house, and this time it won't be to kill an owl."

I look down at the gun again. He's had people watching me for weeks. I know that what he's saying is the truth. He will shoot the deputies and the Brethren will be angry with me for failing. They might decide I need more time in the barn and Jonathan will go to Cody's house and hurt Taylor or her mom. I nod. "Okay, I will. Please, I'll do whatever you want."

Will shakes his head, his hand coming up to the doorframe like he needs to steady himself. He takes a deep breath and walks outside.

"Good." Mr. Brown stands up, stashes his gun in the front pocket of his coat, and then hands me my coat. Together we walk out of the trailer.

The Community has gathered along the road and so have the Rangers. They're all twitchy, standing much too close to one another. Up ahead of them the deputies are standing by their cars. They seem a little twitchy too. I look for the sheriff. He's not here. But I don't need to worry about him anymore. He's an Outsider. Outsiders are evil and not to be trusted. Pioneer's voice overrides my own in my head. I can't hear myself anymore. I have to concentrate on what Mr. Brown says. I have a flash of Cody's face and I almost stop walking. My head still isn't right. My thoughts are so jumbled. But no, I can't think about him. I don't belong with him. I belong here. *This is my home. This is my home. This is my home.* My brain keeps getting stuck on the phrase. I think because they made me say it in the barn. Every time it repeats, I feel more and more certain that it's true.

"Good morning," one deputy says loudly. I remember him from the hospital. It's the guy who likes candy bars . . .

Steve. Seeing him is like a punch to the gut. That small part of me that wasn't washed away last night is telling me to run to him, to beg him to take me out of here, but Mr. Brown is pressed to my side and his hand is in his pocket, the one with the gun, and that voice is no match for the fear that spikes inside me, intense and overpowering. I'm relieved when the voice goes quiet.

"We're here to speak with Lyla Hamilton." Steve eyes the crowd. His gaze passes right over me—probably because he still expects me to have hair.

Will's dad steps forward. "Can I ask why you need to talk to her?"

"It'll only take a few minutes, if you can just get her," the deputy says, not answering the question at all.

There's a moment where no one moves and Will's dad and the deputies just stare at each other. I'm not sure what'll happen now, but I can't stand the tension in the air, the feeling that at any moment the men will start fighting. I see Will's dad and a few others casually put their hands inside their coat pockets. There are only a handful of deputies against more than thirty armed men, if you count the Rangers. I'm not supposed to let the deputies get hurt. I'm supposed to make them leave.

"I'm here," I say. I come forward enough for them to see me. Mr. Brown shadows me. If Steve and the others are surprised that I'm now as bald as everyone else, they don't show it. I make my way toward them, being careful not to walk too fast. If I seem eager, it'll only make Mr.

Brown nervous, and I want to be obedient. I want to do exactly what he says. My heart beats hard inside my chest. I can't fail.

Steve steps in between me and Mr. Brown when we get close enough. "I'd like to speak with just her."

I look back at Mr. Brown. He's grinning like this request doesn't bother him at all, when I know that it does. He doesn't want me where he can't hear what I'm going to say. I'm worried too. I don't trust myself.

The deputy leads me over to their cars—lined up one after another like dominoes—and situates himself so that my back is to the group and he can keep an eye on everyone else. "What's going on, Lyla? What'd they do to your hair?" he asks so quietly that even I have a hard time hearing him.

"I wanted to come home and everyone else's hair is gone. I thought I should cut mine too," I say, and I'm not sure, but I think maybe it's the truth. "How's Cody?" The words come out of nowhere before I can stop them. I cringe. I'm failing. There'll be punishment if I don't try harder.

"He was pretty sick. He and his dad both, but they're being discharged from the hospital today."

I fidget, balance on one foot and then the other. My whole body is tense. I can't relax it. Does he see? Does Mr. Brown? I can't fail.

"Look, Lyla, an anonymous letter showed up at the

Culver Creek Tribune this morning. Whoever wrote it claimed responsibility for the food poisoning. I can't go into detail about it with you, but it warned that there would be another attack soon. And the obvious first suspects for who wrote it are these people." He shoots a look over my shoulder. "This is not where you want to be right now. So get your things and I'll take you back to the sheriff's house, okay? The Crowleys want you to come back. They're worried about you."

Now I know he is lying. One thing I do remember from last night—or was it the night before?—is being chased out of the hospital by Outsiders, and Cody's mom and Taylor letting them.

"I'm staying here," I say. "This is where I belong."

"You're wrong. Listen, I don't think you get what I'm saying. It's not safe here anymore. So go on now and go get your things."

"I'm not leaving," I say louder. "This is my family. I belong with them. Now leave me alone, Outsider!" I yell this last bit as loud as I can so that the others will hear. I shrink away from him and go stand by Mr. Brown. I look up at him, anxious to make sure that I did it right, that he's happy with me.

Steve studies me. "You don't really believe that." But he looks nervous now, like he's not sure.

"You have a warrant, Officer?" a voice yells from somewhere to our left. We look up. Standing between the trailers now are all of the Rangers. They glare at the deputies. Jonathan's right up front, leading the pack along with Brian.

Steve looks like he'd like to strangle them. "Well now, why would I need one of those? You have something to hide here?"

The Rangers bristle in unison. If they were a pack of dogs, their hair would all be standing on end.

"No, but we know our rights and theirs. Unless you've got a warrant, we're going to have to ask you to get off this property. Now," Jonathan says. He squares his shoulders and folds his arms across his chest.

"Come on, Lyla," Steve says quietly. It's obvious that he doesn't want to spark a confrontation that ends badly like the raid, but he seems unwilling to move because of me. It makes me want to shake him. I can't fail and he's making it almost impossible for me.

"Why would I leave with you? I'm home. Can you please just go away and leave us alone?" I say this as calmly and serenely as I can. Inside I am screaming—every part of me, even the small part that wants to go with him no matter what. I'm not sure how much more I can take. My head hurts so bad. I need quiet inside my head, I'm desperate for it.

"No, I can't," Steve says. He looks worried. I shake my head and try to look disgusted, then open my mouth and say something I know will make him mad enough to leave.

"Go back to your candy bars and leave me alone! I can't

bear to be around any of you for one more minute. You're just dead men walking. I was such a fool to think any different, I know that now." I drop to my hands and knees, move my arms so that my palms are open to the sky, and begin to chant.

The Brethren will save us.
Pioneer guides and protects us.
We will look to them alone
In all that we do
In all that we say
In all that we believe.

It takes only seconds from when I start for the others to drop down beside me and start chanting too.

The Rangers move closer. They have their phones out and are holding them up to us and the deputies. They're filming us.

"You heard the girl. She asked you to go. You have no warrant, and without her, no reason to stay. Do these people have rights here or not, Officer?" one of the Rangers says, his phone trained on Steve.

Steve's face goes red. He opens the car door just behind him and takes out a canvas bag. "I brought you your clothes just in case you decided to stay." He drops it in front of me.

I ignore it. Steve stands still for one second more, and then he gets into his car. The other deputies follow. I keep chanting as I watch them drive away. With the others behind me doing the same, my head feels clearer. I sigh with relief and close my eyes. It takes me by surprise when tears slide down my cheeks.

We go inside a few minutes later and Mr. Brown begins to empty the contents of my bag. He piles the clothing neatly as he goes, but not before checking every pocket he comes across. I want to hug my sneakers when I see them. The only thing Mr. Brown finds that he doesn't like is the bag full of makeup. His eyebrows knit together as he pokes a finger inside it. "See, even now they're fighting for your mind by appealing to your vanity." He holds the small bag out in front of him like even touching it is dangerous as he heads for the door.

I take my clothes and shoes back to my room and shut the door. I practically rip off the clothes I'm in, the ones that Mrs. Brown helped me into—I'm not even sure whose they are; I just know they aren't mine—and sigh out loud once I'm back in my own. I sit on the floor to pull on my favorite shoes, but there's something wrong with the lining along the bottom of the right one. It's curling up oddly in the toe. I take it off and begin to inspect it. It's in backward. I take it out and start to put it back in the right way when I notice the neatly folded square of paper taped inside. My heart beats a little faster. I stare at it. This is bad, this is wrong. I need to take the shoe to Mr. Brown, I need to throw it out the window. I scoot away from my shoe like it might grow teeth and bite me. I open my mouth to call to my parents, but then close it again. The pieces of my brain that have been fighting with each other all day are at war again, but this time that tiny voice isn't so tiny. I don't like it and yet . . . I can't make myself ignore it completely. All at once I lunge for the shoe and peel back the tape and unfold the paper, scared the entire time that my bedroom door will swing open and Mr. Brown will be standing there.

Lyla,

What happened at the restaurant wasn't your fault. I know that Taylor made you feel like it was and you went back to the Community because you thought you had no place to go, but that's not true. I can be your home if you let me.

I'm hoping that you're on your way to the house with Steve now, but if you're not, I had Steve leave you my phone. It's hidden beneath the pile of rocks in the clearing just across the road from the trailer park and to the right of the clump of pine trees there. Get it as soon as you can. Then call me, no matter how late it is. We need to talk. Please don't let this be goodbye.

Cody

I feel like I might shatter into a dozen tiny pieces. *I can be your home if you let me.* These words shoot straight to my heart and stick there.

I reread his letter again and again, saying the words to

myself as I go. Every time I start again, my head feels a little clearer. That little voice I've been battling all day gets louder. He isn't mad at me. He wants me to come back. It shouldn't matter. Mr. Brown said that they would try to lie to me again. I know I should believe this and make myself throw the note away, but I can't. After a while I start to realize that when I'm reading the note, I can't hear Pioneer's or Mr. Brown's voices in my head anymore. The only voice I hear is mine. And it's telling me to go get that phone.

I have eyes everywhere. You can't run from me.

—Pioneer

TWENTY-FIVE

The day passes quickly, mostly because Mr. Brown keeps everyone really busy all day. It takes a lot longer to complete each task because everyone's weak from fasting, and this gives me hope. If they're slowing down from hunger, there's a chance that they'll get so tired that they won't be able to keep watch tonight. I keep Cody's note inside my shoe, beneath the lining. I can feel it against my arch and it works like a talisman, warding off the worst of my fear. Getting Cody's phone will be dangerous and I am terrified of getting caught. I won't survive another recentering.

I wait until everyone has gone to bed before I walk over to the window, pull the paper-thin shade away, and press my face to the glass. The light outside is coming from the trailer behind ours, a porch light on the wall by the door.

I dress quickly in my darkest clothes. Then I put on my dad's black knit cap, pulling it low over my head until it's just above my eyebrows. I leave my coat behind because it's too bulky and the nylon makes swishing noises when I walk. I need to be as quick and quiet as possible. When I'm as layered as I possibly can be and still able to move freely, I tiptoe out into the hallway. Listen. The paper notes on my wall flutter a bit in the breeze. I listen harder. Soon I can hear my dad snoring a little, that familiar rumbling intake of breath and the soft blowing sound that comes after it. One of my parents moves, the bed squeaks, but no one calls out or appears in the doorway. I edge out of my bedroom inch by inch on tiptoe, careful to step only where I think the floor won't creak. Still, it does some, little sounds that seem much louder, bigger at this hour. I get to the front door and work at the lock, slowly, slowly turning it to the left until it unlocks. The snicking sound it makes as it does makes me jumpy. I wince and open the door just enough to slip through it before carefully closing it again. I almost go back inside because already I feel so exposed, watched.

The night is full of noises. I can hear a truck somewhere in the distance, rumbling like a growling animal. I can't tell if it's on the road out past the trailers or somewhere closer. I inch my way down the stairs and make my way down the side of the trailer. I look around the corner, scan the road and the trailers beyond for any sign of someone else. Everything is so still that I start to panic. It's so deserted that I'm sure I'm walking into some kind of trap. But if I am, it's too late to go back inside, they already know I'm out here, disobeying. I take a deep breath and head straight for the copse of trees I hid in the first night I was here, sure that I'll be tackled by Jonathan or Brian or Mr. Brown before I get halfway there.

I don't breathe again until I'm there, plastered against a tree, so close that the bark scrapes my cheek. Just as I'm starting to catch my breath, a hand goes over my mouth.

"Don't scream," Will says in my ear. "It's me."

It takes a second before I stop struggling, before I understand that he's trying to be stealthy too. I relax and he takes his hand away.

"You're leaving," he says.

Since he's caught me out in the woods in the middle of the night, there's no point in denying it. "Yes."

His face is sad but resolute. "Okay," he says.

"Really?"

He looks back at the trailers. "You were so . . . broken when you came out of those rooms. I wanted you back, but I never, ever wanted that."

One of the trailers' porch lights goes on and I can hear the creak of a door opening. We crouch down in the brush.

"Mr. Brown's got people on guard duty up in the loft, and there's a few of us in those trees and over by the vans. If you keep to these trees and stay low, you can make it out to the road." Will hands me something. "Take these with you."

I look down at my hand. The shears from the barn are sitting in my palm. Accepting them makes me feel like somehow I'm inviting a confrontation with the others, but

I curl my fingers around them anyway. If the Community's taught me anything, it's always be prepared for the worst. I slide the shears into the back of my pants so that the handle rests on the waistband, then cover them with my sweatshirt.

I look up at Will. "Thanks." And then because suddenly I can't stand to leave him in this place: "Come with me."

He shakes his head. "I can't. Not yet."

I open my mouth to convince him to go, but then one of the porch lights on the trailer closest to ours goes on.

The trailer's door opens and a man steps outside. He's holding a gun. I think it's Heather's dad, but I can't be sure. I watch as he studies the other trailers, the road. He must have heard us somehow.

Will nudges my side with his elbow and leans in so he can whisper in my ear. "I'll take care of him, now go."

He kisses my forehead and I don't pull away. I put my hand on his cheek and smile at him instead.

"Thanks."

He stands up, wipes off his jeans, and walks toward the porch without looking back. He doesn't try to be quiet at all, in fact he makes lots of noise. The man turns his face in our direction. It *is* Heather's dad.

"Hey, you see anything?" Will asks. "I just got relieved from guard duty, but I can help you look if you heard something."

Heather's dad scratches his chin. "I thought I heard voices out here."

Will chuckles. "Yeah, that was me. I was talking to Brian. He just headed up to the loft for his shift."

Heather's dad yawns. "You want some coffee? I could put some on to brew. Might warm you up?"

Will walks up to the trailer. "Thanks, that would hit the spot." I wait for them to go inside and then I head toward the road, feeling the metal shears poking into my back a little with every step. My breath puffs out ahead of me, then disappears quickly. The wind is picking up and there are clouds above me now, thick ones that hint at more snow. They're blocking out the moon, making it hard to see where I'm going. I hold on to the trees as I go so I won't fall. My hands are tingling and half frozen. I forgot to grab gloves. I alternate sticking one hand in my sweatshirt pocket and then the other, but they stay painfully cold. By the time I find the phone and figure out how to call Cody, I probably won't be able to punch in the numbers.

The road is a flat black snake weaving its way through the fields ahead. At this hour there aren't any cars, and Will said that all of the men guarding the Community were farther back, closer to the barn, but still I stay nestled in the trees and watch for any sign that someone else is out here. When I'm sure that it's just me, I trot across the road. The rocks are right where Cody said they'd be.

I crouch beside them and immediately spot the bundle Steve left for me. He'd put Cody's phone in a ziplock bag and then wrapped it up in a towel to make sure that it wouldn't get wet. Once I have it out of the bag, I look it over. I've seen Cody use it a bunch of times, but I've never used it myself.

There's a little taped piece of paper on the back that has a long list of directions on it. Time feels like it's slipping away. I sigh and begin to complete each step. Press the button on the side to light up the phone. Swipe a finger across the front of it to unlock the screen. Find the phone symbol. (Cody drew one on the paper, tiny with a smiley face on one end.) I squint at the paper to follow the rest. Before long the phone is ringing, and almost immediately someone answers it.

"Lyla?" It's Cody, his voice thick with sleep. It feels like forever since I heard it last.

"Are you okay?" I say. I need to see his face, put a hand on his cheek to make sure, but I can't.

"Yeah, I'm fine. I'm home. Dad's home. We're good. And we don't blame you, Lyla. Taylor feels awful about what she said, I mean she should, but you know, she only said it 'cause she was scared."

I feel like I might burst into tears.

"It's you I'm worried about," he adds. "What were you thinking, going back there?"

I lean up against the tree nearest me and grip the phone a little harder. "I didn't know where else to go. I thought maybe if I went back they'd leave you and your family alone."

Cody makes a frustrated sound into the phone. "But you have no problem letting them hurt you? I heard about your hair. What else have they done to you?"

"I'm okay," I say.

"No, you're not. Steve said you looked bad this morning and that you were chanting and acting strange. Look, I'm coming to get you. Now." I can hear him moving, the sound of rustling sheets and stuff getting knocked around.

"I'll be there in fifteen minutes," Cody says, and I can hear him opening his car door and shutting it. "Wait out by the road for me."

I open my mouth to argue with him, but before I can I hear a noise on the road, a car coming. I can see the first faint beams of its headlights.

"Someone's coming, I have to go," I say as I sprint across the road and dive back into the trees.

"Fifteen minutes," Cody says, and I hang up and put the phone in my jeans pocket because I can't figure out how to make the light turn off.

I work my way as deep into the shadows as I can and hunker down against a tree. The sky is changing now, the dark becoming more gray than black. It makes everything crisper, easier to see, which means I'll be easier to spot too. The headlights get brighter. I try not to freak out. It could be anyone out there, but then the lights move past me and I can see the vehicle behind them. It's one of the Community vans and it's slowing down, pulling off onto the hard-packed dirt. The driver's-side door opens and Jonathan gets out. A thrill of terror runs through me. I wish I'd hidden farther in, but it's too late to move now. I don't like that he's stopped out on the road. *What will he do when Cody shows up?*

I have to find a way to get to Cody before he ends up here. I can't call him, because the phone's light will give me away. If I could only find a way to move to the left and work my way farther down, maybe I could run parallel to the road in the direction of town. The trees don't thin out right away. If I go fast, I'll be able to get far enough away that Jonathan won't see me leaving when I finally pop back onto the road.

I am just about to risk moving when I hear another car. Another of the Community vans pulls up next to Jonathan's. The door opens and Mr. Brown and Brian get out. I can feel the terror taking over now. They're going to find me, I can feel it. My teeth start to chatter and I have to clench my jaw hard to make them stop. I put my hand on the shears.

Mr. Brown walks over to Jonathan. "Are you ready, son?"

"I've been ready for a long time," Jonathan says.

"Good. Very soon you will officially earn your place as one of the Chosen." He claps Jonathan on the back.

"Three hours left to get everything in place," Jonathan says. "You have the rest of the fuel?"

Brian holds up a red gas container. "There's more in the van. I managed to get the last ones filled today."

Jonathan moves to the back of his van and opens the double doors. I can't see him anymore, he's hidden by one of them, but I watch Brian move around to where he is and hand him the red container. Mr. Brown goes back to his van and pulls out more red cans. They make a sort of assembly line from one van to the other.

Every minute that goes by, I get more and more panicked. Cody will be here soon and I can't move.

"That's all the cans. Brian, come help me with the other package," Mr. Brown says. Jonathan disappears into the back of his van. I watch as Brian follows Mr. Brown back to the other van again. Mr. Brown climbs in and the van rocks a little. There's a shout of surprise or pain and then a moment later someone else emerges from the van, falls out of the back into Brian's arms, knocking him to the ground.

"Hey!" he hollers. The person on top of him scrambles up. It's a woman. Her hands are bound and there's a gag in her mouth. Still, I can hear her muffled screams. She almost trips, then finds her footing and starts to run past the vans, out into the road. It's Mrs. Rosen. They took Mrs. Rosen. That's why she never met with Jack or came to get Will and the others.

Mr. Brown hurtles out of the van. "Get up and get her!" he hollers, and Brian pushes up off the ground and takes off.

"Jonathan!" Mr. Brown shouts, and then Jonathan's out of his van with a rifle in one hand. She's not going to make it. I will her forward, but already I'm sure that this is it. They're going to kill her. Mrs. Rosen appears on the other side of Jonathan's van. She's running, but there's nowhere for her to go. I can't see her face, but I can tell by the way that she keeps looking back that she knows it.

There's a loud bang. It echoes out into the almost morning, scaring a bunch of birds from the treetops over my head. They rise into the air, a swirling, panicking mass that quickly wings off to the left and disappears.

Mrs. Rosen turns around. Her coat front is covered in bits of down tinged red with blood. Behind her Jonathan lowers his rifle. At close range like that, he had to have blown a terrible hole in her chest, but I can't see it from here. She looks down at her chest and her body falls forward. I feel like I'm seeing everything in slow motion, but then she's on the ground before I can blink. I can feel the thud her body makes in my chest.

I look over at Jonathan. He raises the rifle once more, aiming it at her. He waits for her to move, and when she doesn't he closes the distance between them.

"Stupid cow!" he yells before kicking her body with his boot.

Mrs. Rosen's body shudders just a little before going perfectly still.

I bite down on my lip. Hard. I want to scream. I want to run, but I can't. They'll shoot me too.

"We should've killed her two days ago," Jonathan says. "Mistakes like that can derail everything. We can't afford them anymore."

"Pioneer wanted her to die with the others today. Are you questioning his instructions?" Mr. Brown asks.

Jonathan shakes his head. "No, no, I'm not. It's just . . ."

"We can discuss this later. Get her off the road quickly. There could be a car coming any minute."

Jonathan opens up the van doors and stoops down. For one heart-squeezing moment I can't really see him and I have this awful conviction that he's scrabbling across the ground like a beetle, scurrying toward me on all fours. But then he stands up and starts dragging Mrs. Rosen's body to the van. I can hear her shoes scrape across the ground. The sound makes me want to vomit.

Jonathan lifts her up, favoring his bad hand as he does. His bandage is more red than white. He inches her upward a little at a time until her backside leans against the van's bumper, and then he lets her upper body fall backward into the van itself. Brian comes up beside him and throws her legs in after her. The van is all white, but now there's a long swipe of blood across the side where Jonathan put one hand to steady himself. Mrs. Rosen's blood. Jonathan shuts the van doors again and shakes his head, runs his bloody hand through his hair. He kicks at the tire and then looks around, up the road in both directions. He's making sure no one's around.

I have to hide better.

Get lower.

Now!

I try to readjust, to make myself small, and make a tiny move backward—right onto a fallen tree branch. It gives immediately, the cracking sound every bit as loud to me as the gunshot. I wince and look up. Just in time to see Jonathan startle and peer into the trees. I know he sees me when he lunges forward to grab his rifle. I don't know what to do. So I do the only thing that comes to mind.

I run.

If you aren't with us, you are against us,
and I will not mourn you one bit when you die.
—Brian Wallace

TWENTY-SIX

I hurtle through the trees, leaping over fallen limbs and trying desperately not to fall. Still, I fall twice, my feet slipping on patches of snow. I scramble up and look back. He's coming.

Fast.

I face forward and lean over to try to propel myself faster, my eyes focused on what's just ahead of my feet so I don't fall again. I can't, he'll have me if I do. I can hear him crashing around behind me, the sounds getting louder and louder. Much too close.

He shoots at me once. The bullet takes out a chunk of the tree trunk to my left. Bark hits my sweatshirt, a light tap on my shoulder. I scream—one short burst before I'm out of breath. I suck in more air and try to go faster. *I need to go faster.* I can see the top of the barn up ahead. I'm getting close to the trailer park now. *But can they help me? Will they want to?*

The trees begin to thin and the ground becomes less

treacherous. I full-out sprint, putting every ounce of my energy into it. But then so does he.

I can see the first trailer. The lights are on. I open my mouth to scream.

There's a sudden breeze behind me and then Jonathan slams into my back. All the air rushes out of me. I hit the ground. My chin knocks against a tree root and my teeth clack together. There's pain, sharp and bright inside my head, and I can taste blood.

I claw at the ground. Several of my nails tear off as I struggle. I keep trying to grab hold of something. Anything. The ground is too hard and cold to give me traction. Jonathan's breath is in my ear. I feel his mouth brush against my skin and his spit on my cheek. I grunt, try to take in some air so I can yell, but he's pressing my chest into the ground and I can't get my lungs to work right after the fall.

He yanks me onto my back and puts one hand over my mouth. It's cold and wide and rough against my lips. Then he puts his other hand around my neck, his palm pressing hard under my chin, and starts to squeeze. He settles his weight more fully on my chest. My heart thunders in my head. I kick my feet against the ground and slap at him with my arms, but I can't get a good hold on him through his jacket. Panic rushes through me like a speeding train. I can't get away. I can't *breathe.*

Black spots start to drift in front of my eyes—a nightmarish blizzard of them. I can barely see. I keep kicking, but it's getting harder and harder to. Jonathan moves his hand off my mouth and adds it to the one around my neck. He squeezes so tightly that I feel the cords of my neck shift. I'm pressed so hard into the ground that my lower back is burning. It must be on top of a rock or root or something that keeps jabbing into my skin.

I can't move my head. He's all I can see now, his face ringed in black where my vision is already failing. He's not looking at me at all. He's looking above me, toward the trailer park. The last thing I see before the whole world goes black is the underside of his chin.

I'm feral when I come to, all clawing hands and kicking feet. But he's not on top of me anymore. I'm not where I was, in the trees. I'm staring up at a quickly blueing sky, my hands resting on blacktop. I don't know how long I was out. I try to turn my head to see if I can make better sense of where I am—the road maybe—but the pain is a live thing, writhing and screaming inside every muscle there.

I move my eyes to the right, but I can't see anything. There's a dark spot on my right eye that blots out most of my vision. It's red along the edges. Is my eye bleeding?

I bring a hand to my neck, but I can barely touch the skin. It's like someone rubbed it with sandpaper, then doused it in rubbing alcohol. Tears roll down the sides of my face. There's noise somewhere close by, a flurry of slamming doors and footsteps. We must be back by the van. Very, very carefully I sit up. The world tilts violently and I have to lie back down. Mr. Brown is above me a second later, his face tense and angry.

"What were you doing out here?"

I try to answer, but I have no voice. Literally. All I can do is wheeze.

"You're never going to be right again, are you?" He runs a hand through his hair. His nose is bright red from cold. His hands are shaking. "She has to go with you," he says.

Jonathan and Brian are here now too.

"I know." Jonathan grabs me under my arms and pulls me to a sitting position before I have time to protest. My whole existence revolves around trying to keep my neck still. I whimper as he jostles me into his arms and walks with me the few feet to the van. The road's empty in both directions.

Brain's opened the back doors to the van again. Inside is a pile of empty white bags with the words AMMONIUM NITRATE on them, a crowd of large blue plastic barrels, the red gas cans, and several propane tanks lined up like soldiers, all turned in the same directions. Beyond them, mashed into the far right-hand corner, is Mrs. Rosen. I can't see her face because her head is tucked into her chest like she's just dozed off. There's a puddle of blood under her legs.

Jonathan leans into the van and dumps me onto the floor. My hands land on Mrs. Rosen's legs. Her shoes poke into my chest. I move out of the way, try to scramble back out of the van, but Brian's got a rifle pointed at me. "Don't," he says. He makes me lie on my stomach so Jonathan can tie my hands behind me. The ropes are so tight that my fingers tingle. Then he leaves and Jonathan shuts the van doors and I'm trapped inside.

I press myself against the side wall and work my way up into a sitting position. Up front Jonathan settles into the driver's seat. There's a wire mesh screen separating the front of the van from the back. He looks back at me through the rearview mirror. "It's locked from the outside. You can't get out."

He starts the van and the radio blares on. That song about "walking in a winter wonderland" fills the car—so bright and cheerful and completely wrong right now that it hurts to hear it. He pulls out onto the road, swinging the van wide so that he can head in the opposite direction, toward town. I fall against Mrs. Rosen before I can steady myself. Her body topples over into the blue barrels and her head lolls back. She doesn't look like she's sleeping now. My eyes fill with tears and the red film on the right one makes everything in the van look drenched in blood.

The only way they're gonna feel something, the only way they're gonna get the message, is quote: "with a body count."

—Timothy McVeigh, Oklahoma City bomber and protester of the Waco siege

TWENTY-SEVEN

"Where are we going?" Every word is a knife in my throat. I wince.

"Town," Jonathan says. He turns down the music and I maneuver so that I'm kneeling behind him again, my head on the mesh screen and my hip resting on Mrs. Rosen's shoulder. I try not to think about it.

I look out at the road. A car appears, coming from the opposite direction. I watch it speed past, a blob of pea green that's gone so fast I barely have time to register that it's Cody. *If Mr. Brown and Brian are still back there on the road* . . . I shake my head. *They won't be. He'll be okay. He has to be okay.* But I can't make myself believe it when my jeans are wet around the knees from Mrs. Rosen's blood.

"What are you going to do?" I ask Jonathan.

"Prove myself worthy, make a statement that's so loud and clear it can't be ignored," he says. "You don't need to know the details. Not yet. Let's just say that most of my life has led up to this day."

We're in town a few minutes later. It's early still, but there are cars everywhere. Hanging above the street is a sign with the words WINTER FESTIVAL written in red and green letters. My stomach somersaults. The van slows down as we approach the traffic light near the diner, and Jonathan looks back at me. "Try to scream or attract any attention and I will shoot you." He holds a small black handgun up and presses it to the screen to show me that he's serious. He keeps it low enough that people outside won't see it, but high enough that I can.

I watch as a trio of men walk in front of the van toting a Christmas tree, followed by a mom struggling with a double stroller. Jonathan waves at them and the mom gives him a harried smile; she doesn't see me behind the screen. He's going to do something at the festival. Hurt all these people. He doesn't have to come right out and say it for me to know. I yank at the rope around my wrists, but I can't get loose and even if I could I'm locked in the back of the van. There's nothing I can do.

When the light turns green, we make our way closer to the park where the festival is. Cody's mom had a map tacked up in her dining room that showed where all the game and craft booths will be. The festival spans the whole park and the parking lot beyond it that belongs to the grocery store. There are supposed to be groups from Culver Creek High School and both the middle and elementary schools performing there this morning. The whole town will be in this one spot for the next four or five hours.

Jonathan steers the van into the parking lot now. There are a few spots left open, but most of the lot is blocked off for the ice-skating rink. There are already racks of skates waiting. Cody and I were supposed to work there today. Toward the grocery store itself are several sets of risers. No one's on them yet, it's too early. The program won't officially start for another hour, but the parking lot is still full of people heading into the festival. We take one of the last parking spaces that face the risers and not the road.

"Now what?" I ask.

"Now we wait." Jonathan turns the van off. He pulls out a phone and sits it on the dash before fishing a first-aid kit from the pile of books on the seat and setting it on his lap. I read the titles, looking for something, anything that might clue me in to why we're here. *The Anarchist's Cookbook*. I've never heard of it or the half-dozen other books strewn across the seat. I blow out a frustrated breath.

Jonathan undoes his bloody bandage while I watch, transfixed. I'm finally going to see what's underneath. I'm not prepared for how badly injured his hand is. The skin is puckered and, even after all these days, an angry pink. In some places the skin is actually peeling off.

"Chemical burns," he says. "Not from the owl like you thought, though that stupid bird did try to take a chunk out of me. Hard to avoid them, given what I've been building. Hurts like crap, but it was worth it. I did better than most guys doing this for the first time. I could've been burned worse, or blown my fingers off."

I can't follow what he's saying. *How does a fire blow off your fingers?*

Jonathan rebandages his hand and then picks up his phone again, stares at the screen before he puts it back down. "Soon," he mutters to himself as he peers out the front window.

Phone. I still have Cody's *phone.* I move away from the screen and sit back on my heels. My hands are tied behind me, which makes it hard to get to my pocket, but I manage after nearly twenty minutes of contorting my body to make it easier to reach. I am sweating and sore, and the parking lot is getting loud with people by the time I manage to finally fish the phone out and let it drop on the floor beside me. It makes a small thud and I freeze.

Jonathan turns around. "What are you doing?"

Can he see the phone? My heart hammers in my chest. "Nothing."

Suddenly there's a ringing and I shriek, sure that it's Cody's phone going off, but it's not, it's Jonathan's. He swivels away from me and I pick Cody's phone back up. Its screen is shattered. Bits of it are missing. It must have happened when he tackled me in the woods. I swipe my finger across it anyway and a sliver of glass cuts into my skin but the phone lights up.

Jonathan's phone stops ringing. "Hello?"

I don't have much time. I press my finger to the screen, but I can't get it to work. I think maybe it's too far gone. I slip the phone back into my pocket.

"Lyla, I think you should hear this too," Jonathan says from up front. He holds his phone up to the wire mesh screen.

"Little Owl."

It's Pioneer.

"I'm disappointed in you, Little Owl. I thought you'd come around." He makes a tsking sound into the phone. "After all the hard work I've done to bring you home, you still aren't obedient. Tell me, what's a good shepherd to do if his sheep refuses to come home? How many times does he save her from the wolves? I've tried my best to keep you out of harm's way, but there's a limit to my patience, child." He sighs. "You've left me no other choice. I'm going to have to give you over to the Brethren and let them sort you out."

There's a beat of silence while he lets this sink in.

"Jonathan?"

"Sir?"

"Is everything prepared?"

"Yes."

"And your heart's right, brother?"

"It is. I'm ready to play my part." Jonathan's face is bright, excited.

"There's a seat of honor for you among my people. All you have to do is claim it now. You will have a special place in history after today."

Jonathan's eyes well up with tears. He's so choked up that he can't speak.

"Give Little Owl a front-row seat today." Pioneer's voice manages to sound sweet and ominous at the same time. "For me."

"Sir, yes." Jonathan stares at the phone and then at me. "I promise I will."

"Then let the end finally come."

The line goes dead.

Jonathan wipes at his eyes and puts the phone back on the dash.

"What is he making you do?" I ask.

Jonathan whirls around. "He isn't making me do anything. I want to do this. For so long I didn't understand my purpose. I used to think it was the Rangers, but it wasn't, it wasn't even close. They were just a way to get me here. I mean, I didn't know, I didn't see it until I met Pioneer . . . I could feel the rightness of what he was saying about this world in my gut."

"What are you going to do?" I say as loudly as my throat will allow me.

He grins. "What I've always been meant to do. Start the apocalypse."

I look back at the big blue barrels beside me and the yellow tubing striping the van walls. This is what a bomb looks like? The only thing I picture when I say the word is a black ball with a string coming out of it—something cartoon-like and almost comical. This looks like stuff out of a hardware store. Utilitarian. And somehow this is what makes it feel real to me.

"Don't do this. Pioneer's wrong. The sheriff was right to raid us. Pioneer's not a prophet, he's just a man. If there were any Brethren at all and they were powerful enough to save us from the end, why aren't they powerful enough to start it themselves?"

Jonathan hits the screen with the flat part of his hand. "Shut up! You may have turned your back on your family, but I won't. You can't corrupt my destiny. I won't allow it." He opens his door and gets out. He slams it closed and then he's at the back of the van. I open my mouth and scream, but my voice is still so weak that it's not loud enough to be heard outside the van. He hops into the back and shuts the doors and I turn and kick at him with my feet. I land a heel into his chin and the skin splits along his jaw. His eyes go wild and he throws himself at me, punches me in the stomach and the head. I feel my bottom lip swell up. My vision, already red around the edges, doubles.

I'm afraid he's going to shoot me, but then I realize that he can't. If he does, he could blow us both up. Instead he ties my feet too. Then he grabs a black military-style vest from behind one of the barrels and what looks like a clock from the far corner of the van. The clock's connected by wires to something I can't see. He lays it down beside him and very carefully puts the vest on, then takes a rectangular box out of one of the pockets and puts it into his pants pocket instead. Outside somewhere a band begins to play. The program is getting ready to start.

"What's that for?" I say just to keep him talking, to stall for time.

He looks up at me and grins. "It's an insurance policy."

It's a bomb too, only he's wearing it. Which means . . .

"You're going to blow yourself up?"

"If I'm brave enough to make this sacrifice, Pioneer said that the Brethren will spare me too." When he says it, I can see that familiar glassy, faraway expression in his eyes. He said in the barn that he didn't believe in the Brethren, but here, now, it seems like maybe he's changed his mind.

He picks up the clock thing and presses a button. The numbers start to scroll backward. He set it for ten minutes. That's all the time I have left to get out of here, and my hands and feet are tied. I'm going to die.

"I'm going to lock you in now." He turns and slips out of the van. "This is it," he says more to himself than to me, and his face lights up. Then the doors shut and he's gone.

The clock keeps ticking down. 9:30, 9:29, 9:28 . . .

Think, Lyla, think! There has to be some way to get out. I wriggle down onto the floor and put my feet up to the van wall. I pull them back and then slam them against the wall. *Boom! Boom! Boom!*

Outside, the band has started playing "Rudolph the Red Nosed Reindeer" so loud that I'm sure no one can hear my kicks. Still I wriggle against the floor and pull my legs back to go again. *Boom! Boom! Boom!*

I kick again and again, but when the clock goes under five minutes I realize that it's no use, that I have to figure out a way to get out or I'm going to die and so are a lot of other innocent people. I need to get my hands free. *Now.* I lie flat on my back, panting. *Think, Lyla!*

Something sharp is sticking me in the back.

The shears. I've had them this whole time. I turn on my side and use my fingers to inch my shirt up so I can grab them. My fingers slip a little, but then grab hold.

4:00, 3:59, 3:58, 3:57 . . .

I inch the shears out and they drop to the floor, and I have to wriggle backward a bit to reach them. It takes more time than I'd like because I can't see them. I can only feel around on the floor. Finally my fingers touch the steel and I almost cry out in relief.

3:25, 3:24, 3:23 . . .

I get a hand around each handle and then lie on my side, lifting my legs as close to my hands as I can. My thighs threaten to cramp as I try to open the shears—one handle in each hand—and get them positioned around the rope binding my legs together.

2:52, 2:51, 2:50 . . .

It takes two tries to position the blades around the rope and not my skin. There is a thin line of blood running down my left leg, but I bring the handles together and then apart, very slowly, each opening and closing of the shears an ordeal. My thighs cramp, but I can't rub it out or stop, so I keep cutting even though my leg muscles are screaming.

2:00, 1:59, 1:58, 1:57 . . .

The rope breaks and I drop the shears, stretch my legs out, and uncramp.

1:20, 1:19, 1:18, 1:17 . . .

I have to do my hands now, which will be harder. I am almost out of time, and the knowledge just about derails me, but somehow I pick up the shears again and bring my legs under me until I'm kneeling. I look over my shoulder at the barrels and find a place to wedge the shears tightly. Once they're in place, the blades spread and facing out, I run the rope around my wrists over one of them. It's sharp and nicks my wrists and forearms every time I don't aim exactly right. The rope is loosening, but slowly.

1:00, 0:59, 0:58, 0:57 . . .

I'm talking to myself. "*Come on, come on,* COME ON!"

Outside I can hear people singing. The van reeks of gasoline. The ropes around my wrist are thin—one of them should have given way by now. I'm not going to make it. I don't want to die like this. Not like this.

All at once a piece of rope gives and I'm able to slip out of them. I'm free! The van doors have a latch on the inside. It opens easily and I scooch out of the van without stopping to check the clock again.

RUN!

I don't say this word. It's more like my whole body screams it. I push off of the ground and sprint away from the van, toward the grocery store, where at least a hundred people are gathered. There are kids on the risers ahead of me, preparing to sing. I recognize a familiar set of glittery braids in the second row. Jack. Down below her in the crowd, I see more familiar faces. Principal Geddy, Mrs. Ward.

"Bomb! There's a bomb! Get away. Get away!" I yell as loud as I'm able. It's a real yell this time, ragged and hoarse, but loud. Mrs. Ward turns toward me, and when she sees my face and how I'm hurtling at her, her eyes go wide and she begins to yell too.

"Bomb. Run! Everybody, now!"

I pass Mrs. Ward and start pushing the people closest to me onto the grassy strip alongside the market, trying to get them as far away from the van as possible. I look back to see Mrs. Ward pushing Jack ahead of her, then slowing to help an older woman.

There's a flash of light, and then it's like all the sound gets sucked out of the world before the boom that follows, which is so loud that I feel it shake the ground under me. A massive black cloud shoots up into the air, and then I feel a flash of fire on my skin as something slices across my side. The shockwave hits me next, and I'm thrown off my feet face-first into the grass. I look up in time to see a tire catapult past me, the rubber on fire. The grocery store's windows shatter and pieces of debris slam into it. Smoke washes over me in a cloud and I put my hands over my head. One by one bits and pieces of debris rain down from the sky.

I will take vengeance; I will repay those who deserve it.
In due time their feet will slip. Their day of disaster will arrive
and their destiny will overtake them.
—Deuteronomy 32:35 (discovered on Pioneer's cell walls
shortly before the Winter Festival Bombing)

TWENTY-EIGHT

I'm still alive. The smoke begins to clear and I'm still alive. I look up at the risers, where just a few minutes ago kids were getting ready to sing. There are people lying across the parking lot in scattered groups. Some are moaning; others are very, very still. I don't see Jack or Mrs. Ward anywhere. My side burns and I put my fingers on my sweatshirt. There's a long gash in it and my shirt underneath. My skin is sticky, and when I touch it, it's enough to make me hiss through my teeth. I don't think the wound is deep, but it hurts almost as much as my throat.

I make myself stand up and take a few steps. I don't know where I am at first. The whole parking lot looks like a war zone. The van is nothing but a burnt-out shell and the cars that were next to it are pushed over into the grass. All of them are still on fire.

I can just make out the white festival tents beyond the

wide stretch of parking lot. Most are still intact. I can see people there too, most of them staring in this direction.

Jonathan.

He's somewhere over there. They have to be his next target. I stumble forward, picking my way through the debris as fast as I can. My leg keeps vibrating, my thigh muscle twitching under my jeans . . . but when I put my hand over it, I realize that it's Cody's phone inside my pocket that's moving. I pull it out. The screen's all lit up. It takes me a minute to remember how to answer it. Finally I do and hold it up to my ear.

I can't hear anything over the ringing in my ears.

"Cody?" I shout into the phone. "There was a bomb. Get your dad." I don't bother with turning off the phone, I just slip it back into my pocket and keep going.

I'm not sure what I'll do if I find Jonathan. He's got the bomb strapped to his chest. How can I get him to stop without setting it off? There are so many people here, more than were over by the courthouse. The only thing I know to do is to get them as far away from the festival site as possible. I run up to the two women closest to me. When they turn my way, I stop in my tracks. Mrs. Dickerson.

I take off past them before they can stop me. I look back once and they're both still standing on the sidewalk gaping at me. It takes me a minute to understand. With my bald head and red eye and swollen face, I must look like one of Cody's monsters come to life.

I look around. There are still so many people. I can't get them all out of here, not on my own. It's hopeless. I turn in a circle, my eyes landing everywhere but focusing on nothing. *Where is he?*

A siren splits the air loud enough that I can just hear it over the ringing in my ears. And then another and another until the whole sky seems to be screaming. A line of vehicles, every one of them with flashing lights, speeds down Main Street. They drive right up onto the grass between the tents and the parking lot. I watch as the people jump out and make their way to the bomb site. The entire sheriff's department must be here, as well as all the firemen and EMTs. Thank goodness most of them weren't at the festival earlier. If they had been, there wouldn't be anyone to help the wounded and . . .

I suck in a breath. *Jonathan was waiting for them to show up. This next bomb is meant for them.* I take off in their direction, silently willing my feet to move faster, but I've already been running too long and can barely pick my feet up anymore. I weave in and out of pockets of bystanders, yelling as I pass for them to run to the diner and away. "There's another bomb!" I'm yelling more forcefully than before. I'm right about what Jonathan's planning, I can feel it. I thunder past the tents. The aroma of fried food and cotton candy hangs heavily in the air, a reminder of what this day was supposed to be.

I see the sheriff almost as soon as I get close enough to the vehicles to see people's faces clearly. I open my mouth to shout his name, but then I realize that Jonathan could be somewhere nearby. If he realizes that I'm coming to warn them, he might set the bomb off early. I clamp my mouth shut and push forward. It feels like I'm moving through quicksand; every step is getting harder and harder. My body is slowing down.

I practically fall into the sheriff when I finally reach him. He grabs my arms to steady me. His eyes go wide. I can tell he's horrified by how I look. He doesn't even seem to know it's me at first, but then he pulls me into his arms and hugs me tight to him. I almost lose it and start to cry.

"It's Jonathan. He set off the bomb and he's wearing another one. Here." The sheriff leans over and talks into the round black thing clipped to his shoulder. It crackles. I can hear someone else's voice coming out of it, answering him.

"You have to go, please! There's no time." I pull on his arm and try to drag him away.

I look everywhere, my eyes scanning the road and vehicles and festival tents and people. Jonathan is out there somewhere. I can feel it.

It isn't until he's just a few yards away that I finally recognize his black hat and vest. My heart starts pounding. It makes me feel like even my body is on a countdown timer, beating out the last few seconds before the next explosion. Jonathan's hand moves up toward his vest pocket.

"He's over there!" I shout, and the sheriff grabs his gun, wheels around, and points it at him.

"Don't move!" he yells as he steps in front of me, putting his body between me and Jonathan. Jonathan's hand moves a little closer to his pocket.

"I said, DON'T MOVE!" the sheriff hollers. His voice is loud, but his face is deadly calm.

A dozen deputies have formed a wide arc around Jonathan, their guns trained on him. "Get back, get back," they hiss at the festival-goers standing too close. The people scramble out of the way, running until they're across the street. The area is slowly beginning to empty out, but Jonathan doesn't seem to care. All of the people he wants to be close by are. He smiles just a little. For one very tense moment, everyone waits to see what he'll do.

"I'm the First Horseman of the Apocalypse!" he shouts.

"You don't want to do this," the sheriff says.

Jonathan cocks his head, his eyes wild. "Oh, but it's already done." His fingers twitch, and I flinch and get ready for the next boom.

There are a series of bangs. Jonathan's head snaps back. A spray of bright red dots pepper the tent just behind him. His hand straightens out but never makes it to his pocket. Then he's crumpling, his knees giving way all at once. I wince, waiting for the bomb to go off when he hits the ground, but it doesn't.

Jonathan's face is sideways on the ground. His eyes are open. I can't shake the feeling that he's staring right at me as he dies.

Hmm. I wouldn't do anything I'd feel guilty about.

—Charles Manson

TWENTY-NINE

Deputies surround Jonathan's body and begin to push people back as far as possible. At first I'm not sure why, but then I understand. The threat's not gone. Jonathan's still wearing a vest of explosives. Dismantling it presents a new kind of danger.

"Dad!" Cody is running in our direction. He stops short when he notices me. Unlike everyone else, he knows who I am right away. His arms come up like he wants to wrap me in them, but he isn't sure how to touch me without hurting me. I don't wait for him to figure it out. I throw myself against his chest and hold on to him as tightly as I can.

"Get Lyla out of here. Take her to the hospital. Then find your sister and your mom; they're supposed to be here somewhere." The sheriff pauses. I know he has to be frantic not knowing where they are. He puts a hand over his eyes. "If you find them, you call me that second."

Cody nods and the sheriff turns back toward the field.

"Be careful," I croak. My voice seems to be leaving me

again, but this time because it's so thick with so many emotions that I can't speak past them. In a matter of months, I've grown to love this man and his family. "If you get hurt . . ."

"I'll be fine. Don't worry about me." He gives me a soft smile. "Do you have any idea how brave you are?" he asks.

I shake my head. "I'm not brave. I've been scared all this time." It feels good to say it out loud. I don't think I've admitted it to anyone since I left the Silo.

"Being brave doesn't mean you're not afraid; it just means you're able to act in spite of your fear," he says. "And you do that extraordinarily well." He pats my head, and even after he takes his hand away, I can still feel the warmth of it.

Cody carries me down the road to his car, his arms so tight around me that I can feel his fingers pressing into my arms and legs. I feel a little silly being carried this way, like some kind of damsel in distress from one of those books he caught me looking at when we first met. But it's also kind of nice. Strange how his arms can make me feel safer than any shelter could.

"I stand against . . . these smooth tongued prophets who say, 'This prophecy is from the Lord!' . . . I did not send or appoint them, and they have no message at all for my people," says the Lord.

—Jeremiah 30:32

THIRTY

The bomb killed ten people. It doesn't sound like a lot considering how many it could have been, but still, it's a staggering number. And this close to Christmas, it seems all the more tragic. It's a time for family gatherings, not funerals.

The entire town feels like it's blanketed in sorrow. The streets are full of people gathering together, hugging and crying and trying to figure out a way to carry on. There are stuffed animals and flower bouquets strewn along the length of the park and the grocery store parking lot, lying under strings of white Christmas lights. The town discussed taking down all the Christmas decorations, since no one felt much like celebrating it, but in the end they were left up for the kids.

It's been exactly one week since the bombing. It's only five o'clock but already it's completely dark outside. We're gathered out in the road just beyond the park, standing in front of the diner where just a week and a half ago Jack and I ate lunch. She's with me tonight, as are Cody and his family and my dad.

A temporary stage has been erected in the street. On it is a cluster of people, each holding a picture of one of the bombing victims. Mrs. Ward died trying to help several students get to safety. Her sister and husband stand together, each with a hand on her photo, their faces pale and sad and so, so angry. Mrs. Rosen's husband is in the center of the group. I can barely look at him, there's so much pain in his eyes. He holds her picture as if it's the heaviest thing in the world.

We stand and listen as one by one the mayor reads the victims' names out loud. It's overwhelming, hearing them spoken together this way. I try to memorize each name, hold it in my heart so that I never forget them. It seems like the least that I can do—that we all can do tonight. Several people walk through the crowd handing out small white candles with little paper circles around their bases. One by one people light them and pretty soon the entire street is awash in candlelight.

There's a light tap on my shoulder. I turn around and Will's behind me. He's wearing his baseball cap pulled low over his face and a scarf over his mouth. I haven't seen him since he handed me the shears and told me to leave the trailer park. He looks at me, his eyes wide, scared. He must be afraid that I hate him now that I've had time to process what happened and the part he played in it—the way I was afraid that he hated me after the raid.

"Can we talk a minute?" he whispers.

I glance at Cody and he lets go of my hand. I follow Will to the small alleyway beside the diner.

"I came to say that I'm sorry about everything. I wanted things to go back to the way they were so badly." He looks up at the sky. "I don't have a life anymore, Lyla. You were it. I just . . . when you were gone, I felt like I didn't know who I was. Before the raid I was so sure about my future. I could see my whole life mapped out in front of me. And then it was all gone and nothing seemed right anymore. I kept hoping that if I followed Pioneer, if I listened to what Mr. Brown told me to do, I could get it all back . . . get you back. I didn't think about anything else." He swallows, and I can see tears rolling down his cheeks. His eyes are bright with them. "Mr. Brown and Brian . . . I didn't know what they were doing with Jonathan. I didn't even wonder until I saw what they did to you that night. What does that say about me, Lyla? If I'd just opened my eyes . . ."

"Hey, no, don't do that." I put my hand on his arm. "Everybody wishes for a good, safe life. I still wish for that too, but bad things happen and you can't see far enough ahead to stop them." Even as I say it, I feel the truth of it. Bad things happen. The Community was founded on the idea that if we kept away from the world, the bad stuff wouldn't be able to touch us. But it turns out that no matter what you do or where you go, the bad stuff finds you. It isn't about preventing it; it's about finding ways to make it to the other side when it does.

I look out at the crowd. People are huddled tightly together, families, strangers, and neighbors. No one's standing alone tonight.

"My family is leaving the Community," Will says. He looks down at me. "My dad's uncle has offered to help us make a fresh start. He's been trying to get in touch with us for a long time, but I think maybe after all of this my dad was finally open to it. He's got us on a flight to Texas tomorrow morning."

He's leaving? I never thought that he would be the one to go. I always thought it would be me.

"I came to say goodbye," Will says. The way he looks at me hurts. I'm probably never going to see him again. I'm not ready for this. I can tell he isn't either. "I'll always love you, Lyla," he says, his voice full of resignation.

I want to hug him, to hold on to him for a little longer, but it's time for both of us to let go. I look up at him, at those blue eyes of his, and all I can see is the boy I met when I was seven, the one who taught me so many things and could always make me smile. No matter what happens to him after today, no matter how far apart we are, I will carry that boy in my heart for the rest of my life. I nod at him and smile, tears blurring my vision. "I hope that you can start over, Will. I want you to be happy."

He nods. "I want that for you too."

He backs away and disappears into the candlelit crowd before I can say more. Before I can tell him that I will always love him too.

Once upon a time I thought my happy ending hinged
on the destruction of this earth and the vision of one man.
Now I know that my future is dependent on me
and what I choose to believe about it.

—Lyla Hamilton

(taken from her statement to the press at the trial of Alan Cross)

THIRTY-ONE

It's early morning and I'm crouched beside my bed, desperately trying to find my other shoe. Today I will see Pioneer for what I hope will be the last time.

I'm scheduled to testify at his trial in a few hours. That is, if I can find my shoe. It's there, finally, behind the stack of library books I've checked out from school. I fish it out and sit on the floor so I can put it on. I look around the room.

I'm still sleeping in Taylor's room, but now it looks different. There's more of me here than there used to be. Behind my bed are travel posters—Paris, Ireland, England, all of the places I plan to see now that I know that I can—as well as a bulletin board containing a dozen photographs of me with Cody, Jack, Taylor, and several other kids I have begun to think of as friends. After so many years spent in isolation, I want to explore every place and possibility, to meet as many people as I can. The world is one wide-open field, and it's all I can do not to run across it.

I breathe in, hold it, and then breathe out to try to calm my nervous stomach. I've seen Pioneer on TV a few times over the past few months, but I haven't seen him in person, not since the day he was arraigned in the courthouse, and I haven't heard his voice since the Winter Festival. His voice used to be enough to paralyze me. I wonder if today it will still have the power to do that. I don't think so, but I won't know for sure until we're face to face.

The drive to the courthouse is a long one. Pioneer's trial was moved three counties over in order to make sure the jury is as unbiased as possible. I'm not sure how it makes any difference, since he's been national news for months, but I'm not complaining. It's been easier to breathe these last few months knowing that he's no longer nearby.

Cody, Taylor, and Cody's mom—she wants me to call her Nora now—leave me to go sit in the courtroom with Jack. I'm being held in a separate room until after I testify so that I don't hear what's happening inside before it's my turn to talk.

The sheriff is with me. He says I can call him Stan, but somehow it doesn't fit the way "Sheriff" does.

My dad didn't come today. It isn't that he didn't want to. It's just that he'll be testifying too and he couldn't get off of work for both days. The sheriff helped get him a job with a construction company in Culver Creek. It's not exactly what he used to do before we moved from New York City, but it's more than he could have hoped for, since he hasn't had a regular job for almost eleven years. He left the Community not long after the bombing, once he found out exactly what happened to me during my recentering. Now he lives alone in an apartment near the diner. We eat dinner there together at least twice a week. He's lonely, but neither of us is ready to live together just yet. There is a lot we have to work through on our own—and together, I guess—before we can.

My mom didn't leave the Community. She still lives in the same trailer as before and still follows Pioneer. Her trailer is one of four still left on the property. Mr. Brown's family, Brian's mom, and Mr. Whitcomb's wife live in the others. They are all that's left of the Community. There's no one left to lead them now that Mr. Brown and Brian are in jail too. But they stay anyway. Admitting Pioneer was wrong means that they all were—all those deaths become meaningless.

Dad goes to visit Mom, but I don't go with him. Maybe I will someday, but for now . . . I can't stand to see her keep clinging to the past. I'm not sure that she'll ever be able to let it go, and it makes me so angry. I don't want to hate her, but I'm pretty sure that if I see her in that trailer with Pioneer's pictures still tacked to the wall and Karen's shoes still tucked under her bed, I might.

The sheriff and I wait to be called. He brought a deck of cards, and we play hand after hand of gin and crazy eights. After a while he clears his throat. "You ready for this?"

I shrug. "I have no idea. I think so."

The sheriff nods and then we grow quiet again, immerse ourselves in the game. A little while later a woman pokes her head through the door.

"Lyla Hamilton, they're ready for you."

My stomach plummets to my shoes, but I get out of my chair and follow her into the courtroom. As soon as I'm inside, my eyes find Pioneer. We stare at each other. He looks the same as the last time I saw him, gaunt but intense. He's still capable of commanding everyone's attention. Every person in the room is watching him watching me.

My legs shake as I walk across the room. I sit in the chair I've been led to and wait for things to start. Pioneer leans forward.

"Little Owl," he says with a smile. I wait for the familiar thrill of fear that always comes when he calls me this, but it doesn't this time. I stare right at him, wait. Still I feel nothing. I look over at Cody and Jack and smile.

Without warning, Pioneer jumps out of his chair and tries to get past the table and make his way to me. His lawyer grabs his arm, pulls him back. He's not smiling now. There's something else in his face, something I never saw there before.

Fear.

And it's because of me. The last time he talked to me,

he thought I was going to die, but just like him, I managed to survive.

What I say now helps determine what happens to him next, and he's scared. He thought that he would be out of jail by now. Maybe he thought the Brethren would get him out, perform a miracle, but they haven't, and now after what I say, and what the prosecutors are able to prove, he may be stuck in there for the rest of his life.

He's just a man. He really is just a man after all. The truth of this finally sinks in and I smile. I can't help myself. Knowing this isn't enough to calm my nerves completely, but it is enough to give me some peace.

Pioneer looks at me, his eyes widening, and I can almost see him beginning to understand. The last, thin rope of fear that's been tethering me to him drops away, and for the first time in a very long time, I am free.

ACKNOWLEDGMENTS

To my God, who gave me a passion to write and the opportunity to pursue it as a career. I am truly humbled by all of the wonderful blessings that you've given me.

To the readers who loved *Gated* in ways that both touched and surprised me. Knowing that you embrace Lyla and her story so wholeheartedly has meant the world to me.

To my agent, Lucienne Diver, who knows when to hold my hand and when to set me straight and does both with aplomb and skill. You are amazing, and I am thankful every day that you are in my corner.

To my editor, Chelsea Eberly, who has worked tirelessly to get this book ready for the world and polished into something I can be proud of. You are a rare breed of both editor and friend who can rock a red dress like nobody's business. I love working with you.

To Lauren Donovan, who has done an incredible job spreading the word about *Gated* and *Astray,* as well as getting me gigs that I only ever dreamed about doing. I owe you a thousand doughnuts at least.

To my publicist, Sadie Trombetta, who took on the task of promoting *Astray* with great enthusiasm and mad organizational skills. You are a powerhouse!

To Jocelyn Lange, who loved this book enough to sing the creepy cult song in it to people in the Random House Children's Books office, which tickled me to no end. I only wish I'd been there to see it. Thank you for championing *Astray* to the rest of the world.

To Nicole de las Heras, cover designer extraordinaire, who has gone above and beyond to find just the right cover for this book. Your attention to detail and care in creating something eye-catching have meant so much.

To the Lucky Thirteens, who have made navigating the publishing world much, much easier. You all have saved me from more meltdowns than I care to fess up to.

To the Gunning for Awesome girls—Natalie, Kim, Michelle, Amy, Gemma, Ruth, Corinne, Lori, Deborah, and Stephanie—you have become some of my truest friends. I am so glad we get to be on this publishing road together.

To my truly talented critique partners, Jennifer Baker, Krystalyn Drown, and Stefanie Jones, who have read and reread this book and have been brave enough to be truthful, yet kind enough to keep me from doubting my vision.

To my parents, who still give out the best hugs. Thanks for loving this very stubborn and determined girl and being the biggest cheerleaders a writer could ever have.

To Trish and Alan for showing my books to every person that steps foot in your home and buying more than your fair share of copies! I am fortunate to call you family.

To Tom, Erika, Lauren, and Kiersten. I'm overwhelmed by your continued support and love. You guys have championed my work and me and there are no words for how I feel about you all.

Finally, to my husband, Jay, and my two incredible girls, Samantha and Riley, who remind me of what's really important. You three inspire me to be a better person every single day, and I love you with all my heart.

ABOUT THE AUTHOR

AMY CHRISTINE PARKER writes full-time from her home near Tampa, Florida, where she lives with her husband, their two daughters, and one ridiculously fat cat. Visit her at amychristineparker.com and follow her on Twitter @amychristinepar.